Never Again,
No More 4:

What Goes Around

Never Again, No More 4:

No More 4:

What Goes Around

Untamed

www.urbanbooks.net

Urban Books, LLC
300 Farmingdale Road, NY-Route 109
Farmingdale, NY 11735

Never Again, No More 4: What Goes Around

ISBN 13: 978-1-64556-327-3
ISBN 10: 1-64556-327-8

First Mass Market Printing December 2022
First Trade Paperback Printing September 2021
Printed in the United States of America

10 9 8 7 6 5 4 3 2 1

Distributed by Kensington Publishing Corp.
Submit Orders to:
Customer Service
400 Hahn Road
Westminster, MD 21157-4627
Phone: 1-800-733-3000
Fax: 1-800-659-2436

Never Again, No More 4:

No More 4:

What Goes Around

Untamed

Acknowledgments

Lord, I can never say thank you enough. This talent is yours; I simply borrow it. Thank you for allowing me to do what I love, and I pray you increase my gift. I promise to keep applying it as you see fit.

To my number one fan, bestie, and love, my husband, Chris, your sacrifice for these late nights and early mornings, weekday through the weekend, and deadlines and events never goes unnoticed. I love you, but more importantly, I appreciate you. Twenty years in, and we ain't going nowhere. Good marriage for life!

To my heartbeats, Kiana, Christian, and Kameron, teamwork makes the dream work. You all have grown up and jumped on Team Everything Untamed. Thank you for everything, from the check-ins to the assisting to the jokes and hugs. We all we got.

To my angel baby, Da'Ja, Granny, Grandma, Keisha, Annie, and Mama—my host of angels—the watchful care you all give is always felt. Love you always and rest well.

Acknowledgments

My A1s ain't nothing like y'all. I don't need no big cliques, just my small tribe: Kesha, Sabrina, Chinek, Chia, Kisha, Vulyncia, Kiana D., and Tam. JC, Black, and Xodus.

To my ridahs in the literary world who have my back and my front, I couldn't do this without you. That includes Diane Rembert (Frienddd), Robert, N'Tyse, K. Reshay, TK, Eye CU, Sip and Flip Book Club, Danesha Little, Your Oral Diktion/Black Love Poetry Series and, of course, Urban Books!

To the readers, listen, thank you for continuing this *Never Again, No More* journey with me. These characters get loose in Part 4, so get ready. In my Durrell "Where the money reside" voice, I say, "'Cause we gon' go, we gon' go where the story reside, where the story reside, where the story reside, where the story reside, so let's tap, tap, tap in, and that's on—Untamed got a fire book series."

Previously from

Never Again, No More 3

Ryan

I was beginning to wonder if this relationship was even worth the fucking trouble anymore. I loved Charice, I did, but the fact remained that the more I looked at shit, the more it was apparent to me that she had feelings for Lincoln. She could tell me she didn't until she was blue in the fucking face, but one minute she couldn't stand him and the next she was sitting in his house. Yeah, I understood how the story went down. The delivery company fucked up the address, and she assumed Lincoln was being cruel. I got that. What I didn't get was why my wife was in his house, especially since I didn't observe one damn delivery truck in his yard when I drove off. Okay, so she said he told her the story about how he was awarded custody of London. Yada. Yada. Yada. Who cares? I felt sorry for Lauren, but that was Lincoln's business and Lincoln's problem. The true question was, Why did Charice care? I'll tell you why. She still had feelings for that nigga.

LaMeka

Suddenly, there was an awkward silence between us. He stood there rocking back and forth, with his hands in his pockets, and I stood there with my arms folded, nervously sliding glances between him and the floor. What could I say to Gavin? "Oh, by the way, I like you and all, but let me tell you everything going on in my life and how I'm considering getting back into a relationship with my babies' father?" Yeah, I didn't see that going over too well. We'd kept it strictly professional at work, or rather he had. To be frank, besides hello and goodbye, Gavin spoke to me only about work-related issues. He'd even stopped calling me, but I knew for a fact that Misha was calling him and keeping him on ice, so to speak. How'd I know? Well, besides that same little birdie telling me she was doing so, I have to admit that I'd actually reached out to Gavin once. I missed his companionship, friendship, and his sense of humor. Hell, I missed him.

I am an introvert except with my family, my girls, and Tony. And Gavin was the only person outside of that circle to get me to open up. After Tony hit me with his request, I broke down and called Gavin, but he didn't answer. I assumed it was because he no longer wanted to be bothered with me on a personal level, so I left him alone. Now here he was in the middle of my foyer, staring at me, and I at him, with so much to be said, yet so little being said.

Lucinda

"I'm just in shock. It is so true that you cannot judge a book by the cover. Lucinda, you're all right." He nodded, having determined that he'd misjudged me.

It was the first time I saw Mike through different eyes. We were actually more alike than we thought, and I realized I'd misjudged him as well. "Aww, thanks, Mike. So are you," I said as the game started. "But I'm still gonna whip that ass."

We stood there playing *Guitar Hero* for what had to be thirty minutes. Nadia had come back and sat on the sofa, and she was watching us play, and we were laughing it up and having a good time when Aldris floated into the family room with two boxes of pizza.

"Hey!" Aldris yelled loudly to us over the noise.

I paused the game, and we all calmed down with the laughter and talking.

"Hey, baby," I greeted, smiling at him.

"Hey," he said, looking back and forth between Mike and me. "Mike?" he asked, puzzled.

Mike snapped his fingers. "Oh, man, I came over to scoop you up. Remember, you were going to shoot hoops with me?"

Aldris sighed and snapped his fingers. "Oh, yeah, man. I totally forgot. My bad," he said to him as they slapped hands together.

"Oh, no worries. Lucinda's been a great hostess." Mike smiled back at me.

I fanned him off. "*He's* the one that's been a big help."

"Yep, Papi, he helped me study, and he and Mami have been battling on *Guitar Hero*," Nadia said and then whispered. "But Mami's winning."

"I heard that." Mike nudged Nadia playfully. "Sheer luck," Mike hollered.

Aldris nodded. "Oh, okay. Wow. Well, I appreciate it, man. Lu, I was calling you to find out what you all wanted to eat. I see now that you were occupied by the Wii. I settled for pizza."

Gasping, with a balled fist to my mouth, I apologized. "Ooh. I shoulda called you. Mike bought Nadia and me pizza already, but at least we have a meal for tomorrow."

He set the pizzas down on the coffee table. "Yeah, I guess you're right. Well, did you manage to get any work done?"

"Yeah, I did. Thanks to ol' Mike here." I play boxed with Mike. "He watched Nadia for me while I finished my paper and homework. Speaking of work, I have to sign on . . ." I looked over at Mike. "Although I was thoroughly enjoying kicking your tail," I joked with Mike as he moved into one of my play punches. "Stick and move."

He laughed, fist-bumping me, and then pulled the guitar off. "Until next time. You won the last dragon this time," he teased as I did a little victory dance, and then he laughed.

"Y'all are just bosom buddies now, huh?" Aldris commented.

"Man, Lu is a trip. I told her we have to plan fight nights and some tailgate parties when the football season starts," Mike said excitedly.

"Yeah, in that regard, you and Lucinda have a lot in common," Aldris admitted with a shrug.

"Yeah, we know," Mike and I said at the same time. Then we looked at each other and pointed. "Jinx. Double jinx. Triple jinx," we rattled off together, howling.

"Jinxy twins." Aldris put his hands up. "I'm pretty tired. I'd love to chop it up with you, man, but I need to eat and chill and, you know, spend a little time with *my* family."

Trinity

Now that he claimed the Pooch situation was handled, I was on pins and needles even more. He looked at shit from his lens, but I was the one who'd been in a relationship with Pooch. I knew how he operated and how he thought. When Pooch found out whatever plan had failed, he wouldn't stop until he found out the reason and the culprit behind it. What kind of leverage did Terrence have that this scheme wouldn't eventually be linked to him? That was my whole point. I knew that he was intelligent and a forward thinker, but Terrence possessed a different level of comfort than I did when it came to Pooch. He dealt only with the people who dealt with Pooch. I dealt with Pooch. I knew his mindset better than anyone else, and that included Terrence.

The calm that we were now experiencing felt eerie to me. By now, I figured we'd have heard something besides just that the bribe worked. The fact that we hadn't heard anything was what gave me pause. Pooch may not have been as intellectual as Terrence, but he was still a street nigga. They didn't fight fair. And being honest, for all of Terrence's intelligence, Pooch was the one who got him locked up first, because that's how grimy niggas operate.

Terrence wasn't that type of dude. He didn't give a damn about what the next man had going on as long as he could get his. Pooch wasn't like that. He cared. He wanted it all, other niggas be damned. It was that attitude that made me wonder what the fuck was going on behind the scenes that we didn't know about. We'd covered our tracks the first time, but the second time might not be so easy.

Pooch

Man, I was one grumpy muthafucka. A lack of sleep, being locked up, and not locating Trinity were fucking with me something awful. I missed

Trinity. Man, there was so much I wished I could've redone with her. I wished I coulda been a better nigga for her and the kids. She had wanted to do her art shit, and I shoulda let her. She still coulda been my dime piece with her own grip. I'd admit that the main reason I never wanted Trinity to do nothing with her life was that I was afraid of her being successful. If she was successful, then I knew she'd leave a nigga like me, so I'd used my power and money to keep her from doing what she wanted to do. I was wrong for that.

I hadn't asked Flava about her lately, but I was definitely gonna get back to that. It was time to find out what the hell was truly going on with Trinity. Whether I missed her or not, if I found out her ass had been with Terrence this whole time, she was gon' wish I had got that fuckin' triple cocktail concoction instead of this prison sentence. Real talk. But if I found out something had happened to her, whoever had done it wasn't gonna have time to worry about running from me, nor would their family members have to worry about retaliation, because I was gonna meet that person's muthafuckin' ass in the same hell I was gonna send them to. I was definitely gonna get the triple cocktail if that was the case, and I wasn't gon' mind one bit. Hell, I'd strap up in the seat and stick the needle in my arm my damn self.

Welcome to

Never Again, No More 4:

What Goes Around

Chapter 1

Trinity

For the most part, my life was great. I had my husband right beside me, loving me, supporting me, and taking care of me and the kids. My career was in full swing, and I was working on my degree, so that I could progress. I didn't need or want for anything. But I was still feeling a disconnect in my life. Ever since Terrence had accused me of sleeping with his cousin, Big Cal, I had felt so hurt. I got that he had risked a lot, especially when it had come to helping Big Cal and his other cousin, Thomas, infiltrate Pooch's Dope Boy Clique and take them down, but hell, I had risked a lot, too, by sneaking off with the kids and leaving with Terrence, so why would I want to be the one to jeopardize it? I understood that he felt he couldn't trust anyone. Cool. I got that. But it really seemed like he was saying he couldn't trust *me*, and that was a problem.

I'd done a good job of pretending not to let it worry me, but over the past couple of weeks, I'd spent more time at the art gallery instead of staying at the house, because I wanted to be away from Terrence. Being made to feel like I was a whore when all I'd ever been was a straight-up, down-ass chick did something to me. Especially when the person who made me feel this way was supposed to be my better half.

"Trinity, we've got an issue with your Ecstasy collection. Two of the portraits came back from production with marks," my manager informed me.

I looked up from my computer. "Give me about five minutes, and I'll be right out."

"Sure. Oh, and I have the invoices from last month for you to go over when you get a chance."

Once I acknowledged her last statement, she placed the invoices on my desk and left. I wasn't trying to be rude, but I was finishing my research paper for class, so I could submit it to my professor.

Ding. My work cell phone alerted me that I had a message. I looked at the screen and saw that it was from Big Cal.

Biguc1: You still there?

TatsByTrin: Yeah, I told you I was typing my paper. I can't really talk now anyway. I'm at the office, and I have a couple of shipment issues to deal with.

Biguc1: Well, don't be frustrated. My cousin can be paranoid at times. He loves you, Trinity, and I can't blame him for keeping his eyes out on you. Besides the fact that he loves you, you're a dime-piece girl, and any man would be happy to have you on his arm. So, don't take offense to it. Count it as a blessing.

His words spread a feeling of warmth and comfort through me, and I giggled at his assessment.

TatsByTrin: Of course. LOL. I gotta go. Good talking to you. You're always there for me.

Biguc1: LOL. True. I'll always be there for you. Like a good neighbor, Big Cal is there. LOL.

TatsByTrin: LMAO. Clown. Holla at you later. Be good.

Biguc1: Peace. Stay sexy, lovely lady.

After I placed my phone down, I signed off my work computer and went to deal with the marred pictures. After that issue, there was another one and another one, and before I knew it, I was tied up for at least another hour handling business. It didn't bother me, but I did want to finish my paper before Terrence came to take me to lunch, and now I wouldn't have the time.

"What's up, people?" Terrence said, walking into the gallery.

"Hey, Terrence," everyone replied in unison.

My baby looked all kinds of fine. His dreads had just been freshly retouched, and his goatee lined up, and his outfit was fresh. I swore only he could make a pair of black cargo shorts and a fitted, gray V-neck T-shirt look sexy.

He walked over to me and kissed me on the lips. "What's up, sexy?" he whispered.

"Aw," the ladies sang.

"You all are so silly." I smiled, looking back at them.

"Girl, please. I wish I had a man to call me sexy," Jalise, my operations manager, joked as they all high-fived each other.

Terrence wrapped his arm around my shoulder. "Well, I do have a cousin named Aaron you can have."

I put my face in my hands and couldn't help but to laugh. If only they knew why he had said that. I playfully nudged him.

"Girl, Mr. Right will come. Don't rush it. The wait makes it that much sweeter." I winked at her. Then I turned to face Terrence. "I'm just wrapping up a few minor issues. I'll be ready in a few. You can sit in my office and wait if you want."

"Cool. Handle your business, businesswoman." He kissed me on my forehead before he turned and headed back to my office.

Owning my own business wasn't easy, but I wasn't going to complain. Fuckin' with Pooch, I would've never been able to have anything to complain about. I did not know what in the hell had ever possessed me to enter into a relationship with that fool anyway. All I knew was that I'd lived and learned, and I was so glad that Vernon "Pooch" Smalls was out of my life.

When I thought about all my good fortune— everything I'd accomplished and the person I had become—I knew it was not only because of me, but also because of Terrence's continued love and support. So at the end of the day, it was hard to be upset with him. Hell, the man wasn't perfect, and he did say that he never intended to doubt me. As I thought it over and listened to how the women that worked for me all wished they could have a man like mine, I decided that Big Cal was right. I'd read too much into what had happened, and I needed to let it go. With that thought, I decided to call it a day and went to the back to get my husband so we could eat lunch. Then I'd take him to our favorite hotel and make passionate love to him for dessert.

"Ready?" I smiled at him as I walked into my office.

He looked up. "Yeah."

After closing down my office laptop computer, I packed it, the invoices Jalise had left on my desk, and my work cell phone in my shoulder bag. Then

I gave myself a once-over in the mirror. Perfection stared back. I opened my purse, slid on my bangle bracelets, and reapplied some lip gloss; then I tossed the lip gloss back inside before I grabbed my things and walked out with Terrence.

"All right, ladies. I'm gonna call it a day. You all hold it down, and if you need me, hit me up on my cell," I announced.

Terrence threw up his hands as he followed me out. "See you, ladies. Have a good one."

A minute later I slid into Terrence's Range Rover, put my head back, and closed my eyes, relaxing to the sound of Kem's latest CD flowing through speakers. Suddenly, Rick Ross came crashing through the airwaves. I looked over at Terrence, who was nodding his head to the music, and got slightly irritated that he had taken me out of my sensual mood. Hell, with this damn Rick Ross, I felt like I was getting ready to go bust out somebody's car windows.

"Can we switch it back to Kem, babe?" I asked him, my head still on the headrest.

"Nah. I'm feeling Ricky Ross right now," he said plainly.

Wow. Okay then. "So, I was thinking maybe we could do something else for now and go to Oceanique or L2O later," I said, trying to block out the music and switch the subject.

"I was kinda feeling like I wanted some Kuma's today."

That made me sit up. "Kuma's?" I asked, turning to face him. "You came and got me from the gallery to go to Kuma's?"

"Best Chicago dogs and burgers around. They have some good Italian beef sandwiches too. You know you love Kuma's."

Cutting my eyes at him, I crossed my arms. "Yeah, I like Kuma's if the kids are with us, but I thought we were making a nice little moment out of this. Ain't nothing sexy about digging into a greasy Kuma's burger."

Without even taking his eyes off the road, he shrugged. "Kuma's fries are better than Mickey D's."

I hit my forehead. "That is so not the point, Dreads. I don't want Mickey D's or Kuma's. Damn."

"Okay, well, where would my *princess* like to go?" he asked. The sarcasm practically dripped from his lips.

My head tilted as I gave him the side-eye. He'd never called me a princess before. I didn't know what that or his abrupt attitude was all about. "Um, like I said, I was hoping to skip the lunch and spend a little time together, and then go home, change, and head over to Oceanique or L2O for dinner. We could still make it if we put in reservations now."

"Well, I'm hungry now. Can't we just go where I want to go for once?"

I looked at him as if he were crazy. He'd never been so rude, and it was highly uncalled for. "You happen to like Oceanique and L2O."

"Yes, but neither is open now, and I want some Kuma's."

"Fine. Why can't we go to Fire House Grill? It's a nice little spot that we can eat at now, and we love their food."

"It ain't Kuma's."

"It's not, but it *is* a compromise," I said, tossing out my own jab at his relentless behavior.

Gripping the steering wheel, he steeled his jaw and then grunted. "Kuma's can be a compromise too if you'd let it be."

Throwing my hands up in exasperation, I quipped, "Why not Mickey D's, then?"

He rubbed his belly. "Damn. They *are* running a special on their Double Quarter Pounders with Cheese."

"Oh, hell no," I mumbled. "Fine, Dreads. Let's go to *Kuma's*," I said, stressing Kuma's to show my annoyance.

"Cool. Thanks, babe."

Shocked by his nonchalant attitude and bad-mannered behavior, I looked at him and rolled my eyes. Confession time. My relationship with Dreads was a lot different than my relationship with Pooch. Pooch had given up that bread, true enough, but he had been very clear that he was in charge and that it was his way or no way. With Dreads, I was spoiled. Point blank, period. With Dreads, it wasn't his way. It was whatever I wanted or needed. I was used to that from Dreads. Don't get it twisted. I gave him his space and let him be the man of the house. Yes, we were partners, and our decisions were mutual, but I always allowed him to be the man. Still, as my man, Dreads spoiled the hell out of me, so his little stance about going to Kuma's was something I wasn't used to.

I tried not to let it spoil my mood, though, because I wanted to get him alone, tell him that I forgave him, and put it down on him like it wasn't nobody's business. Part of me felt like he would still go to one of the restaurants I wanted to go to, but when he never picked up his cell phone to make the reservation, and we pulled up at Kuma's, I knew he was serious. Instead, I tried to make the most of it. I sat at one of the few vacant tables and pulled my Dolce & Gabbana shades above my head as Terrence went to get our food.

"Gurl, is that a Coach bag?" asked some chick on the other side of me. I turned to see her and two of her friends staring at my purse in awe. "Where'd you get yours from? Chico? That definitely looks like a Chico bag. He gets the shit that looks real, like for real for real," she said, high-fiving one of the females.

I shook my head. "Naw, boo. This is real. It's a Birkin bag."

"Bur who?" the girl asked.

Her friend hit her on the arm, with a wide-eyed stare. "Gurl, you know the shit that Jay-Z be talkin' 'bout in his songs that he be gettin' for Beyoncé. Them bags."

The girl who'd asked me about the bag turned from her friend and faced me again. "Damn. Where you get a fake . . . um . . . one them bags from? Chico only deals with Coach and Gucci," she said. The other two girls nodded, waiting for my answer.

Exhaling slowly, I really had no words. I'd come so far from this . . . environment. "It's not a fake. It's real. I got it when my husband and I went shopping in New York."

"Damn," they all sang in unison.

"What kinda weight yo' man pushing? He must be, like, a true supplier to be gettin' you shit like that," commented the girl who'd recognized the brand of my purse.

Ghetto birds. I couldn't help but to snicker. "My man doesn't push weight, darling. He has a job, and it's legit. He's a real estate investor," I said curtly.

"Ooh. Oh, okay. Excuse me, then, girlfriend," she said with her nose turned up.

Miss Head Ghetto Bird and her crew looked at each other, and I turned back toward my table. "Can we say boujee?" she joked in a fake whisper to her friends as they giggled.

I wanted to bring ghetto Trinity back on them and cluck her ass in the head, or even bring out a little of the educated Trinity and let her know the word was *bourgeois*. But I digressed. I wasn't with Pooch. I was with Terrence, and he was a gentleman, so I was going to be a lady, even if I was at damn Kuma's.

When Terrence came back with the food, the girls looked at each other and said in unison, "D-boy."

Terrence looked at me strangely, obviously having overheard their assessment of him, but I shook my head, signaling that he should not ask. "I got us some burgers and fries." He smiled as he placed a burger and fries in front of me and then sat down across from me.

"I see." I lifted the greasy burger with the tips of my thumb and forefinger, placed it back down, and then grabbed a napkin to wipe my hands.

"Girl, stop. Act like you remember that you're from the hood," Terrence chastised with a smirk on his face.

Pointing my manicured nail at him, I said, "From the hood, but I don't live there now, and I certainly don't have to act like it. And why do you wanna act like it? You are far removed from that type of environment yourself, and your occupation certainly calls for you to be different. Ain't this what you preach to Terry about every day?" I said, patting my fries with a napkin to get the grease out.

"Yeah, but I'm proud of my past. It made me the man I am today. I may not be proud of everything I've done, but I'm still the same hood nigga from the ATL. I just happened to make it."

"Ain't nobody denying their past or being ashamed of it, but I left the hood for a reason. Ain't nothing wrong with acting civilized. It's called growing the hell up," I said and stuffed a fry in my mouth.

Terrence eyed me for a second, shook his head, and took a drink of his soda. For the rest of the time we were there, I may as well have been talking to the damn table. His answers were short and to the point, and most of them consisted only of yes or no, so I shut up, and we ate in silence for the last few minutes. So much for feeling the romance.

He stood up and stretched. "You ready to take it to the house?"

"Yeah," I agreed, throwing my napkin over my half-eaten food.

"You barely touched your food. You must not have been hungry. I'm glad I spent only twenty bucks on a meal instead of two hundred if you were gonna eat like a bird," Terrence said as I stood up.

Completely irritated, I shouted at him, "I didn't eat it because I didn't want Kuma's."

The girls snickered. "Boujee," they chorused again as we walked by. Now I was blowed. I turned to face them.

"Look, *gurl*, the word is 'bourgeois,' that's *bursh-waa*, and if that's what I am, then so be it. At least I know the real from the fake, and I know how to pronounce Birkin, which is something your little ghetto ass may never have," I said with plenty of attitude.

"Hold up now, boo," snapped the ghetto bird who had been silent.

They all stood up, as if they were about to tag on my ass. I turned to look at them with my hands on my hips, ready to get it on and poppin'.

Terrence plastered on the brightest smile. "Ladies," he said, "let it go. She's just a little upset with me. Don't take it personally. She's a little bourgeois. She's used to white tablecloth dinners and shit. Let me make it right with y'all." He pulled out a grip of money.

"Damn. Where are you pushing, man?" the loud-mouthed one who had spoken to me asked him. At this point, they all looked at my husband as if they could eat him up.

He pulled off three one-hundred-dollar bills and handed each one of them skeezers a Benjamin.

Then he shook his head. "I don't push weight. I'm legit. You all do something nice for yourselves with that and have a good day," he said and walked up by my side.

Their blushes were sickening. "Bye, boo. Thank you," they all said together.

"And if you ever get tired of her bourgeois ass, come find me. I love Kuma's. Wit' yo' fine ass," the head ghetto bird with the loud mouth said to him.

Before I could run up on that ho, he wrapped his arm around my shoulder, winked at them, and began to walk me out to the Range Rover. I pushed him off me. I was so fucking blowed.

As soon as we got in the truck, I gave his ass *the business*. "What the fuck was that all about?"

He shrugged and started the SUV. "What did you want me to do? Let them jump you?" he asked as he backed out.

"Let them jump me!" I yelled in disbelief. "No, you're supposed to get an attitude with them broads and help me tag team them bitches."

"So we can all go to jail, and then Pooch will know exactly where the fuck you are. That's bright, Trinity. And you say you don't act ghetto no more," he said sarcastically.

My eyes narrowed to slits. I was seething. "I can't believe you just came at me like that."

"Li'l mama, calm the hell down."

"I will not!" I yelled, turning in my seat to face him and go off. "I get a lame-ass twenty-dollar meal, and you peel off a hundred dollars for each of them broads as if it wasn't shit."

"For me, it ain't shit," he yelled back. "I'm a fucking multimillionaire. Damn," he said, as if I weren't aware. "Besides, you was the one poppin' off on three chicks like you were being followed by a team of fucking security guards. This is Chi-town, Trin, not Evanston, and these females will get at you."

"So your form of protecting me is to pay them off and flirt with them? Winking your eye and shit at them nasty skeezers."

He scoffed, his irritation evident, before he smoothed his hand over his goatee. "Boy, oh, boy. What a fucking day." He shook off my comment. "Look, if you want a nigga to go off about every little thing, then you shoulda stayed with Pooch, but you know how I am, and I don't change for nobody."

My mouth dropped open. I was stunned speechless for the first time in my life. I couldn't believe how he was acting, let alone the fact that he'd just told me some shit like that. It was as if he didn't even care about me. Did I even matter enough to him that he cared whether I stayed with Pooch? Apparently not. This could not be my husband. I had to be stuck in a remake of *Invasion of the*

Body Snatchers or something. As pissed as I was, I didn't say shit to him. Honestly, I couldn't, because anything I would've said at this point might have landed us in divorce court. I looked out the passenger's-side window while I collected myself. We were off to a bad start, but that didn't mean we couldn't end on a good note. And given these past two weeks, we needed a good note.

I was so upset that I forgot to tell Dreads to go to a nice hotel, but it was cool, though. Consuela always took Tyson with her to run errands on Thursdays, so I figured she wouldn't be home when we got there, which was indeed the case, judging from the note she left, stating they'd be back after 3:00 p.m.

Good. It was only 1:15 p.m. Maybe I could coax him into a nice quickie. Dreads ran upstairs to our bedroom, kicked his shoes off, and sprawled across the bed, and I jumped into the shower. Since time was of the essence, I was in and out, smelling fresh and sweet, and my body oiled down, in fifteen minutes. Rather than put on a teddy or a negligee, I came out completely naked and crawled on the bed. After straddling his back, I kissed his cheek, which stirred him awake.

"I know we were beefin' a little bit ago, but let me make it up to you," I whispered in his ear. "I know what to do to make it right."

He turned on his back and put his hands behind his head. "Oh yeah?"

I smiled at him. "Yeah."

I bent down and kissed him, but he seemed hesitant, as if he wanted to kiss me but didn't at the same time. Still, I pressed on, moving from his lips to his neck and wrapping my fingers in his locks. He let a small moan escape but stopped there, as if he were trying to hold the rest in. I noticed he wasn't holding me or caressing me. Nothing. I lifted his shirt to kiss on his hard abs.

"Baby, you're so tense. Let me loosen you up," I said and unbuckled his belt, then took it off. After easing down his shorts and boxers, I gripped his manhood in my hands and massaged it.

"Mmm. Oh yeah," Terrence moaned as he closed his eyes and began to relax a little.

"That's it." I slid his manhood into my mouth.

"Ahhh," he moaned. "Trinity."

"Yes, baby?" I moaned in between sucks.

"Trinity, stop."

"I promise I won't make you cum like this," I whispered and looked at him seductively.

"No, stop. For real."

"Huh?"

He sat up. "Just stop. I can't do this right now."

"What the fuck is going on? What the hell do you mean, you can't do this right now? It's been two damn weeks since we've had sex."

He stood, pulled up his boxers and shorts, and sat on the edge of the bed, with his head in his hands. "I can't do this."

My frustration bubbled over. "Do *what*?" I asked, throwing my hands up.

"Us," he said softly. He looked up at me, and his eyes were glossy. He swallowed a lump in his throat. "You don't love me, Trinity."

"What? Where? Huh?" I asked, so confused that I couldn't even finish one question to ask the next.

"I was just a way out of your relationship with Pooch."

"No. I've *never* felt like that. I love you. Where is this coming from?"

"You lied to me," he screamed. "You were in your office, chatting with Aaron. Talking about our relationship to my *cousin*. Come on, man. How could you tell him what we discussed in confidence about our marriage?"

That was when it dawned on me, and I gasped. *My cell phone.* When I had sent Terrence into my office, I had left the text messages up on my phone. *Damn. Damn me straight to hell.* It all made sense now. His off-color comments, his attitude, his mood—everything.

Tears sprang to my eyes. "Baby, I'm sorry. I was just so upset that you thought that I would do you dirty. I needed someone to talk to who'd understand. I can't talk to Lucinda, LaMeka, or Charice like I want to, and I was just so mad at you. Please don't be upset."

Terrence glared down at me, and his disappointment was evident. "Then why not talk to me about it?" he asked angrily, beating his chest. "I've never gone to Aaron and confided in him about anything about you, because we're married. You're *my wife*, Trinity! Not some gawddamn jump off. And you treatin' me like a nigga off the street. I feel like I come second to Aaron in my own damn marriage."

Hearing the hurt in his voice, I realized how wrong I was and how absolutely right he was. I would've been pissed if he had talked to any of my girls about our marriage instead of talking to me. I wiped my tears before I spoke again. "Baby, I shouldn't have done that to you. I was so wrong for that, and I won't ever do that again, but please believe me when I say that Aaron and I are just—"

"*Friends?*" he blurted, as if he were tired of hearing the word. "Yeah, so you keep saying, but what the fuck was he doing calling Princess 'his' baby? And what the fuck was he doing signing off with 'Stay sexy, lovely lady'? And since when are you all messaging each other? I thought it was only emails and the occasional phone call. What's the real reason you even left Pooch?"

"Wait, what?" I asked as I grabbed my robe from the chair beside our bed and wrapped it around my naked body. "I mean, we have each other's phone number. Every now and then, he'll message me, and we'll talk. I never put stock into it, but where are you going with this whole Princess and Pooch deal?"

"I'll be frank." He placed his hands in his pockets and closed the space between us. His jaw tightened as he stared at me with such intensity. His next words nearly pummeled me. "Is Princess really Aaron's child or Pooch's?"

Shockwaves ripped through my core, causing a heavy flow of tears to stream down my face before I could blink them away. "Oh, my gawd. I can't believe you asked me that. Princess is *Pooch's* child. You know that. I've never slept with Aaron."

He shook his head, as if he didn't believe me. "So you keep saying, but all your actions and his say different. Then you made the comment that you left the hood for a reason. Was I your meal ticket out of the hood, so you can be away from Pooch? Is that all I was to you?"

"What?" I asked in disbelief. "Hell no. Come on, baby. You know I left Pooch because I was . . . *I am* . . . in love with you, and I was pregnant with your baby."

"Was or am in love, Trinity? Which one?" he yelled angrily.

"I am. I *am* in love with you."

That declaration seemed to take some of the steam out of Terrence, because he turned away from me and paced for a few moments. His shoulders slumped before he plopped down on the bed. "I don't know. I don't know what to believe," he said, more to himself than to me.

Thick emotions gathered in my throat, and I swallowed hard to hold myself together. Then I sat beside him. "Believe in me, baby. Believe in us." Gently placing my hand on his chin, I turned his face so that he could see the sincerity in my eyes and hear it in my words. "I would never do you dirty, and I'm not lying to you. I wanted to use today to make it up to you. Honestly, Big Cal helped me realize that I was being too hard on you about assuming that he and I had ever been together. I know it's because of what happened and how close Big Cal and I are. I'm so sorry for making you feel like there was more between us, and I'm sorry for confiding in him about our marriage. I was wrong for that." I took a deep breath. "I'm so, *so* sorry. Please forgive me," I begged as I leaned on his shoulder.

After a few minutes, Terrence stood up and slipped his feet in his tennis shoes. "I don't know, Trin. I need some time to think. I'll be back." He headed to the door.

I jumped up. "Dreads, wait," I called out, and he stopped in his tracks. "Baby, *please*. Let's not do this. This is us. We've been together so long. You've been my heart since I was fifteen. It's always been you for me, even when I was with Pooch. You know this. You were my first kiss, my first love, my first lover, my first baby daddy, and you're my first and only husband. Please," I pleaded.

Exhaling, he slowly turned to face me. "Yeah, I have been all of that to you, but we ain't kids no more, Trinity. Maybe a part of you wants something or *someone* new. I don't know. What I do know is that I have to leave this house before my head explodes." With that, he walked out of the bedroom and slammed the door behind him.

I couldn't believe what had just happened. I stood frozen in place for a few minutes, as I heard Dreads's Range Rover pull out of the garage. I felt like I was moving in slow motion as I went to our closet and threw on some old clothes. I pulled my hair up into a ponytail and lay across our bed and clutched my pillow. A few minutes later, the tears I could not hold back began to slide down my face again and onto the bed as I wailed from all the pent-up emotions inside me. My cell phone rang, and I answered it quickly, hoping it was Terrence.

"Baby?" I asked in a tear-strained voice.

"Trinity?" Big Cal's voice came crashing through the receiver. "What the fuck is wrong? Is everything okay?"

"Yeah. Um. Everything is cool." I managed to get out. "Listen, Big Cal, I gotta go. We don't need to talk."

"What? Why the fuck can't we talk?" he asked angrily. "Wait a minute. Where is T?"

"Gone."

"Gone? Gone where?" he asked, upset.

I shrugged, as if the gesture were visible to him. "I don't know."

"Did y'all fight? Did he hit you? Did he say something to you?" He fired off this succession of questions faster than I could answer.

After taking a deep breath, I said, "Big Cal, please just leave it alone, and leave me alone. I gotta go. Bye."

For the next few minutes, my phone buzzed off the chain, but I refused to answer. Once my tears stopped, I rolled over, with heavy eyelids, and picked up my phone. I'd missed seven calls from Big Cal and none from Terrence. I put my phone down and closed my eyes. As I drifted off to sleep, I couldn't help but wonder if Big Cal cared more about me than Terrence did.

Chapter 2

Terrence

Love made you do crazy things. I didn't want to believe that Trinity would do me dirty, but right there on her cell phone were the messages between her and Aaron. Talking about us—about me. What the fuck was I supposed to think? Every time I looked around, those two were acting closer than close. Always talking. And me? Hell, I was on the outside, looking in. He was my cousin, and she was my wife, but neither one of them talked to me about the shit that was bugging them. Now, Aaron was real quick to get me involved when he thought Pooch was going to get out and fuck up his and Thomas's life, but did my cousin let me know that my wife was confiding in him about our marriage? Hell no. It wasn't even that the conversation was all that bad—well, not until that eloquent ending that my cousin wrote. The point was that after all we'd been through, my wife couldn't come to me, and my cousin couldn't tell me that she was going to him.

I was hurt beyond belief. I felt betrayed by them. True, it ain't like I caught them sleeping together, and Trinity continued to deny that they had done that, but I could go only by their actions. Whether they had had sex or not, their actions told me that something was brewing between them. I could just feel it. I didn't get married to be at war with my wife, and I sure as hell didn't get married to compete with another nigga for her attention and affection.

I rode around the Chi for about an hour, just thinking and bopping my head to any type of gangsta rap that hit the airwaves. Still, the more I tried to clear my head, the more hurt I felt and the angrier I got. Before I knew it, tears were rolling down my face.

"Shit," I said aloud, wiping my face.

I'd never cried a day in my life until Trinity. There was always something that would break a man down. For me, it was my wife and kids.

"Come on, T. Man the fuck up," I coached myself out loud as my bottom lip began to tremble. I just didn't want to face the possibility that my wife had feelings for my cousin. "Fuck."

My cell had been buzzing like crazy, so I pulled it out to check who was calling. I figured it was Trinity, wanting me to come home so she could cuss me out for leaving, but I was wrong. I had ten missed calls, and every last one of them had been from Aaron. Humph. Coincidence? Not a chance in hell. I dialed his cell phone number.

Aaron's voice came through after the second ring. "T?"

"Yeah, man. What's good?" I said, trying to straighten out my voice.

"What the fuck is wrong with Trinity?" he asked without hesitation.

Scoffing, I pulled the phone back and side-eyed it before placing it back to my ear.

"Ain't shit wrong with her. Why?"

He paused. "Don't lie to me, man. I called her, and she sounded so distraught—"

My temper flared and went from simmer to sizzle in one second flat. "Why the fuck are you calling my wife? Huh? What the fuck goes on in my household and in my marriage is none of your muthafuckin' concern, Aaron. She may be your fucking friend, but she's my wife. I advise you to remember that, nigga."

"You muthafucka. Who the fuck do you think you're talking to like that? I helped you get your fucking girl back so she could become your wife. Or have you forgotten that?" he yelled.

"No, nigga. Have *you* forgotten it?"

"You muthafuckin' trippin'," Aaron said, then sucked his teeth.

"No, muthafucka, you trippin'. If you need to contact anybody in my household from this point forward, it better only be me."

Aaron laughed. "You are really fucking jealous of my friendship with Trinity, aren't you? What? You're so fucking insecure that you can't stand for another man to be involved in her life? Remember, nigga, when you was locked up, it was me who looked out for her and had her back. Me. Not you. *Me*. I was the one who had to watch that nigga Pooch degrade her and treat her like shit, while trying to encourage her by letting her know it was gonna get better. And if it weren't for me, you'd still be in that damn gray box, looking at yo' wifey from a wallet-size picture frame. So don't fuckin' come at me wit' no bullshit about my friendship with Trinity. I've been there for her, and I always will be there for her."

That nigga had really just tried me on my manhood and my gangsta. Both of which was legit as a muthafucka. I flipped open my glove box and saw my .45-caliber pistol resting in there. Cousin or no cousin, I was about to handle this shit, on the real. Trinity was my wife, and wasn't no nigga gonna tell me how he was gonna interact with my wife regardless of my feelings. I had that ass. Oh yes, I had that ass.

A sinister chuckle escaped me. "Is that so?"

Aaron sucked his teeth. "Yeah, muthafucka, it is so."

"A'ight. Bet. I see you, nigga."

"I see you too, *nigga*. Anytime. You know where I'm at. All day, baby. All day," Aaron said and then hung up the phone in my face.

I pulled over at the nearest gas station. That nigga didn't know I was right around the corner from his house. I pulled out my bullets and loaded my gun. He officially wanted it with me, so he was gonna get it.

Not even two minutes later, I pulled up at his house. I stepped out, with my gun in hand, headed to the door, and tapped on it. Thomas answered the door.

"'Sup, cuz—"

"Where's Aaron?" I asked, pushing my way inside.

"What's with the gun?" he asked, clearly getting nervous about the situation.

"Where's Aaron?" I asked again.

"Yo, T, what's wrong?"

"Tot, I don't have time for this. Where is your brother?"

"He's taking a dump."

"Good." I walked to the bathroom with him on my heels.

"Bring me some damn tissue, Thomas. Fuckin' wit' Terrence done made me forget it," Aaron shouted at the door.

I opened the door and pointed the gun at him. "Oh, bitch, you gon' see angels, but it damn sure ain't Angel Soft."

Aaron jumped, grabbed the towel rack with one hand, and the sink with the other. "*Oh, shit. Fuck!*" he shouted as I fired off a shot into the wall above his head. "What the fuck are you doing?"

"Coming to see you, nigga," I yelled, then aimed and squeezed the trigger, pumping hot lead through his shoulder.

He clutched his bleeding shoulder, in pain. "You *muthafucka.*"

Just then, Thomas grabbed my arm and tried to wrestle the gun backward out of my hand, which sent a bullet flying into the hallway wall.

"Let me go, bruh!" I screamed at Thomas.

"Come on, man," Thomas demanded as I struggled to get free. "What the fuck is wrong with you? We family," he added, trying to reason with me.

The mention of the word *family* clicked inside of me. An image of my grandma flashed across my mind, and it was just enough of a reminder to stop me from fighting against Thomas and to lower my gun. Once he realized that I wasn't a threat anymore, he let my arm go, and I shrugged away from him.

"We stopped being family when your bitch-ass brother decided he was gonna push up on my wife. Claiming to be her friend and shit. The way he talked to me on the phone and shit . . . Hell naw, I've been there. He's in love with Trinity."

My words came out scorching hot. Hotter than the lead in Aaron's bleeding shoulder. Thomas stood there wide eyed and obviously oblivious to what had transpired between Aaron and me.

"I'm gonna kill your ass," Aaron growled as sweat poured down his face and blood seeped through his fingers "Shit, it hurts."

His words made me remember exactly why I was on some "Fuck this family" bullshit. I raised my arm and aimed right at his head. "You first, nigga. Send my regards to Grandma."

Thomas ran in front of his brother. "I ain't gon' let you kill Aaron. He was wrong for what he did, but I ain't gon' let you take out my brother. I love you both, but this is *my* brother."

"Move, Thomas."

"No," he said sternly. "If you gon' kill him, kill us both."

"My beef ain't wit' you."

"And I ain't beefin' wit' you. But this is my brother, and y'all are my fam. I will ride or die for both of you."

With Thomas standing in the way, I couldn't pull the trigger. Had Aaron's face been in my line of sight, I would've, but I could not shoot Thomas. He was the baby of the family, and he'd always admired and looked out for me, more so than

Aaron had. He had treated me as if I were his big
brother too. I couldn't do that to him. I loved my
family—all of them, even Aaron. That didn't mean
I wouldn't make an example out of his ass over my
wife, though. It just meant that Thomas saved his
life. My point was made. *Leave Trinity alone.*

After lowering my gun, I put the safety back on.
Thomas and Aaron sighed with relief, and I backed
up and leaned against the doorjamb as Thomas
grabbed a towel so that Aaron could put pressure
on his wound.

"Ugh," Aaron shrieked from the pain. "Terrence,
I swear it's gon' be me and you. Ugh."

"Shut up," Thomas yelled at Aaron. "That's
family, and Trinity is his wife, bro. You was outta
line. Trinity ain't your fuckin' assignment no more,
and she ain't your woman. What the fuck is wrong
with you?"

"Ugh." Aaron grimaced. "Just get me to the
fucking hospital. I'll deal with this nigga later."

"I love you, cuz, but you better stay away from
my wife and kids. Final warning," I said just before
I turned and left.

I was halfway home when my cell phone rang.
I expected it to be Thomas, but it was Trinity.
"Yeah? What's up?" I answered.

All I heard were sniffles. "So, this is it, huh?
You're really done with us? You haven't called, and
I guess you ain't coming home."

Her sadness shredded me. Pinching the bridge of my nose, I gave a deep sigh before I spoke. "Baby, I'm coming home. I just needed some space, and I needed to handle something."

"Handle what?"

"Nothing."

"What have you done, Terrence?"

"Nothing."

"Liar," she said softly.

She knew me, so there was no need to pretend like she wasn't right. "We'll talk about it at home. Just know that I love you."

A grateful sigh sounded through the phone. "I love you too, baby. I love you so much."

The sweet and sincere tone of her voice made me smile. "You do?"

"Of course I do. Only you. I've had poor judgment with some of the things I've done, but, Dreads, baby, you're my husband. No one comes before you, and no one ever will."

A single tear fell from my eye, and I felt like such a bitch. My grandma used to say women brought the female out in a man. I had never understood that until now. I cleared my throat of the emotion. "No one will ever come before you, either, li'l mama, and no one will ever come between us. That I mean. I'll see you at the house, baby," I said, and then we said our goodbyes.

Now that my clearer head had prevailed, I decided to make another phone call. I dialed Thomas.

"How is Aaron?" I asked when he picked up.

"Other than mad as hell, he'll survive. It was a flesh wound. They're stitching him up now." He paused. "You know he gets top-notch service, since he is the man," Thomas joked.

"Yeah," I agreed somberly. I paused for a moment before offering an apology. "Listen, I lost my cool, and I'm sorry. Still, your brother is trippin' over my wife, man."

"Yeah, I know. He keeps telling me that Trinity is just his friend, but I'm starting to think otherwise myself. He's just too protective of her. Something's up. I just don't know what."

"Well, find out," I ordered. "I don't know what it is, either, but I have to know. In the meantime, just know that I'm cool, and I'm sorry."

"You may wanna tell Aaron that. That nigga is the one in the ER with anger management issues, not me."

"True. Call me when you two are outta there. I'll talk to him."

"A'ight. Bet. Go home and sex your wife, cuz. You need it."

I laughed. "You ain't lying. Later."

It felt good to feel like I was back on track with my wife. After today's crazy turn of events, I could honestly say that I believed Trinity when she said she had never slept with Aaron and was only his friend. Something was up with Aaron. I didn't know what the deal was, though. It was weird, because he claimed only to be her friend, and he had never truly pushed up on her, but he reacted to her as if he were her man. Maybe he was going senile. Whatever it was, I was a little concerned about having him around Trinity, because that shit just wasn't right. But since I had no control over whatever was wrong with Aaron, there was one thing I was going to make right. I placed a call.

"Hello, Mr. K." Consuela's voice came through the phone. "Is everything okay between you and Mrs. K?"

"Yes, Consuela. Thanks for asking. Have you picked up the kids from school?"

"Yes, sir. I'm about a block away from your house now."

"Good. I apologize, but I have a last-minute favor to ask—"

Her giggles interrupted my question. "Yes, I can stay and watch the kids for you," she said.

"How'd you know I was gonna ask that?"

"I'm an old wise woman, Mr. K. I know when a man has some making up to do."

Her accuracy made me laugh. "Can you stay until midnight? I'll pay you double overtime."

"For double overtime, you don't even have to ask. I'm in."

"Thanks, Consuela. And please—"

"Don't say anything to Mrs. K. It's a surprise," she said, as if reading my mind. "I already know, Mr. K."

"You've been around us a long time." I noted. "Thanks again."

"No problem."

We hung up, and I dialed another number. A woman picked up.

"Is it too late to get a reservation for tonight? My wife and I are frequent guests. The Kincaids," I asked the maître d' at L2O.

"No, sir, Mr. Kincaid. We have a seven-forty-five reservation available, if you would like."

"Perfect. Dinner for two," I told her, and she secured our slot.

It felt good to know that I would end that day on a good note for Trinity, given how it'd begun. My next call was going to be to housekeeping at our condo. I'd acquired the building and sold it, but I'd decided to surprise Trinity, and so I'd kept one condo for us for when we needed to get away from the kids, like tonight. After dinner, we'd head over there for some romance, with a bottle of Moscato on chill, rose petals on the bed, and a bubble bath by candlelight. Then, later on, I'd hit her with my heavyweight knockout bouts. Oh yeah, it was going to be a good night for my wife.

Chapter 3

Lucinda

"Wake up, birthday girl," I whispered to Nadia.

"Yes! My party is today. Jumpin' Jamboree. Jumpin' Jamboree," she said repeatedly while jumping up and down on her bed.

Her excitement tickled me as I watched her with glee. "Yes, it is. We have to get up and get dressed because Mommy has some errands to run before we get there. It's already ten, so let's go, kiddo."

After I planted a kiss on her forehead, Nadia threw her arms around my neck. "I love you, Mami," she said sweetly.

I wrapped my arms around her and squeezed her gently. "I love you too, *hija.*"

"And I love you both," Aldris said as he strode into Nadia's bedroom and walked over to us.

"*Daddy,*" Nadia shouted as she hugged his neck. "Let me show you what I'm going to wear to my party."

With the skill of a cheetah, she leapt off the bed and ran to her closet. She pulled out her brand-new jean capris with the matching button-down, belted top and her brown slide-in mules.

"See, Papi," she squealed as she ran back and jumped onto her bed. "Isn't it just to die for? Mami says I have to bring socks, but I am going to be *so* cute."

Nadia's happiness about her day was infectious, and Aldris had the same giddy grin on his face as I did, and then he chuckled at her declaration. "Yes, my little *niña*, you are." He turned to me and added, "She definitely gets her fashion sense from you."

"Like mother, like daughter. What can I say?" He wrapped his arms around my shoulders and pulled me in for a hug. "I have to get dressed, so I can go pick up her cake, the balloons, and her gift. Can you make sure that she is ready when I get back?"

"I got this," he said and kissed me.

"Ooh." Nadia giggled at our public display of affection.

"What'cha lookin' at, nosy?" Aldris said as he dove onto the bed and tickled her.

"I'm gonna leave you two and get dressed. Don't play for too long, you guys. We have a party to make," I shouted over their playful banter before I left the room.

The giddiness I felt after leaving Nadia's room felt nothing short of amazing. I had to admit that Aldris had been making a big effort to get our family back to the way we were. He was doing better about including me on decisions concerning Jessica, and he was spending a lot more time with Nadia. He left no room for complaints, and for the first time in a while, I allowed myself to settle into the fact that this blended family would actually work.

Today was both Nadia's and Jessica's parties, and I had full confidence that Aldris was going to somehow make this thing work. I took a quick shower, and after I jumped out, I pulled my curly brown hair up into a ponytail. Then I put on my skinny-leg denim jeans, black Nine West flip-flops, and my double-layered black-gold tank top.

When I came out of the bedroom, Aldris met me in the doorway. He licked his lips. "You're looking good, Mama."

I kissed him. "Thanks, baby, but I have to go. I wish I could've given you a little loving before it was time for me to leave," I said sexily to him.

He playfully popped me on the ass. "I'll handle that later," he assured me with a wink.

I giggled. "Oh, yes, you will. See you in a bit."

We kissed again, and I left to go gather the items for Nadia's party. It seemed like everybody in Atlanta was at every stop I had to make. By the time I ran around to get the cake, the balloons, and the motorized scooter that Aldris and I had got Nadia for her birthday, I was damn near ready for somebody else to actually take her to the party. When I got home, it was nearly 12:15 p.m.

"Hey, the stores were jammed packed today," I said as I ran into the house, completely exhausted. "Is Nadia ready?"

Aldris stood up, with his wallet and keys in hand. "All save for her hair."

I hit my head. "Jeez, Louise. I have to do her hair."

Aldris walked up to me, pulled me into his arms, and gave me a reassuring hug. Cocooned in his embrace, I felt a calm fall over me instantly. "It's a party. Do a simple ponytail and call it a day. Do you need my help with anything else?"

His soothing words put everything into perspective for me. I was overhyped for no reason. "No, go ahead. I know you have to get to Jessica's party. I don't want you to be late. Everything I need is already in the car."

"Okay, give me a kiss," he said, and then he bent down and planted a nice juicy kiss on my lips. "A'ight, Mami. You and my little lady get there safe and enjoy yourselves. I'll see you soon."

"A'ight, Papi. See you in a bit."

"All right, baby." He patted my rear end again. "I can't wait for later on. My gawd," he joked before he left.

Hurriedly, I put Nadia's hair into a ponytail, and then we headed out the door. I wanted to get to Jumpin' Jamboree to make sure that the food and drinks were good to go and that the decorations were set up. Admittedly, I was a little over the top about the party since this was actually the first one that I was able to throw for Nadia at an actual party establishment. All her previous parties had been at the park or at my mom's house because I hadn't been able to afford Chuck E. Cheese's, Putt-Putt's, or Jumpin' Jamboree's price tags. While I had made every birthday party fun for Nadia, it was also a painful reminder that I couldn't give my daughter the few desirable experiences that she wanted. So, this year when she'd asked me to give her a Jumpin' Jamboree party, I was all over it. That was a big deal for both of us.

When I got there at a quarter to one, the rented room space looked amazing. Everything was decorated in the *Raven's Home* television show theme. My mom and Ms. Lily were there when I arrived, along with LaMeka and her kids, Mike and his kids, and some white guy.

"Hey, everyone," I greeted when I walked into the jump area.

"*Abuela*, Grandma Lily," Nadia said, running up and hugging her grandmothers.

While the grands doted on Nadia, I walked over to LaMeka and Mike. "Hey, you guys." I hugged each of them. "Mike, I'm so glad you were able to bring your kids."

"Oh, yeah. I wasn't gonna miss Nadia's party. Nothing against Jennifer or Jessica, but you know Nadia is my little buddy. So where's Dri?"

"At Jessica's party. He'll be here in another hour or so."

"Okay, cool. You need any help with anything?"

"Yeah, I do. First off, did you meet my homegirl LaMeka?"

He nodded. "Kinda. We spoke."

I turned to LaMeka. "This is one of my besties, LaMeka, and LaMeka, this is Aldris's best friend, Mike."

LaMeka looked at me kind of funny, and Mike laughed. "Yeah, I'm the one that gave Lucinda a hard time when she first started dating Aldris," he confessed.

"I thought so," LaMeka said, shaking his hand. "So I guess you two have mended things."

"Oh, yeah," Mike and I answered simultaneously. We spun around to face each other and quickly called, "Jinx, double jinx, triple jinx."

"Man, give it up. Isn't it bad enough that I've already whipped your ass three times on *Guitar Hero*? You can't win with me," I joked.

"Whatever, Lu. I got you this Friday, though. You damn sure ain't gonna beat me at *Madden*."

I fanned him off and looked at LaMeka. "And that's what he said about *Guitar Hero*."

He and LaMeka burst into laughter.

"You two are some damn clowns," LaMeka said.

"Yeah, he is," I said, playfully nudging Mike. "And where are my babies?" I asked, looking around for LaMichael and Tony Jr.

"Child, you know they are already in the inflatable with Nadia," LaMeka said and pointed them out. "I have someone I'd like you to meet." She pulled the white guy forward. "This is the man I was telling you about, Gavin Randall. Gavin, this is one of my best friends, Lucinda."

Talk about stunned. I was shocked out of my mind. He really was white. I thought she had meant "white," as in having a really bright complexion, like Tony, but this dude was really Caucasian. But, hey, whatever floated her boat. I was just thankful it wasn't Tony on her arm. White or not, dude was fly as hell and fine as hell too. *Go, Meka. Go 'head and get down.*

I shook his hand. "Pleased to finally meet you. Please enjoy yourself. You're in the clique now. My fiancé, Aldris, will be here later on. This is his best friend, Mike."

"Nice to meet you. LaMeka tells me about you, Charice, and Trinity all the time." He shook Mike's hand. "Nice to meet you, bruh."

Mike nodded. "Likewise, man."

I offered Mike the keys to my car. "I have the cake, some balloons, and her gift in my car."

"I got you," he said and took the keys out of my hand.

"I'll help," Gavin offered. The two of them walked out to get the rest of the party items.

"Well, he did a complete three-sixty," LaMeka said once they were out of earshot.

"Yes, he did, and I'm glad. Lucinda is a great person," Ms. Lily said from behind.

LaMeka and I both turned around, and I hugged her. "Thanks, Mama Lily. I'm so glad you could make it." I waved my hand at LaMeka. "This is one of my best friends, LaMeka," I said.

Ms. Lily hugged her. "You're in the wedding, aren't you?" she asked.

"Oh, yes, ma'am. I wouldn't miss these nuptials for the world."

"Are you going to Jessica's party?" I asked Ms. Lily curiously.

"I'm not dealing with Al's attitude. I will probably go there once he gets here," she said. Their relationship had been rocky ever since she had begun dating again. Well, that and the fact that Aldris had caught her and her beau, Mr. Franklin, having sex.

After taking her hand in mine, I caressed it lovingly. "I understand. It'll be all right."

My mom walked up and hugged me from behind. "Ay, *hija*, you're stealing my company?" she asked, referring to Ms. Lily.

I turned around and hugged her back. "No, ma'am. I'll let you two ladies have at it."

"Aw. You two make me wish I had a daughter," Ms. Lily cooed.

"You do," I assured her and hugged her.

LaMeka whipped out her camera and hollered, "*Moment*." All three of us posed, and she snapped away.

The party was moving along just fine. Within ten minutes, there were eighteen children at Nadia's party, and they were all having a blast. Mike, Gavin, LaMeka, and I all sat around joking and watching the children play. LaMeka and Mike took great pictures for me and even caught me clowning and jumping on one of those inflatables with Nadia.

I kept eyeing the time, and after about fifty minutes, I wanted to call Aldris, but I decided to give it a minute. I didn't want to seem too pushy. It was Jessica's day too, but when five minutes after two arrived and he still hadn't shown up, I had to make that call. At least I needed to make sure he was okay.

While everyone was in the jump area, I stepped into Nadia's party room and called him. No answer. *Shit*. "Hi, Aldris," I said to his voicemail.

"Baby, call me. I'm getting a little concerned. I hope you're okay and all is well. Nadia is going to be eating in the next twenty minutes or so. Give me a call. Love you." I hung up and walked back into the jump area, where LaMeka and the crew were.

"Hey there, stranger," Ms. Ana, Raul's mom, said to me.

Gasping, I hugged her tightly. "Ms. Ana, it's so good to see you. I'm so glad you could make it."

"I was determined not to miss my *niña*'s big party. Where is she?"

"Playing with the other kids. My mom and Aldris's mom are in the play area, watching over them."

"Okay, well, I'm going to grab a seat in there with them." She hugged me again. "It's so good to see you."

"You too," I said, gripping her tightly.

"Is that her other grandma?" Mike asked when I sat back down.

"Yes. The resemblance is shocking, isn't it?"

Mike and Gavin both nodded in agreement.

"Is her dad coming?" Gavin asked me.

"Hell would freeze over first," I answered.

"Gotcha." Gavin put up his hands, as if he were backing away from that conversation.

"Did you talk to Dri? It's getting kinda late," Mike said.

I shook my head. "Nope. I left a message."

"I'll try him," Mike said, then got up to go and call.

To no avail. He returned a minute later and shook his head.

I pretended like I wasn't bothered by Aldris' tardiness, but it was quickly chipping away at me. I kept myself occupied by trippin' with LaMeka, Gavin, and Mike, but with every minute that passed, I got more pissed off. Even Aldris' mom tried to call him, and she didn't get an answer. At 2:20 p.m., when Mike came back and told me that he hadn't got an answer for the second time, I decided to step away and call again. And—surprise, surprise—I got his voicemail again.

"Aldris. This isn't funny. You need to give me a call or something. You promised me and Nadia you'd be here. Now come on. She'll be cutting her cake at exactly two forty. Bye."

"Still no answer?" Mike said from behind me.

I shook my head in frustration. "No."

"Hey, it's okay. He'll show up, and I'm sure with a good explanation," Mike said and hugged me. "Don't get upset."

"I'm trying, Mike. I am."

After I took a beat to shake off my rising anger, we walked back to the party room, where my mom and Ms. Lily had herded the kids. Mike, Gavin, and LaMeka helped me set up the plates with the pizza and the juice drinks. After I made sure everyone had enough pizza and juice, I slipped off to call Aldris again.

"Aldris. It's two thirty-eight. I'm about to bring out Nadia's cake in two minutes. In exactly two minutes, you better be here," I seethed angrily to his voicemail and hung up.

My eyes hawked the clock and the entrance as I paced around until 2:41 p.m. It was then that LaMeka approached me. "Honey, do you think we should wait any longer for Aldris? It's coming up on a quarter till, and they'll charge you extra if you go over your party time."

LaMeka's words were the realization that Aldris had broken his promise to me and, worst of all, to Nadia. That searing pain caused emotions to well up, and tears threatened to spring forth from my eyes. Quickly, I swiped the single tear that managed to fall. It wasn't that I was sad. I was mad as hell. The only problem was I refused to show that to anyone, so I had to tamp down my emotions.

"No, let's go ahead and do this."

LaMeka sat the cake on the table, stuck in the number seven candle, and lit it. Then I crowned Nadia with her birthday tiara.

"All right, everybody, are we ready to sing 'Happy Birthday'?" I asked, making a big effort to be excited. All the kids hollered yes, so I directed everyone. "Okay, everybody, on the count of three,"

I said. Then I did the countdown, and everybody sang "Happy Birthday" to Nadia.

After the song, Nadia leaned on me and whispered, "Where's Daddy?"

Right then, my heart ripped in half. Unless Aldris had been involved in an accident and was laid up in Grady, unconscious, he was going to have hell to pay with me. I promised I was going to stick my foot so far up his ass that he'd need a team of surgeons to physically remove it. I was that serious and that angry.

Piss me off, shit on me, and dog me out even, but he had crossed the wrong muthafucking line when he'd walked over my baby girl's feelings. Now that . . . that was a deal breaker. Now I was in "Fuck 'em" girl mode, because the shit had definitely hit the fucking fan. Nobody—absolutely nobody—hurt Nadia. I hadn't let her raggedy-ass father get away with treating her like trash, so I damn sure was not going to allow Aldris to do the same.

"Um, I'm sure he's on his way. For now, just blow out the candle, and don't forget to make a wish," I whispered.

She closed her eyes, made a wish, then blew out her candle.

I rushed out the door with my cell phone in hand and called Aldris one final time. "You missed the party. Thanks for remembering her on her

special day like you promised you would, asshole,"
I said angrily, my voice full of sarcasm. Then I
hung up and turned my cell phone off.

Since time was of the essence, I passed out cake
hurriedly as Nadia opened her gifts. With about
seven minutes to spare, the attendant, LaMeka,
Gavin, Mike, and I began packing up and cleaning
the area as the children's parents began picking
them up. At 3:01 p.m., we were all in the parking
lot and set to leave.

LaMeka hugged me. "I'm sure he has a really
good reason, honey. Don't get crazy. I know you.
Hear him out. Do you need me to stay with you?"

I shook my head and looked back at Gavin and
Mike, who were chatting it up. "No, Mami. You
go ahead and kick it with your little Caucasian
persuasion," I replied, attempting to joke around.

She laughed. "He's Cablanasian."

I looked at her, puzzled. "What? I've never
heard of that."

She laughed and playfully slapped my arm with
the back of her hand. "Girl, Tiger Woods."

"OMG, girl. Not Tiger." I laughed as it dawned
on me that Tiger had made that crazy statement
about his racial makeup. "Gavin is pretty cool,
though. I'm happy for you. White, Cablanasian,
or whatever, he's got my vote. He's great with the
boys," I said, noticing how he held LaMichael in

his arms and how Tony Jr. stayed right by his side as he talked with Mike.

"He is. We'll see where it goes, though. For now, I'm good."

"And that's all I wanted to hear. You go ahead and spend some quality time with your man, *chica*. I'm good," I assured her.

Ms. Lily was worried and upset with Aldris and decided to go search for him. I hugged my mom and Ms. Ana goodbye before loading Nadia in the car. Mike decided he'd follow me to the house to help me unpack. I was so happy that Nadia fell asleep as soon as I started driving, because I couldn't take it. I had so many pent-up emotions that I just let it all out. I was surprised I was able to see my way home, because I was a bucket of tears by the time I arrived. When I got out and opened the front door, Mike was right behind me.

"My kids are asleep, so I'm just gonna help . . ." He looked down at me once I got the door open, and saw my tear-stained face. "Aw, Lucinda. Damn."

"No, no. I'm good," I said between sniffles. "Just go home with your kids."

He grabbed my hand and walked me inside. "Sit down."

I plopped on the sofa, and Mike walked into the hallway bathroom and came out with the box of Kleenex. "Here, take this. I'm going to bring Nadia in the house and get the things out of your car."

Dazed, hurt, and confused, I sat there as he brought in my Sleeping Beauty and put her in her bed; then he brought in all the food, the cake, and the gifts. I was so distraught that I just sat there in total silence, crying.

Mike walked over and kneeled down in front of me to bring his six-foot, five-inch frame closer to eye level with me. "Do you want me to stay until he gets here? Or I could go looking for him for you."

I shook my head no as I toyed with my Kleenex. "You have your kids today. Spend your time with them. This is my situation to handle with Aldris."

"All right," he said begrudgingly and stood up. "I'm sure everything will work itself out, Lu. Aldris loves you and Nadia."

I stood up and walked him to the door. "Yeah, just not as much as he loves Jessica and, hell, for all I know, Jennifer."

Mike rubbed his face. "Man. Well, I can't tell you how to feel. It's just something you and Dri gonna have to get through together. I hope that you do."

"Thank you." I offered him the only thing I could muster up, a half smile. "You've been such a good friend to me, and it really means a lot. You don't realize how much."

A silent beat passed between us before he brought his hand to my face and rubbed his thumb on my chin. "That's what friends are for."

His kind gesture caused me to thrust myself into his arms for a much-needed hug. Only instead of it being a brief hug, he held me for a few moments, and I allowed him. I knew it probably wasn't the best idea to let another man hold me like that, but I needed the comfort. His powerful and masculine arms encased me, as if to assure me that I was safe there. It was the first time I noticed Mike's physique. No muscle was left uncut. His facial features were smooth, and he had a strong jawline and a neatly trimmed goatee. I pulled away from him, and he cupped my face in his hands. His eyes held such sincerity.

"Lucinda," he said softly, then closed his eyes and breathed out.

"What?" I asked faintly.

He put his hands down and opened his eyes before stepping back. "It'll all work out for you two. I'll try to hit up Dri later. Take it easy, Mama," he said, then turned to leave.

"Bye, Mike."

He threw up deuces as he kept walking until he made it to his still-running Lincoln Navigator. I walked outside and watched him. He jumped in the SUV, waved goodbye to me, and backed out of my driveway.

Once I walked back inside and sat down, I realized that I actually wasn't as upset as I had been earlier. I had Mike to thank for that. He'd managed to calm me down in a way no one except Aldris and my mother had ever been able to do when I was that pissed off. I just prayed that the sense of peace that I was feeling would last me until I saw Aldris. I wanted to believe that something horrid had happened to Aldris, but in my gut, I knew that it hadn't. In my gut, I knew that he'd drawn the line in the sand, and it was me and Nadia on one side and him, Jennifer, and Jessica on the other. I sat in the dark, silent family room with that thought and twisted my engagement ring around.

Chapter 4

Aldris

I know what you're thinking, and you're wrong. Dead wrong. I did not skip out on Nadia's party. I have a perfectly good reason as to why I missed it. In fact, you may even laugh a little bit. Well, maybe not, but you'll understand. I promise you will. Just please, let me explain. I kept rehearsing those words in my mind as I sped all the way to the house.

I hit myself in the head and then gripped the steering wheel so hard that even my black knuckles were turning white. "How could I miss Nadia's party? Lucinda is gonna kill me. Nadia has probably cried her eyeballs out. I'm so fucked. So royally fucked," I said aloud to myself.

I swore, if it wasn't for bad luck, I don't think I'd have any luck at all. I couldn't even imagine how far off the Richter scale Lucinda was going to be today. I contemplated stopping to buy some full-body armor and a thick Bible to shield me with the whole armor of God from the wrath of Lucinda Rojas. One thing was for certain, she did not play about Nadia. Period. You had better believe that if you wanted to be a part of Lucinda's life—whether you were a friend, family member, or her man—you were going to have to love her daughter. You couldn't help but respect that, and it was one of the reasons I loved her so much.

Not only was this Nadia's special day, but it was truly special for Lucinda too. She'd confided in me that this was the first time she could afford to have Nadia's birthday party at a kid party establishment, so I knew it was a big deal for her, and rightfully so. I loved when Lucinda chalked up a new accomplishment in her life. No matter how small it may have seemed to others, I knew it was a big deal for her. A huge deal. That was why I knew the ramifications of my actions were astronomical, so I prayed for the best when I finally got to the house.

"Hello?" I said, answering my ringing cell phone, which was plugged into its car charger.

"What happened to you today?" my mom demanded angrily.

"Ma, it's a long story. I didn't mean to miss the party."

"Well, how about you shorten it up for me?" she said, obviously irritated.

"Listen, Ma, I wish I could, but I need to talk to Lucinda first, and I'm trying to prepare myself for that battle. Please let me talk to you later about it."

"You, my son, are messing up. I just want you to know that."

"I hear you, Ma." I tried to mask my annoyance. I didn't need her to confirm shit that I already knew.

"Don't *hear* me, Aldris. *Feel* me, as you young people say. Lucinda is your future wife, but you won't have her if you keep down this path you're on," she preached.

At this point, I couldn't mask my irritation anymore. "*Ma*," I whined.

"Okay, whatever, Al. You wanna complain about my advice? Fine, I won't give it, and you don't have to take it, but I wasn't married over thirty years for nothing."

"It's not like you remember that you were married in the first place," I said, letting these words slip out. "Oh, shit, Ma. I'm sorry."

"Goodbye, Aldris," she snapped, using my full name, and hung up in my face.

Great, man. You're just fucking up with everybody, I said silently to myself as I hung up.

As soon as I did, my cell rang again, and Mike's info came across the screen. I answered the call. "Hey, man."

"What are you sounding so down for? Lucinda is the upset one."

"Listen, I already know. I'm less than five min-utes away from my house, and I know she's gonna act a fool, so I really don't need it from you." After my mother's rant, I didn't need to hear it from my boy too. "And since when did you become such a fucking advocate for Lucinda? I would've thought you'd be happy to see us having rifts. One minute you hate her because she was a stripper, and the next you're fucking bosom buddies, battling on the Wii and having Friday night fight parties to-gether."

"I've long forgotten that foolishness, and you know it. You just want somebody to pet you right now in your wrongness, and I'm not gonna do it. Your girl was so fucking heartbroken that I'm embarrassed for you. I told you once before that Lucinda loves you. She's a good person, and she deserves so much better than what you're giving her now. You're gonna fuck around and lose out. Believe that, bruh."

"Wow. Look who is really growing the fuck up! Now, how is it that you can tell me how to handle my issues with my girl, and you can't even find one of your own? Oh, I know why. 'Cause you're a dog. That's why. I'm not doing anything to push Lucinda away, because I do love her. But I don't owe you or anybody else an explanation. I'm going home to give that to my girl, so you can be easy.

You don't have to worry about *my* girl. I got this, pimpin'."

"Amazing. Okay, playa, you go 'head on and handle that, then," Mike scoffed with an attitude.

"A'ight, *playa*."

"Later," he said abruptly and hung up.

My phone rang one more time as I was turning into my neighborhood. I picked up on the second ring. "Hey, Jenn."

"Hey, did you make the party in good time?"

"No, after I left, there was a stalled vehicle. Lu is pissed off."

"Oh, shit. Do you want me to call and try to explain it to her? I mean, maybe she'll be a little more understanding if someone can vouch for you," she said sincerely.

"No, I think the last person she'd want to hear vouching for me right now is you. It's best if I do this alone."

"You might be right about that. Are you at home?"

"Getting ready to pull onto my street as we speak."

"Let me let you go, then. I hope it works out for you."

"Me and you both."

I pulled into the garage and parked next to Lucinda's car and took a deep breath. I knew I was in for some serious explaining, and I felt like I was about to be in the fight of my life. Slowly, I got out of the car and looked at my watch. It was 3:35

p.m. *Damn. Lord, please help me,* I thought as I unlocked the door.

When I walked in, the house was completely quiet. Nothing was on. I didn't hear a peep, a woot, or a holler, and I didn't know whether to be grateful or to be prepared to bob and weave. Moving slowly from room to room, I searched for Lucinda but didn't see her. I kept moving through the house until I reached our family room, where I found Lucinda lying back on the sofa, staring straight up at the ceiling.

"Lucinda?" I called out to her. "I'm home, baby."

"So I see," she said quietly, her hand across her forehead, as she continued to stare blankly at the ceiling.

Placing my hands in my pockets, I leaned against the wall. I was so scared to move, I didn't even take off my baseball cap. "Um, can you sit up, so I can talk to you, please . . . if you don't mind?"

Her eyes closed, and she blew out a deep and weighty breath, then sat up and planted her feet on the floor. She clasped her hands together and propped her chin on her hands. Her curly hair was loose and in disarray, and she kept shaking her right leg.

"Yes," she said, clearly not beat for the bullshit.

Somewhere from deep within, I found the courage to walk up so I could face her, but I stayed my distance. "Let me just first say that I am so sorry, Lu. Where is Nadia, so that I may personally apologize to her?"

"She was asleep in her room, but my mother came and picked her up not long after we got here."

"Understandable."

She looked up at me and waited to hear what else I had to say.

"Well, I guess I should get straight to the point. I know what you're thinking, and you're wrong. Dead wrong. I did not skip out on Nadia's party. I have a perfectly good reason as to why I missed it. In fact, you may even laugh a little bit. Well, maybe not, but you'll understand. I promise you will. Just please, let me explain." The words flowed out exactly as I'd rehearsed them in the car.

She slowly flung her hands outward to indicate that I should continue.

I scratched my head, because Lucinda was way too calm for this. This had to be the quiet before the storm. "Okay, well, I was leaving the party at exactly one fifty so that I could have time to get to Nadia's party in time. Before I left, Jennifer wanted me to eat some cake and watch Jessica open the gift we got her. So, at one fifty-five, I kissed Jessica on the forehead and left. I was five minutes up the road when I remembered that I left my cell phone on the table by the empty pizza boxes, so I had to go back. By the time I got back there, grabbed my phone, and started heading to Jumpin' Jamboree, it was close to two twenty. I saw your missed call, but my battery was damn near dead, so I couldn't even get the call to connect. On top of that, my charger had fallen on the passenger's-side floor, so I couldn't get it to plug my phone in." I looked down at the floor and then continued.

"At that point, I hauled ass to get to the party, and I'll be damned if two college girls' car didn't stall in the road and completely block traffic. Another guy and I pushed their car onto the side of the road, and by the time I got back into the car, it was two fifty-five. I knew I probably wouldn't make it, since I still had a good distance to go and traffic was a beast. I got to Jumpin' Jamboree at, like, five after three, praying that maybe you all were still there, but the people at the front desk said I'd just missed you guys. I ran back to the car, grabbed my charger, plugged up my phone, and listened to your messages. By then, I already knew I was pretty much in for it. And by the tone of your messages, I am. That's my story in a nutshell," I said and then breathed for what seemed like the first time since I had started explaining. I knew it sounded crazy as hell, but on everything I loved, it was the truth.

She sat there for a few minutes, as if she were contemplating my story. Then she stood up and folded her arms.

"Do I have the word 'dumbass' stamped on my fucking forehead?" she asked and then stared at me in silence. She stared at me as if she were expecting an answer.

Fuck. I opened my mouth to attempt a response, but before I could say a word, she interrupted me.

"You really expect me to sit up here and believe that you were doing all of this trying to get to Nadia's party? Hell, I would've expected you to at least give me the fucking decency to admit that you put my feelings and Nadia's feelings on the fucking back burner for Jessica. At the very least, I could've said you were honest," she hollered.

"Lucinda, I'm telling you the truth. I swear to God, baby," I pleaded as she began pacing the floor.

Hurricane Lucinda was brewing, and I knew that I was about to be caught in the middle of the storm.

She threw her hands up. "Really? The truth? Aldris, if you were only five minutes up the road and it took you only five minutes to get back, why the fuck did it take you nearly fifteen fucking minutes to get the damn cell phone? Huh? Then it conveniently wasn't charged, and your charger was unreachable. Then two poor souls needed your help to get their car out of the roadway. Were they stalled horizontally across all the lanes so no-fucking-body could get past them? I mean, really, dude, you deserve a fucking medal. No, no, better yet, I'm going to the Pope to ask him to declare you

for sainthood. Saint Aldris Sharper the First." She
rattled all this off so fast, I could barely keep up.

"Lu, baby, I don't know why it took so long to
get back from the phone. I had to find a parking
spot, and you know how crowded Putt-Putt is
on a Saturday afternoon. The two young ladies
were blocking me and the man behind me, and it
would've been a bitch trying to get around them.
You know people in Atlanta don't believe in letting
nobody in their lane to hold them up. I figured it'd
be quicker to move them. I was just trying to get to
the party. Yes, my phone's battery was low, and my
charger was unreachable. I'm telling you the whole
truth. I don't know what else to say," I told her,
pleading my case.

She stood there with her arms folded and her
eyes misting. "Aldris, do you want to know why
this is so fucking unbelievable to me?"

I threw my hands up. "Yes, I'd love to know
why."

"Because it makes no fucking sense!" she
screamed. "Even if I took what you just said and
actually believed this cockamamie story, there's
one thing that just doesn't seem right. You are a
very bright and intelligent man, so to me, there
was one logical solution for all of this, and it seems
you would've thought of it."

Seriously, I was lost, so I asked, "And what is
that?"

"Why didn't you just bring your ass to the party and call Jennifer about your phone from Jumpin' Jamboree? Every adult at the party had a cell phone. The facility has phones you could've used. You would've been at Nadia's party way before they left theirs, so Jennifer could've just kept the phone for you. Had you been courteous enough to call me and let me know you were on the way, you would've had your fucking phone, and better yet, you would've known that it wasn't charged. This is the same shit that I've been screaming about—a failure to communicate."

I had to lean back against the bookcase, because she had knocked the wind out of me with that one. In hindsight, she was absolutely correct. I couldn't even be mad or argue, because that was exactly what I should have done.

"Baby, you're right. I'm so sorry, and I can't apologize enough for this. Please believe me when I say that it didn't even dawn on me to do that. If it had, you know I would've done that. It makes perfect sense, and it was the perfect solution, but I'm not perfect, and I made a mistake. I realize that I really fucked up, and I want to make it up to you and Nadia. Can you please forgive me?"

The deathly glare she threw my way made me want to never miss making a phone call again in my life. When I saw tears streaming down her face, I knew we were approaching a category 5 storm. "Of course it didn't dawn on you. When it comes to common courtesy and putting Nadia and me first, it *never* dawns on you. You feel like you're free to do whatever you want to do when it comes to Jessica and Jennifer. Meanwhile, you throw us on the back burner at free will, and we're just supposed to sit back and accept these two new people in our lives, and this new situation, without showing any type of emotion about it because you say so."

"Wait. Whoa. Wait a minute. I've never tried to force you to deal with this—"

"Yeah, right. You don't want me to confront Jennifer, because that's Jessica's mom. I'm not supposed to tell you that you're not giving Nadia enough time, because then I'm trying to make you choose between your daughters. I'm not supposed expect to come first, because then I'm not being understanding of you having to develop a relationship with Jessica. Anytime I have ever tried to stick up for Nadia and me, you've always accused me of being the bitch, just not in those exact words. And the only thing I've asked is for you to be courteous of our feelings and to keep me first, because as your future wife, I deserve that."

"You do deserve that, and I am trying like hell. I'm not gonna get everything right, but it's hard enough just trying to deal with this—"

The interruption was instant. "So you expect me to just roll over and deal with whatever you dish out?"

Exasperated, I bit out, "I look for you to *support* me."

"Fine! Then *support* me too," she screamed, her hands flailing in the air. "Give me courtesy calls, make it to appointments and parties when you're supposed to, and treat me like I'm the wife instead of your chick on the fucking side."

By now, Lucinda was damn near hysterical. I couldn't bear to watch her unravel, and I knew that I had to put whatever frustrations I had aside to bring calm and somehow repair the cracks in our relationship. We were standing on shaky ground, and my mother's words pounded in my head: *Lucinda is your future wife, but you won't have her if you keep down this path you're on.*

After easing up to her, I gently wrapped my arms around her and held her close. She fought against me, but the more she fought, the tighter I held on. I couldn't think of anything else to do. I didn't realize how much she had bottled up on the inside, and hearing all of this had made me feel even worse. Every time she'd needed me, I'd let her down, and now I'd let Nadia down too. I didn't want to be *that* man, but I was.

"I'm so sorry, baby. I didn't realize it. I'll do better by you. I swear."

My words lingered in the air as I continued
to hold and rock her. After a few moments, she
stopped resisting and caved in to my embrace. A
wail like I'd never heard before escaped her throat
and ripped through my soul. I'd been the one that
had protected her from Raul and had consoled
her through the debacle with her father, yet now I
was the one that was hurting her. It tore me up on
the inside to feel as though, out of everyone, I had
broken her. I'd broken her when I had promised
her that she never had to worry with me. I felt like
the greatest disappointment in life. Not just to her,
but to myself. Her next words were enough to
make me crumple to my knees.

"I just want to know that we matter to you,
Aldris," she whimpered.

I pulled back a few inches and held her face in
my hands. "You do. You both do. And I'll show it to
you. I promise, baby."

My desperation for her to feel how sincere
I was caused my own tears to fall. Finally, she
reached up and hugged me around my neck, and
I squeezed her body close. So close, we seemed
melded together. I was basking in this moment
when I suddenly felt her body go stiff as a board,
and she pushed me back.

"You smell just like Jennifer's fragrance."

"Huh?"

"Don't fucking lie to me. I remember that smell. She had on the same perfume the first time she came to our house. Why do you smell like Jennifer, Aldris?" she stormed, on the verge of being livid.

"I don't know what you're—"

"You have lipstick on your collar and a lipstick print on your neck, Aldris."

She pointed to the side of my neck. Then she stepped back, with her arms folded across her chest, as if waiting for whatever excuse I could drum up to support my reason for this offense. Truth was, I had none, because at the moment, I had no clue what she was referring to or why she even thought I had evidence of lipstick stains on my collar and neck. My mind was focused on the here and now; I was still trying to correct my wrong about the party. I struggled to catch up with the accusations. As my mind scrambled, it suddenly hit me.

Shit. When I'd got ready to leave Jessica's party, I had hugged Jennifer, and she had brushed her lips against my neck during the hug. I hadn't thought anything of it at the time, and I had never even thought about Jennifer's lipstick. I sure as hell didn't want to tell Lucinda about that hug, given my track record with Jennifer. Now I couldn't hide it. I had to come clean.

"When I got ready to leave, I hugged her. That's it."

She shoved me into the bookshelf so hard that some of the books fell off. "You hugged her? For what? You know what? I'm so sick and tired of your and Jennifer's inability to keep your fucking hands off each other. You said the last time you wouldn't touch her again."

"It was just a friendly—"

"It's always friendship and innocence with you. Just like you calling her 'baby' at the family gathering was innocent too, huh?"

"Huh? What? I don't even remember calling her that."

"Oh, well, I most certainly do. Let me refresh your memory. 'Baby, that thing was so dry, I had to drink a gallon of water just to swallow it, and two gallons once it hit my stomach.' I let that shit slide because the girls were there, but oh, believe you me, had they not been there, I would've pulled out my blade and cut both of y'all's asses every which way but a loose."

Why me? I hit my forehead. *Damn.* Now that she mentioned it, I remembered saying that. I mean, it was a figure of speech. She'd taken it way out of context. "Lu, it was just an inn—"

"Oh, please! Fucking spare me the 'innocent gesture' comment, Aldris. The bigger issue is that now you can't even keep your damn promises to me. Jennifer comes before me with even that? If that's the case, take your ass over to Jennifer's house and be with her. Because you damn sure respect her more as your woman than you do me."

Attempting to step around the books and recover from being knocked backward, I put my hands up to block any further strikes. "Wait a minute. This is getting outta hand."

She shoved me again. "You've been outta hand," she roared.

I reached for her, trying to show that I was peaceful and that this was unnecessary. "Lucinda."

She snatched away from me and hollered, "You will not disrespect me. Get out!"

"What?"

"Leave me alone, Aldris. I can't even think right now, and I need for you to go," she said angrily, her voice low.

Defiance took over me. Ain't no way I was leaving with our shit jacked up like this, and I definitely wasn't about to get kicked out of my own house. "We need to talk about this—"

She picked up a book and threw it at me. "I'm beyond talking!" she screamed and hurled two more books in my direction. "Get away from me!"

"Baby," I yelled as I dodged books and then figurines. "I'm sorry."

"Leave now!"

Distraught and not wanting the situation to escalate any further, I grabbed my keys and left.

Before I pulled out of the driveway, I sat in my
car for a minute, wondering how our relationship
had gotten to this point. The last thing Lu needed
to see was the slightest evidence that I'd broken
a promise or what she presumed was a sign of
unfaithfulness. I hadn't even been thinking about
this when I hugged Jennifer, but I had broken
a promise to Lucinda when I did that. What the
hell was up with me and my foresight these days?
Couldn't God just spare me this once? Everything
that had happened up to this point was completely
innocent, but I always ended up looking like the
guilty party.

I drove around aimlessly, going over and over
everything in my mind, wondering if my relationship was even salvageable. My scrambled thoughts
led me to stop at a sports bar and grab a beer or
two or three. I sat at the bar for hours. After four
tequila shots, three beers, and a Hennessy and
Coke, I felt right—and the bartender wouldn't
serve me any more alcohol anyway—so I paid my
tab, left the bar, and sat in the car for a while. I
didn't even know if I could go back to my own
house. Hell, with that alcohol in my system, I
didn't think it would be a good idea for either one
of us if I returned to the house. I understood why
Lucinda was pissed, but if she threw something at
me in the state I was in, shit was gonna get ugly

real quick. Ain't nothing worse than that ball of C-4 at the house mixed with a sloppy drunk.

I was just about to close my eyes when my cell phone rang. I took the call. "Yeah, hello." My slurred words came out sounding foreign to me.

"Aldris?"

"Yeah. Who this?"

"Jennifer. Have you been drinking?"

I knew I had to be drunk when I laughed at Jennifer's question. "Yep. A whole lot."

"Oh my God. Where are you at?" she asked.

I looked up at the ceiling of my car, then to the left and to the right. "At . . . Shit, I don't know. I forget the name of this place. Um, hold up. Let me ask this man walking by." With the phone still to my ear, I rolled down my window and hollered, "Ay, my man. What's the name of this place?"

"Dugan's, man."

"You heard that?" I said into the phone. "Dogans. Dogarts. Domans."

"Stay put," Jennifer commanded. "I'm coming to get you."

The line went dead, and I was left staring at my phone. The next thing I knew, I heard a tap on my window and jumped.

"Shit," I yelled, then I looked out to see Jennifer. I opened the door. "How long you been standing there?" I staggered out of the car.

"I just got here. Can you even walk?"

After three unstable steps, I found my footing but then leaned on the car to keep from falling down. "Yeah, I got it. I could've drove."

"Yeah, drove yourself straight into the grave. Get over on the passenger's side," she demanded. "I'ma drive your car back to my house."

"Now who's drunk? If you're driving your car . . . wait, *my* car . . . then who's driving . . . *your* . . . *mine* . . . How did you get up here?"

She rolled her eyes and pursed her lips. "Mm-hmm. Yeah, you are in great condition to drive. My neighbor rode with me, so she is gonna drive my car. Now go get in." She pointed in the direction of the passenger's side, and I obeyed.

By the time we pulled up in her driveway, just enough of the alcohol's effects had worn off for me to show concern for Jessica, but I was still pretty tipsy. "Hey, where's Jessica? I don't want her to see me like this."

"I'm already on that. She's spending the night down the street, at her friend's house, so you can recoup in peace."

She dialed her neighbor and thanked her for the favor, and then we walked in the house, where I plopped on the sofa.

"Man, I haven't been this wasted since college." I grabbed one of her throw pillows and hugged it.

She hit my feet. "Shoes off my sofa, please."

After sitting up, I kicked my shoes off, and she sat down next to me, crossed her legs, and stared at me.

"So?" she asked.

"So, what?" I asked, leaning my head back and closing my eyes.

"So how about those Hawks?" she scoffed. "What the hell do you think I'm talking about, Aldris? What happened between you and Lucinda?"

"Man, do I have to go into that right now? I can barely think straight. Let alone go back through that horror story. What time is it, anyway?" I rubbed my forehead.

"It's a little after seven."

She stood up and headed to the kitchen. "I'm gonna make you some coffee," she said over her shoulder.

A few minutes later, she came back with a steaming mug, and I sat up. I blew and sipped without looking. "Yuck. It's black." I stared into the cup.

She pointed to the cup. "It's strong. And you need it." She sat back down. "Now that I have your attention, what happened?"

I put the cup down, slid my hands down the length of my jean shorts, and straightened my Polo shirt before I explained the whole story to her. "We went around and around until finally the truth behind her anger came out." I picked up the coffee cup and took a huge gulp.

Jennifer shrugged. "So, what was the truth?"

I felt uneasy telling her, but I was so confused and fucked up with that alcohol in my system that I needed to talk to someone. Maybe Jennifer could kind of help out, being that she was smack dead in the middle of the whole thing.

I leaned forward and looked over at her. "She feels that I put her and Nadia on the back burner for you and Jessica. I mean, she wasn't saying for me to ignore you all, nor was she acting like Jessica was a nuisance in our lives. She was just saying that I tend to do what I want for you all and with you all without regards to our relationship and household. Since I'm not used to being the parent with an outside kid, I kinda like . . . I guess . . . expect her to suck up everything without complaining and support me without my really supporting her."

Jennifer nodded and pushed her hair behind her ears. "I see. Well, are you?" she asked.

"I don't know. Hell, maybe I am. I see some of what she's saying." I shrugged, leaned back, and held my head, which was fucking spinning. Why couldn't I just fucking drink and drown in peace?

"Like what?" she asked.

"Like, I promised her that I wouldn't be caught in a compromising position with you again, and right when she was gonna forgive me for missing Nadia's party, she spotted this on my collar." I pointed to her lipstick.

She leaned over and made an "uh-oh" face. "Oh my. I see it now. I'm really sorry about that."

She turned to face me, with one knee propped on the sofa. "Listen, I never meant to cause a rift in your relationship with Lucinda. We have a past, and well, that past keeps us tied together in the present and future by Jessica. I think what's hardest for her is that you are an involved parent with your outside child. You don't have to deal with baby daddy drama, because Raul isn't around, and she's never had to deal with baby mamas and outside children in regards to her man. It's an adjustment for both of you. You're trying to find your way in this too. And, hell, at least you're trying. Most men don't give a damn anyway. In that respect, Lucinda is lucky, because she has a man who won't abandon his responsibilities. I'm not saying that her feelings aren't valid, because the things she's feeling are very real to her, but at the same time, as your fiancée, she should know where your heart is."

With my head leaned back on the sofa, I allowed my eyes to fall on her. "And I guess that's what she's questioning. Where my heart is."

There was a brief pause as Jennifer's eyes danced around before she swallowed hard. "That's easy . . . with her," she said, shifting in her seat.

"True." I nodded. I looked at how uneasy she'd become. "Let me ask you a question, though. Where is your heart?"

Her eyes fell downward as she fiddled with her hair. "It doesn't matter where my heart is."

With a slight nod, I closed my eyes. "I just need to know that Lucinda isn't reading mixed signals on either side."

The next thing I knew, I felt pressure on my thighs, and I jerked my head forward. Jennifer had straddled my lap, and now she leaned forward so her face was close to mine.

"Then I guess I have to be honest, then," she said.

"Wh . . . what are you doing?"

"I've been fighting the feelings for you brewing inside of me for a while, because I know that you're engaged to Lucinda. But if there's any chance at all that we could get back to where we were, I need to know that, and you do, too, before you make a mistake."

I went to push her off, but she locked her arms around my neck. "Tell me part of the reason you don't mind being close to me is that deep down you want to be," she whispered in my right ear.

"Oh, dear God," I mumbled.

She knew that was my spot. Talking softly, kissing, or blowing on my right ear just did something to me, and my little head reacted instantly.

She giggled. "Mm-hmm. Little big man agrees with me."

Sweat dripped from my forehead from both the situation and the alcohol I'd consumed. Jennifer was making me delirious, as the heat from the moment and the heat from my intoxication threatened to consume me.

"Please. Let's just stop." Why did my voice sound so weak? I wondered.

Rather than move, she kissed my neck. "Do you really want me to stop?" She planted a kiss on my lips, and our tongues hungrily met each other. My animalistic urges shot to unimaginable heights.

"Jennifer . . . oh God . . . baby . . . we need to . . . we need to . . . ."

She nibbled on my right ear, and it was over. Whether or not my relationship with Lucinda was salvageable could've been answered in one word now. No. Within seconds, our clothes were off, and I was dick deep inside of Jennifer. I remembered every curve of her body, and the way her breasts bounced made me wanna cum all over them. We moved from position to position, as if fucking were going out of style. Our final position had me sitting down on the sofa and her riding on top of me. By then we were giving it to each other too good to stop.

"Aldris! Oh gawd, baby. I'm 'bout to cum," she panted as she held on to my neck, and then she let out a wail.

"Ooh, shit. That's sexy," I moaned. "I'm 'bout to cum, baby."

Then she did something she'd always refused to do. She got up, stuck my dick in her mouth, and swallowed all my climactic juices. My body damn near lifted off the sofa. It was so fucking incredible. My eyes got heavy, and all I remembered was floating off in a dreamlike state.

Faintly, I heard, "I love you, Aldris."

"I love you too, Lucinda."

I didn't remember shit else.

Chapter 5

Charice

I never should've moved to New York, I thought to myself. I should've stayed my black ass in Atlanta. I had thought that Ryan actually loved me and that our time had come to be together as a family, when it had been nothing more than him trying to appease his bruised ego.

Yes, Ryan was still pissed about "catching" me at Lincoln's house. My reasoning or Lincoln's explanation didn't matter to him; he was pissed, as if I had broken the sacred rule of our marriage. At first, I had understood him needing time to get over the incident, but a whole week? That was some bitch-assness. I mean, really? You would've thought he had found me in Lincoln's bedroom, legs aimed high in a V-shaped position and squealing in falsetto. I was tired of his possessiveness. It clouded his good judgment, and now he'd stuck his foot completely in his own shit. Treating me like a jump off was not ever going to happen. I'd been through too much in my life—namely, because of him—to let anybody, especially him, take me through anything else. Not for any reason.

I'd been sleeping in the guest bedroom and avoiding Ryan like the plague. Wherever he was, I was definitely trying not to be there, at least until nighttime, when I didn't have a choice. I wouldn't answer his calls when I was out, and when I was at home, I stayed locked up in either our guest bedroom, my office, or my own little sitting area with Lexi and the boys. I hated living like this, but I had to decide whether I wanted to move out on my own or try to salvage our marriage, and at the moment, I was undecided. Aside from everything, he was my husband, and I did love him. I grew up with parents who'd remained married for thirty years, so it was in my DNA to try to make it work. Right now, I just had no will to try.

Surprisingly, Lincoln had never retaliated. He had stayed his distance from our house and me. Even though it'd been only a week, it had been a week of solace. The times he'd seen me, he had only thrown up his hand to gesture a hello and had kept it moving. No stops or stopping by, no conversation, and no staring. He hadn't even attempted to come by with London, whom I'd seen one morning, as they were riding past my house. She and I had waved excitedly; he hadn't. It had been as if he didn't even live just three doors down. I was shocked and impressed by his new attitude. I believed that part of him needed closure for himself, and I was happy that he was able to have that. The only fool who was still harping on the shit was Ryan. Lincoln and I were far past it. So why wasn't he?

My honest belief was that Ryan's extreme behavior over my interaction with Lincoln had more to do with him and Lincoln and less to do with Lincoln and me. At first, I had assumed it was because we were married and because we had agreed to raise Lexi as our own, but now, it struck me as being deeper than that. Of course, I'd always felt like there had been something brewing between those two, but when it had never manifested, I'd chalked it up to male egos colliding. However, Ryan's reactions to me and Lincoln weren't normal. At the end of the day, I was still his wife, and he knew that I was as loyal as they came.

I decided the best way to solve the problem would be to face it head-on. I needed to talk to Lincoln. I needed to find out what the hell this rift was between Ryan and him so that he could grill up and eat it. If my marriage was going to work, I needed this thing between Ryan and Lincoln to cease.

Three loud knocks on the door interrupted my thoughts.

"Yes?" I called out as I rolled over and looked at the clock. Eight a.m. You'd think he'd let me rest, since I was up early this morning, seeing the boys off to school.

"I'm going to a team meeting and then to work out. I just wanted to let you know," Ryan said softly through the door.

I rolled my eyes. "Okay."

He paused for a moment; then he breathed out. "Charice . . . baby—"

"I was asleep, Ryan," I said harshly. "Goodbye."

"Can we at least talk?" he asked, obviously ignoring my last statement.

"Maybe when I'm awake."

"Okay, okay. I'm gone. I love you, Charice."

He waited around for a few seconds for a response that he wasn't getting and then left. As soon as I heard his truck pull out of the garage, I jumped up and went into the nursery. Lexi was sound asleep. My perfect little angel. Lincoln's little twin. I stared at her for a few moments, then went downstairs, where Johanna was.

"Good morning, Mrs. Westmore," Johanna greeted me.

"Good morning, Johanna. How are you this morning?"

She smiled. "Blessed and highly favored, and so are you."

I smiled back. She didn't realize how much her morning devotion and uplifting words always encouraged me. There was just something about feeling the spirit and the goodness in someone else that made you have that same feeling. I admired her strength. I walked around the kitchen island and hugged her.

"Ooh, Mrs. Westmore. You startled me." She held me back.

"I'm sorry, but you just don't know how much I needed to hear that this morning."

She shrugged. "I can only imagine. God puts the Word on me and speaks through me. That is my anointing." She looked at me and pointed, as if something had struck her mind. "You know, Mrs. Westmore, I don't know what you're going through, but everything will be all right. Whatever battles you're facing, just know that nothing is bigger than God. Trust in Him, and He will guide your path, reveal, and provide the true desires of your heart. Just believe God for it. He will never let you down. As my grandmama would always say, 'Your answer is only one prayer away.'"

There I stood, completely speechless. Nothing but God could've possessed Johanna to give that Word today. I believed in God and prayed to Him every day, but I wasn't perfect, and even though my relationship with Him wasn't as strong as Johanna's, I felt as if He were talking directly to me through her. And that was when I knew I had to set my plan in motion. *You've guided my path. Now let's see where it takes me,* I thought to myself.

"Johanna, can you listen out for Lexi for me? I have to make a very important phone call."

"Of course." She walked over to the intercom and turned up the volume to Lexi's room.

I ran upstairs and called Lincoln's house phone. No answer. *Shoot.* He was probably on his way to the team meeting too. I said a little prayer to myself and called his cell phone. I hoped that was still the number, and yes, I did still have it. *Sue me.*

"Hello?" a man answered.

"Is this Lincoln?"

"It is. And who is this?" he said, puzzled.

"Uh, Charice."

"Charice?"

"Please tell me you are not around the team."

"No, I'm five minutes away. I was running late, you know, trying to get used to London's school schedule and all. What in the world brings you to call me?"

Nervousness overcame me, and I bit my bottom lip. "I need to talk to you face-to-face."

"Still chewing on your bottom lip when you're nervous, I see."

Puzzled, I asked, "How'd you know?"

He started to say something, then seemingly changed his mind. "It doesn't matter."

"I am a little nervous," I admitted. "But I really need to know if you can meet me."

"What's this about?"

"It's about something I'd rather discuss in person. Can you meet me or not?" I didn't mean to come off as abrupt, but he had far too many questions, and I had far too little time.

"Pipe down, Ma. No need to get all rah-rah with me. I just asked a question. You've been married to Ryan too long," he chastised. "After this meeting, I'm free. Where do you wanna meet?"

"How about the Starbucks in Vernon Hills?"

"Can we make it the one in Midway?"

"No, we can't," I said a little tensely. "If you and I just so happen to be in the same location, I can at least say that I was doing a little shopping, being that the Children's Place is right next door to Starbucks in Vernon Hills."

"Oh, okay. You're being unofficial right now," he said sarcastically.

"And you're being an ass right now," I shot back. "Why must there be such a love-hate relationship between us?"

"When you stop loving to hate me, then I guess we won't have one anymore." He chuckled.

A gasp fell from my lips. "I'm offended. I don't hate you. I could never hate you."

"Wow. I'm surprised at that. I would ask what brought that change about, but I need to get out of

my car so I can make my meeting. Since our visit is
unofficial, I assume you don't want your husband
to know who I am on the phone with."

"I would greatly appreciate it if you didn't tell
him."

"Cool, Ma. Whatever you want. I'll call you once
I'm in my car. Is this your cell phone number?"

"Yes, I changed over to the nine-one-four area
code."

"I see. You're a proud New York State resident
now. Well, I guess I'm a traitor. My cell is my
only remaining personal link to Texas. I guess I'm
sentimental that way," he joked.

His comment caused me to giggle, as I thought
back to our conversation the night our relationship
began. "Hey, I'm still a Georgia peach at heart."

After a few shared laughs on our unspoken trip
down memory lane, Lincoln got quiet. Then he
said, "On the real, I gotta go. I'll call you after my
meeting. Later, Ma."

"Later, Pa," I joked. I heard him say wow as he
hung up.

I headed downstairs to find Lexi awake, in the
bouncer, and watching Johanna clean the living
room. I played with her for a little while before
heading to my office to answer a few emails and
clean up my inbox. I fed Lexi, and then I got
ready, so that when Lincoln called, I could head
out without any delay. The funny part is that after

I showered, I found myself mulling over what to wear, as if this were a personal visit.

"What are you doing, Charice? Get it together," I told myself out loud.

I decided on my denim, belted halter dress and floral-colored wedges. I put on light makeup, and I unwrapped my hair, happy that I'd just gotten it done, which meant that my long layers still had bounce. After I oiled down and sprayed on Euphoria, I put on my ensemble and finished the look with a big bangle bracelet. I had to admit to myself that I looked good. I grabbed my purse and my shades, then headed downstairs.

"You look nice, Mrs. Westmore. I love that dress. Heck, and the shoes," Johanna said.

"Thanks. Listen, in a bit I'll have to step out. Lexi is fed and should be dozing off soon, so she should be good for now."

"Okay. That'll give me time to eat a little something and start the laundry."

As soon as she said that, my cell phone rang. I answered it immediately. "Hello?"

"I'm on my way to Starbucks," Lincoln said.

"Okay." I hung up. "All right, Johanna. I'll be back in a bit."

On the drive there, I was rather nervous, but once I pulled up, a sense of calm just eased over my body. Perhaps, I was doing the right thing. When I entered the coffee shop, I didn't see

Lincoln, so I ordered a light Caramel Frappuccino and a turkey and Swiss sandwich. Then I grabbed a table in the back and flipped through a magazine as I ate my food.

"You're still addicted to caramel frappes, huh?" Lincoln said as he sat down on the other side of the table with his double-shot espresso and a ham and Swiss sandwich.

"You scared me." I nervously toyed with the napkin in my hand and looked around for any familiar faces. "I didn't even see you come in."

"It's the shades and the snapback. I was sitting in the corner when you came in. I figured if you couldn't figure out who I was, then no one else could, either," he stated before drinking some of his espresso.

"True. And you're still stuck on your canned Starbucks energy drinks."

"Yep." He sat back and looked me up and down. "You fancy, huh?"

"Hair done, nails done, everything did." I finished the song behind a blush.

"Only you would know to finish the lyrics." He gazed at me with the same one-sided smirk he'd always had when we used to clown around. Just as suddenly, his expression turned solemn and serious. "But on the real, you look good. Although, you're a little overdressed for shopping."

Of course, he couldn't help the dig, and I rolled my eyes at his smart-ass remark. "That's how fancy people do it."

"Good one, Ma."

The immediate silence that followed made that previous nervous feeling creep up my spine, so I sat back and sipped my Frappuccino to give myself a little boost of confidence. "I guess I should tell you why I summoned you here."

"That would be helpful."

I took deep breath, and out of nowhere, a few tears sprang to my eyes. Lincoln grabbed my hand and held it.

"Are you okay?"

I grabbed the napkin and dabbed my eyes. "Thank God for waterproof makeup."

His lip twisted at what I'd said, and he shook his head. "You women, I swear."

Even though he was making fun of my obvious theatrics, I couldn't help but laugh. I needed it. My eyes darted to our hands. He still held my hand in his larger one. Rather than pull back, we lingered there in the familiar moment. I was transported back in time, to the days when this gesture was normal, instead of inappropriate. His thumb glided across my fingers, but he stopped when it touched my wedding ring. He moved his thumb back, as if he'd gotten a needle prick, and his eyes bore down at the gleaming diamonds. The Charice original.

"What a rock," he said, lifting my ring finger.

The way he stared at my ring made me a bit uncomfortable, so I slipped my hand away and decided to change the subject. "Um, well, maybe I can start on a different note. I saw London."

He conceded to my request without pressing me about my ring or my marriage. "Yeah, she's been on my nerves to come and see you. Given the circumstances, I don't think it's a good idea, so she's a little upset with me."

"Yeah, I understand. How's she adjusting?"

He sighed. "As best she can, I guess. I haven't had any real battles with her yet. She just doesn't open up to me as much as I would like. She talks to my mom a lot, though, so I get my pertinent information from her on the sly. I know she misses her mom, and I just hope that Lauren gets better, for London's sake. I don't want it to take a toll on London, so I let her have free rein when it comes to communication with her grandma and auntie. She talks to her grandma once a week, and I think she talks to her aunt Rosalyn every day. Thank God for unlimited minutes."

"Well, wait until she's a teen. It's very sweet that you allow her to stay in contact with her mother's family, despite all the struggles you went through with them."

He finished off his sandwich and wiped his mouth. "Thank you. We're still cool on each other, but we sit our personal bullshit aside for London. She's all that matters." He snapped his fingers. "I wanted to tell you that she wants to dance too. I wish you could teach her. It would be the perfect solution. She was enrolled in ballet and hip-hop back in Texas, so I have to find a dance academy for her here. And she loves her room too. Obviously, I didn't tell her who designed it, but she loves it."

"That's great." I beamed. My heart soared from the knowledge that in some way I was able to assist in making her happy. I loved London like my own, and I missed her so much. "I wish things were different, so that I could teach her to dance. I would love to do that. But it really seems like you're definitely adjusting well to being a full-time parent. I'm proud of you."

Nodding, he sat back and took a sip of his espresso. "Yeah, I appreciate that. I have to be there for her. She's the only child I have."

Full of conviction, I looked downward. "Yeah." I sighed and looked at him. "I guess I need to get back to the real subject."

He raised his hands up in the air. "Whenever you're ready."

I took a deep breath and looked Lincoln in the eyes. I felt so conflicted. In a way, I knew I was getting the answers that I wanted and probably needed to hear, but as Ryan's wife, I felt as if I were betraying his trust. I was the one speaking of dividing and conquering. If Ryan knew I was here and for what reason, there would be a divide between us so huge that it had been given a name—divorce. Still, I needed to know. I just prayed like hell I wasn't opening Pandora's Box.

"Um, I realize I shouldn't be telling you half of what I'm about to say, but I have to, because I need answers," I confessed to him.

He looked puzzled and leaned forward. "Go ahead."

"Ever since Ryan saw me at your house, things have been bad between us. He gave me the complete silent treatment for an entire week."

"I'm not surprised. Ryan is a grudge holder."

"But against me, though? For heaven's sake, I'm his wife."

"Hey, you're preaching to the choir."

"Well, anyway, after a week, I simply couldn't take it. I forced him to talk to me about three days ago. Only, he went into an unbelievable tirade that ended up with him saying something totally offensive to me. As a matter of fact, he called me a jump off, or rather he said that he's been straight with me during our entire marriage, and the only time he cheated on me was when I was nothing more to him than a jump off."

"*Whoa*," Lincoln said before his mouth fell agape. He grabbed my hands. "Are you okay? What did you say?"

"I was hurt. I'm still hurting over it. I didn't say much to him, but I did sucker punch the shit outta him."

"As you should've. Damn, I would've paid good money to see that."

Just then, my cell phone rang. I looked down at it. Ryan. I pressed the END button and pushed my hair behind my ear. "Anyway."

"Did you need to answer that?" Lincoln asked.

"No. It was only Ryan. I don't answer his calls. It's ironic, because now I'm the one who is doing the ignoring."

"Wait. In the meeting, he kept going on and on about how you all were doing great and how everything was lovely at the Westmore residence."

"We are so far from that right now. I guess he was just frontin' for you."

He drank more of his espresso. "I guess so. So I hate to ask, but what does this have to do with me?"

"Well, I've come to the conclusion that his reactions are extreme. I understand that, for obvious reasons, he doesn't care for us to be around each other. However, he reacts as if I'm not his wife, as if he's still fighting for me or something. You both know that I am very loyal. I can understand him

being angry at first and even needing some time
to calm down from the situation, but a week? And
then to explode on me like that was just insane. I
feel like there's more to it—"

The shrill ring of my cell phone interrupted my
statement. Ryan again. I pressed the END button
again.

I went on. "There has to be more to this situation between you and Ryan other than beefing over
me. I was wondering what it was, so that maybe we
could resolve it and move on. We have to coexist
for the next few years, and I'd rather coexist in
peace."

Lincoln looked shocked and sat there for a moment. I guess he was stunned by what I'd said to
him.

Then my phone rang again. Ryan again.

"Hold on for a second," I said, putting up my
finger. I answered the call. "What?"

"Can I please get you to come home?" Ryan
asked.

"I'm out shopping."

"Well, it's a bit of an emergency."

"Emergency?" I repeated, hopping up instantly.
"What's going on? What's wrong?"

"Please, calm down. I just need you to get home
as fast as possible."

"I'm on my way." I hung up and then frantically
grabbed my belongings.

"What's going on, Charice?" Lincoln asked, alarm evident in his voice.

"I've gotta go. There's some type of emergency. Ryan won't say what. I'm so sorry."

His hand on my forearm prevented me from walking away from him. "Wait. You don't want to know what the deal is?" Lincoln asked.

I lifted regretful eyes to his and patted his hand, indicating that I needed to head out. "I do, but right now, I have to go. I'm sorry to have wasted your time. I am not the one for emergencies ever since Charity. I'll call you so we can finish this conversation another day."

I was about to walk off when Lincoln stood and grabbed my hand. He turned me around to face him and stared into my eyes. "I hope everything is okay. Call me if you need me. I mean that," he said, genuinely concerned.

He was so sincere. I placed the palm of my hand on his cheek and rubbed his goatee with my thumb as I looked him in his eyes. "You're sweet. Thank you. I will, but I have to go." With that, I pulled my hand away and dashed out of Starbucks.

My heart beat a mile a minute as I raced all the way back home, praying like hell my family was okay. I wanted to call Ryan back, but if he told me something terrible over the phone, I'd probably crash, so I sweated bullets and dodged police and traffic all the way back to the house. No sooner had the garage door come down than I jumped out of the car and ran into the house.

"*Ryan*," I yelled from the mudroom. Silence. After exiting the mudroom, I ran frantically down the long hallway and into the kitchen. *"Ryan!"*

He appeared suddenly, and I ran smack into him.

"Whoa! Baby, where is the fire?" he said.

Filled with panic, I shot off questions with the force of a tommy gun. "What's going on? Where are the boys? Where's Lexi? Where's Johanna? Is it my parents? Your parents? The kids at the center?"

Taking note of my heightened anxiety, Ryan held me close, and my head fell into his chest. I was so upset, I was shaking. "Baby, calm down. It's none of them. I guess I shouldn't have used the word 'emergency.' I should've said that it was important. That is my bad. I'm so sorry."

I lifted my head up, tears in my eyes. "You mean to tell me that I nearly had a heart attack, cursed out five drivers, and ran one red light, two caution lights, and three stop signs just to get here and have you tell me that this is just *important*?"

He looked at me apologetically and nodded. "Yes, I'm sorry."

Angrily, I pushed him in the chest. "I should beat the living shit out of you. Don't do that to me. Do you have any idea how fucking scared I was?"

He held my hands against my will, forcing me to focus on him. "I'm sorry, baby. I really am. Can you forgive me?" he said, giving me those damn puppy dog eyes.

Damn those eyes. Not this time. Folding my arms across my chest, I scoffed, "Those only work on the boys."

He stood back and looked me up and down. "You look . . . you look . . . very nice. Not that you ever look bad, but you are so well put together today for a weekday. No jeans and stilettos. Not to mention you smell so damn good. You have on Euphoria. You usually wear that for special occasions," he said, circling me. He kissed me on the neck from behind. "You are really fancy for shopping."

Shit. Even he had noticed. I had to downplay my appearance. I didn't need his intuitive ass putting shit together in his mind. That was why we were in the predicament we were in now.

"There's nothing wrong with making myself feel better, given how I've been feeling lately. And now you've stopped me from doing the one thing that was lifting my spirits." So what if I threw my style preference for today on his behavior? He'd done worse. I hid my expression behind my hand as I rubbed my forehead. "What the hell is this about, Ryan? What is so important?"

Letting the thoughts behind my ensemble go, he kissed me on the lips and then lightly grabbed my hand. "Come with me," he said, and then he led me into the dining room.

Right beside the big dining table was a smaller table, set for two. It was adorned with a white linen tablecloth, two wineglasses, a bucket of Moscato on ice, two place mats covered with fine china, and two lit candles.

"What is this?" I asked, a bit confused.

Ryan stepped over to the table for two, then spread his arms as if presenting a prize. "This is lunch for two at the Westmore Café," he said and walked back in front of me. "I know that I messed up, but I want to make it right this time."

"Where are Lexi and Johanna?"

"Lexi is with Johanna, who is taking a two-hour lunch break at the mall." He reached for my hand and pulled me close to him. "And I am not training today, so that I can have lunch at the Westmore Café with my beautiful, amazing, intelligent, loving, and stunningly sexy wife," he continued, moving his hands to hold my face in the palms of his hands. "I love you, Ricey, and I'm so sorry for the way I've been acting lately. Most of all, I'm sorry for alluding to the fact that you have ever meant less to me than being a wonderful woman who is the mother of my children."

My eyes misted, and even though he had touched me, it was hard for me to forgive him. What he didn't understand was that even when I had refused to be back in a relationship with him after Iris, his ex-girlfriend, dumped him and publicly humiliated him, I had always held on to the fact that he cared about me. He'd cared even when I was with Lincoln. I knew there was a time when he hadn't loved me, but I had always felt like he cared. But knowing that at one point in his life, he had thought of me as only a jump off had made me question everything else. Jump offs didn't become marriage material to any man unless he was trapped or was trying to appease his ego. Well, even though we had three children together, he had refused to be held down by me or them, so the only reason was to appease his ego. Was I only a ploy to say he'd won over Lincoln?

He kissed my tears as they began to fall. "I'm sorry," he repeated.

Still reeling from his words and my internal struggle, I pushed away from him. "Don't. I know how you really feel about me, Ryan. Jump offs don't become wifeys." I held up my ring finger. "The only thing this symbolizes is that you beat Lincoln, and if that's the case . . ." I pulled off the ring and threw it to him. "You can have it. I'm done," I said, then stalked out of the dining room, with Ryan right on my heels.

He ran in front of me, halting my steps. "No, baby, I messed up. I was angry, and I was saying shit that I shouldn't have said. You're my wife—*my wife*, Ricey—and I love you with my soul. I don't feel that you're a jump off, and I never have." His emotions started to take over, and his eyes misted. "I can't lose you. I can't."

After closing the space between us, he leaned his forehead against mine, and we stood there for what seemed like forever. My heart was so vulnerable to Ryan—hell, it always had been—but my mind was undecided. Husbands shouldn't treat their wives the way that Ryan had treated me. Still, he was my *husband*. That had to mean something. He wouldn't honestly marry me if I didn't mean something to him. I didn't know if that was true, but what I did know was that I loved Ryan. I loved my life—our life. I wanted our marriage to be better than the mockery we were making of it, and I wanted it to last. I could admit that because of his angry outburst, I didn't fully trust him, but I loved him enough to forgive him. I *was* his wife.

Choosing forgiveness, I looked up into his eyes. "If you ever disrespect me again, whether it's about your past, present, or future, I will not be putting that ring back on. That I mean."

He nodded. "Understood."

I nodded in return. "Good."

"So can you put the ring back on now?" he asked, giving me those damn puppy dog eyes again.

Those eyes made me blush despite myself. "No, but you can." I held out my hand.

Gently holding my hand, he leaned forward and kissed my forehead before he uttered, "Proudly." He slipped the ring on my finger and, for good measure, added, "With this ring, I thee wed. I love you."

"I love you too."

Our impromptu vow renewal was sealed with a long and succulent kiss. Then for a long while we stood there, engulfed in each other's arms, as if time stood still. It felt good to be back in this familiar space with Ryan. When we were bad, we were bad, but when we were good, we were the best. No one had the ability to send me on a love high like Ryan, but likewise, no one had the ability to carry me through the pits of hell like him, either. We needed a middle ground because this topsy-turvy highest of highs and lowest of lows could not go on forever. We wouldn't survive that. We couldn't. But for now, we were high, and I wanted to relish the moment.

After kissing the side of my head, he whispered in my ear, "It's been, like, a month. Can we please skip the food? I really need to handle some other business."

"No, wait on it." I giggled.

Although he pouted, he gave in to my request to wait. We walked back into the dining room hand in hand to partake of this lovely meal. He pulled out my chair for me to sit down, then moved to the other side of the table and opened the bottle of Moscato. Once he'd poured some into both glasses, he sat across from me and raised his glass.

"Let's make a toast," he said. I raised my glass as well. "To our future as husband and wife."

"Hear! Hear!" I exclaimed.

We touched glasses and sipped.

"I have one more toast to make," he said, so I raised my glass again. "To my lovely wife, who is so graciously forgiving and forever loving me and my intolerable ways. It gives me great honor to help make her dreams come true, just as she has done for me."

I looked at him, puzzled. "Ryan, what are you talking about?"

He smiled, pulled some paperwork out from under his place setting, and handed it to me. "You, my dear, are the proud owner of your own state-of-the-art dance studio."

I placed my wineglass down, and I flipped hurriedly through the paperwork. He was right. It was an outline of how I envisioned my studio, complete with contracts, the closing papers—everything. "Oh my . . . oh God . . . oh my God," I screamed. "Ryan, how did you? When did you?"

"It's been in the works for a while." He shrugged. "I wanted to make you happy, just like you've made me so happy."

My soul opened up. I couldn't believe he'd done this for me. My lifetime goal was in the palm of my hand, and it was mine. *Mine.* I was in complete and utter shock. My husband—he did love me.

"Look over everything, and if you want to change—"

I jumped up from the table, rushed around it, and hugged him. "It's perfect," I declared, holding him tightly. "Thank you, baby. I love you so much."

"Always?"

"Forever," I reassured him, and then I kissed him passionately.

My kisses moved from his lips to his ear, then down to his neck, and I began unbuttoning his dress shirt. I was on fire for him, and I couldn't wait. *Damn that food.*

"I thought I had to wait on it." He breathed heavily.

I lifted my dress over my head and slid my thong off. "Are you still waiting?"

Ryan lifted me up and put me on the big dining room table. "Hell no. I have a seven-course meal to eat."

In a matter of moments, his pants were off, and my legs were in the V position and dangling over his powerful biceps as I moaned in falsetto. He filled me up to the hilt. His girth was so massive that it damn near hurt, but I knew it was due to the length of time that had passed. Taking me right there on the table had to be one of the sexiest and most memorable moments we'd ever had, but what made it more memorable was Ryan repeating over and over again that he loved me as I came again and again. Once he climaxed, he actually cried.

"Baby," I said, softly wiping his tears.

"I thought I'd lost you, Ricey. I thought I'd lost you," he said in a tear-strained voice. "I love you so much."

"I love you, baby. I'm not going anywhere."

He rose and helped me off the table, and then he gathered our things and blew out the candles. "I guess we better shower and get dressed," he said.

Wrapping my arms around his neck, I shook my head. "No, sir. I'm calling Johanna and asking her to tack on another hour. I refuse to be a jump off, but I can be your freak all day."

Ryan damn near dropped his cell phone while trying hurriedly to dial Johanna his damn self. When she picked up, he pleaded, "Please stay gone another hour, Johanna. Please." I could hear her laughing into the phone.

Once he hung up, I wagged my forefinger in a "Come hither" motion so that he would follow me up the stairs. "Can I be your little freak today, Mr. Westmore?"

"Shit, every day," he said as we ran up the stairs.

Chapter 6

LaMeka

"Hey, you," I said when I answered the phone call from Charice. "Long time no hear."

"I know. I've been horrible these past few months, but shit up here has been fucking crazy, girl. I have so much to tell you. You wouldn't even believe it."

"Yeah, I know a little. I ran into your mom at the grocery store last week. But that makes two of us. I have so much shit to tell you. But first, you." I paused before I asked my question. "So Lincoln is in the NY, huh?"

Her groan was immediate. "Yes, girl."

"Damn. So does he know about Lexi?"

"No, I haven't told him."

"I don't think that you and Ryan should—"

"Please let's keep this on a good note," she interrupted. "This is my first time being able to speak to you in three months. Let's keep it judgment free."

I loved my bestie, but when it came to doses of reality, it was like trying to force-feed a toddler medication. "Fine, Charice. So tell me, what is up?"

She went into the entire story, from Lincoln and London to her marital troubles, all the way up to the dance studio.

"Wow. There *is* a lot going on up there in the NY. So let me ask you this, are you still going to meet up with Lincoln to find out what the rift was about?" I said when she finished.

She hummed, as if she were in deep contemplation. "I don't know. I mean, it's been three days, and everything is so smooth right now. Not to mention Ryan is going above and beyond to prove that he wants this marriage to work." She paused for a moment. "I know I am definitely gettin' my back broke," she said around a fit of giggles.

"Damn. Come through, Mr. Westmore. It's like that?"

"Girl, on the dining room table, on top of the washing machine, in the theater room, in the tub, and in his SUV. Not to mention in the bed. I am so sleepy from these past three days. It is unreal."

"Okay, TMI. Just remind me to eat my food in the breakfast room when I visit. Nasty asses," I joked. "Wait . . . on top of the washing machine?"

"Let's just say spin cycle is the shit during an orgasm," she howled.

"No, ma'am. We're switching the subject right now. My mind is trying to create a visual, and I'm going to throw up if it does."

"All right. Enough about me. Tell me about Tony. I heard that he was awake and out of the hospital."

Confirming the news, I said, "Yes, he is."

Then I went into Tony's story, including his proposal, and I told her about Gavin and our relationship. I also told her about my home purchase and how Tony had found out about Gavin.

"Whoa! What happened after Gavin introduced himself as your man?" Charice asked.

"Tony looked at me as if I'd hurt him to his core. I didn't want to see him like that, so I talked to him as a courtesy."

"What did he say?" Charice asked. "I know he went off."

"Actually, he didn't. He pretty much listened and seemed to accept it. Then he left. I haven't heard from him since. I was going to take the boys over this weekend, though. I've just been so busy with moving."

"Wait, wait, wait a minute. Tony? *Tony Light*? Didn't say anything?" Charice asked again.

"Tony. *Tony Light* didn't say a word."

"That ain't him. Something ain't right. Watch that muthafucka."

"You are so melodramatic at times, Charice."

"And you are so nondramatic at times, LaMeka. I'm telling you. Be on your p's and q's with that dude."

Not up for the debate, I agreed. "I will," I said, hoping she'd drop the subject.

After a brief period of silence, she asked, "How's Lucinda? And has anyone heard from Trinity?"

"Girl, Trinity hasn't been heard from in, like, five months, so I don't know what's up with that chick. You know none of us has a number, so I hope she's fine. But Lucinda, honey, I have to let her tell you about that fiasco going on over there between her and Aldris. Trust me. She's got some mess going on for you."

"Lord, I would've thought she'd be drama free."

"What man you know who doesn't eventually bring some type of drama?"

She laughed. "Very true. Well, I guess I better call her too."

"All right, then, lady. Take care. I love you, boo."

"Love you back," Charice said before we disconnected the line.

"So all men bring drama, huh?" Gavin said, walking up behind me and wrapping his arms around my shoulders.

Startled, I jumped. "You scared the life outta me."

"My best friend's grandma used to say, 'Then you ain't living right.'"

We both laughed at the old adage, and I turned to face him. "Shut up. And stop being up in my conversations. I stand behind every word I said. Men bring drama."

"And women start it."

"Oh, really?" I said, wrapping my arms around his neck.

"Really," he answered as he bent down and kissed me. "You know your mom has the boys out with her, and your sister just left with her dude."

"So, what are you saying?"

"I'm saying the house is empty except for us for, like, the first time ever."

"So I guess we better make the most of it." Stepping back, I lifted up my top. I enjoyed watching his expression as I let my huge breasts topple out after I unhooked my bra.

He bit his lip. "Damn, girl. Mmm."

After gently pulling me toward him by my waist, he began to caress and suck on my twins. Oh, my gawd. This man could drive me fucking insane with his touch. The ironic thing was that Gavin and I had not actually done the "do" yet. With everything that had happened in my life, we had agreed to both get tested before we went there. Happily, we were both HIV and STD free. Besides waiting on the results, with so much going on with me, I'd not been up for it. Gavin was sweet about my not wanting to have sex while the kids or my mom were in the house, and even though I'd been to his house, we ended up falling asleep while watching television most times. We'd been doing some pretty heavy petting, and I knew that one or both of us would implode soon if we didn't get some, even though it'd been only two weeks since we hooked up. That was how badly we wanted each other.

He used his lips and hands to apply just the right amount of roughness I needed from a man, but he also knew how to apply the right amount of softness I needed with his touch. Every time he touched me, my knees buckled. He had a natural ability to be the most sensual person without being unmanly. Sure, I'd only ever slept with two men, but with the way Tony used to brag about his skills back when we were together, I knew he didn't have shit on Gavin just from his kisses alone.

"Mmm, Gavin," I moaned, wrapping my arms around his neck.

He kissed my neck and ear; then he pulled up. "I can't let our first time go down like this," he said huskily, shaking his head.

"Hmm? What? No, baby, I'm ready. I am," I said, panic mode activated. I needed this so badly, and, hell, I *wanted* it so badly.

"I am too, baby, but I gotta do it right, though." He walked into my bathroom, with me close on his heels. He turned around. "Sit on the bed for me, baby. Okay?"

"Okay," I said, then turned and went to lie across my king-size bed.

Soon I heard the sound of water in the tub. Next, Gavin ran out of the room and returned with some items that I couldn't see save for the wine bucket in his hand. Then I heard him in my closet, and he came out with a blanket and placed it on the floor.

"What are you doing?"

"Just wait." He smiled; then he went back into the bathroom.

A few minutes later, the water stopped, and he came out of the bathroom and stood before me with his hand held out. "Now come in the bathroom with me," he said once I placed my hand in his. He guided me inside the bathroom. "This would've been better had I had everything and had more time," he explained.

Laid out by the Jacuzzi was a bottle of Moscato with two wineglasses and a bowl of grapes, and lit candles surrounding the tub.

"Where's the bubble bath?"

A devilish grin crossed his face. "There is none. This isn't a bath, just trust me."

He kissed me and began easing my jean capris and thong down. Once I was completely naked, he undressed himself. Then he helped me into the tub and then got in with me. He poured the wine and handed me a glass as he sat in front of me.

"Thank you."

"You're welcome." He lifted his glass. "To new beginnings and endless possibilities." We touched glasses and sipped together.

Once I sat my glass down, I found out why this wasn't a bath. He took his wine and began to pour it down between my breasts and around my nipples, and then he slowly licked every drop of wine up with his tongue. I was damn near in heaven. This shit felt so good, it had to be illegal in all fifty states. Once his glass was empty, he fed me a few grapes with his mouth.

"You spoil me," I said between grapes.

"I'm supposed to," Gavin replied sexily, rubbing my thighs.

Gripping my thighs, Gavin spread my legs apart so that they were on opposite edges of the tub. He put a grape between his lips, and his face disappeared below the water. The sensation of the juice from the fruit combined with the feel of the grape and the suction of his tongue sent shock waves through my body.

"Ooh, Gavin. I am on fire," I moaned.

After his face surfaced, he licked his lips and winked. "I know, baby," he said, his lust apparent in his bated breaths. "Just relax and let me please you. You taste so damn sweet." He licked his lips.

This man didn't know what he was doing to me. He turned on the Jacuzzi jets, and the warm water pulsated around my sensitive honey pot,

heightening the sensation that was already building. Without further hesitation, he devoured his
feast between my legs. The mixture of the warm
water and the feel of him sent me straight over the
edge. As I gripped the sides of the tub for dear life,
my legs began to quiver ferociously, yet I couldn't
move.

"Ahh. Ahh, Gavin, baby. Ooh, baby," I panted
and moaned. My breathing was so shallow at that
point that I could barely get a word out. "I'm 'bout
to . . . ooh."

"Let it go, baby. Give it all to me. Let me make it
mine."

That was all she wrote. "Ooh, Gavin!" I yelled,
climaxing hard as he drank all of me to the last
drop. I was shocked that the tub was still bolted
down.

He massaged my clit with his hand as my body
slowly calmed and my senses and the feeling in
my limbs began to return. When I finally opened my
eyes, Gavin licked his lips and fingers.

"Good to the very last drop." He winked at me.

"Baby, you are amazing." I was in awe as I eased
my legs into the tub and fell back in exhaustion.
"I've never felt this way. Ever."

"I'm glad, because now I get to make you feel
that way all the time." He got out of the tub and
grabbed a towel; then he helped me out and dried
both of us from head to toe. "Can you walk?" he
asked playfully.

He was playing, but I was a little wobbly for real. "No," I laughed. "You got me weak in the knees."

He laughed. "Okay, baby." He picked me up as if he was about to carry me over the threshold. "Just hold on around my neck," he said as he carried me out of the bathroom into my bedroom.

He placed me on the blanket he'd laid on the floor in front of my fireplace, and then he grabbed a thicker blanket off the bed. He lay down with me and covered us with the thick blanket.

"What are you doing? We have the bed. Besides, I'm freezing," I told him, rubbing my arms. The cool air hitting my skin, which had been warmed by the "bath," was giving me the chills.

He shook his head. "Woman, let me get my romance on."

"Don't get me started on something and take it away now."

"This is all Gavin all the time," he said, turning the fireplace on low to let the light heat warm my body. "We have plenty of time for the bed."

"I feel like I'm on vacation or something, sprawled out on the beach, just me and you."

"Exactly. See, let your man handle this for you. If we can't be on an exotic vacation, I'll bring it to you."

He sat up on his knees in all his naked glory before me. That was when I zoomed in on his package. Lawd, have mercy. He was only at half-mast, and he was clearly thicker and longer than Tony. Whoever in the hell said black men had the girth had never run up on men like Gavin. The Cablanasians. It was actually light brown too. I'd always pictured it being pink or pale white. Well, he was breaking all kinds of myths today, and I was more than happy to be the one to unlock the mysteries.

He leaned down to kiss my neck, instantly sending chills through my body. This man. This man. This man. Lawd, this man. He was about to go back down south when I stopped him. I would not do this with anybody else, but Gavin was different. Not only was he special to me, but he also made me feel special. All he ever did was aim to please me, so I wanted to please him. This time I could find pleasure, instead of disgust, in everything that I gave.

"You don't want me to go there?"

"No, I want to please you—my way," I said shyly.

He looked at me, smiled, and stroked my cheek. "Baby, I want you to be comfortable with anything that you do."

"That's the thing. I am comfortable. I was never comfortable before, but I am with you. So, please let me please you."

Gavin's loving eyes captured me in a trance as his hands caressed my face, stroking my cheek and lips. The words that his lips didn't speak resonated through his heart. He knew this moment was special for both of us, but especially for me. It signified that I was giving myself to him and, more importantly, that I trusted him with my precious body. The fact that he didn't rush it and basked in the revelation made me feel that much more secure in my decision. He brought my face to his and kissed me softly and sweetly. Then we swapped spots. I gently massaged his manhood with my hand, and he moaned. I prayed I wouldn't choke as I went in slow and sensual. What I had learned from Tony, with his evilness, was working to Gavin's benefit. As I sensually worked his manhood in and out of my mouth, his fists grabbed the blanket, as if he were holding on for dear life, and his eyes rolled back. There was no doubt that he was enjoying every minute of it. He looked down at me in sheer amazement as his girth stretched and pulsated.

"Damn, baby. Meka, you just don't know," he moaned. "Your mouth work feels so good. Oh, shit."

He breathed heavily, holding on to the back of my head, as I continued to move up and down on his shaft. I ain't gon' lie. He tasted damn good too. His sticky serum was just like candy to me, and I wanted to taste it all. The hotter he got, the wetter I got, until we both couldn't take it.

He pulled me up, flipped me on my back, and entered me. We paused for a moment and got lost in each other as the realization that we were now one consumed us. We shared a kiss so full of passion that neither of us could stand it any longer. Then my baby went to work. I had never been worked the way he was moving. He convinced me that not only could white men jump, but they had rhythm too. He tore down every myth I'd ever heard and damn near made me peel paint off the walls from yelling. After I'd climaxed twice, he flipped me over to his favorite position—doggy style.

"Oh, damn, baby," Gavin said in shock.

"What's wrong?" I asked, looking over my shoulder at him.

My concern was met with his gorgeous half smile. "I'm in heaven. I've died and gone straight to heaven." He rubbed his hand across my ass, in awe. "To see it in person, damn. You have the sexiest ass I've ever seen in my life."

I tried my best to stifle my laughter, because he was as serious as a damn heart attack. I already knew the ass would get him. It was already rotund in my pants, but seeing it up close and personal was another story. While it was a hindrance to me, men loved it. And Gavin was most definitely a butt man.

As he moved in and out, his eyes rolled to the back of his head. "This shit . . . ooh, this shit. Man, I'm not gonna last."

"Baby?" I moaned.

"Yes?"

"Who's your mama?"

I began throwing my ass back to meet his thrusts, making my ass jiggle like jelly. He started losing control instantly. My baby tried to hold on, but his body began to tense up.

"Oh, baby, shit," he yelled as he climaxed.

He collapsed on my back as his body was rocked by aftershocks. When he could finally move, he rolled over onto his back, and I snuggled beside him. He held me in his arms until his breathing returned to normal. When I looked up at him, he pushed my sweat-drenched hair out of my face.

"So how did you enjoy our first time?" I asked, then reached up to kiss him.

"It was amazing. You're amazing," he said sweetly. "You've got skills, baby. Let me tell you that."

"I try, but I cannot compete with you. I don't believe any of the nonsense that people say about white men and sex anymore, because, baby, you puts it down."

He laughed. "Oh yeah? You liked that?"

Smiling demurely, I planted another soft kiss on him. "I sure did. Let's just say, 'Baby . . . you the fucking best, you the fucking best. You the best I ever had, best I ever had.' Real talk." As I sang that snippet from Drake's song, Gavin bobbed his head to it.

A throaty chuckle rumbled through his chest. "I'm just glad you're on birth control, because the way I unloaded just then, I know them would've been triplets," he joked.

After we finished teasing each other, we lay there in silence, basking in the afterglow of our first moment together. The sex was great, but these were the moments I cherished. When I could be with the person who made me happy, and nothing had to be done or said as long as we were together. It was like my emotions were radiating to him. It was an awesome feeling.

"I'm scared, Meka," he blurted out.

I rose up on one elbow and looked at him. "Of what? Why?"

He sat up on his elbow so that he was looking directly at me and used his forefinger to trace the outline of my cheek. "The things I'm feeling for you when I'm with you . . . not even just then . . . even when we're apart . . . I don't know. It scares me. I've never felt this way about anyone, and I'm scared to feel the way I feel. I'm scared of being scared of how I feel and of messing it up by moving too fast or too slow. Shit. I'm sounding real female right now," he confessed.

Dragging my fingers up and down his arm, I offered him some comforting words. "I know exactly how you feel, because I feel the same way. You don't have to be afraid to tell me how you feel, because I get it. I really do."

He pulled me into him, and we were about to kiss when he pulled back. "Did you hear that?"

"Hear what?" I asked, lost in our moment.

He jumped up and threw on his jeans and T-shirt. "Somebody is out there. It sounded like glass shattering."

As soon as he said that, we heard an alarm go off. "That's my car alarm," he shrieked, and he took off toward the front door.

Hurriedly, I put on my shorts and his wife beater and followed. As soon as I ran out the front door, I saw Gavin rushing up to some guy.

"What the fuck are you doing?" he roared, grabbing the dude.

The next thing I knew, they started fist fighting.

"Baby!" I ran down my front steps toward them. "Get off my boyfriend," I hollered when I reached them. I pushed the guy.

He turned around and knocked me flat on my ass, and that was when Gavin punched him and knocked his ass down on the grass. He had to shake himself out of a daze as he struggled to get up and staggered around.

"Baby, you okay?" Gavin asked as he helped me up.

"Yes. Who is that?" I asked frantically.

"Fuck if I know. This son of a bitch just shattered the back window of my fucking Corvette," he yelled. "You muthafucka!"

The guy had finally shaken off the punch and broke out running when Gavin charged toward him again. I grabbed Gavin.

"No, baby, he may have a gun," I said nervously.

Gavin stopped short, and the guy turned around in the middle of the street and yelled, "Follow me if you want to, white boy. You need to stick to your own kind and leave our women alone."

He took off around the corner, and Gavin and I looked at each other with the same thought. *Tony*. Damn Charice straight to hell. She called it, and I should've heeded her warning.

"Are you sure you're okay?" he asked, giving me the once-over.

"I'm fine. I'm just pissed that dude brought that shit to my house."

"Ol' son of a bitch." Gavin wiped the blood from the corner of his mouth and looked at his car. I walked up behind him and hugged him around the waist.

"I'm so sorry. I hope this isn't Tony."

"Who the fuck else could it be, Meka?" Gavin asked, looking back at me. "The muthafucka asked you to be his girl again, and you didn't do that, so you could be with me. Who the hell else would have such a problem with our relationship that they'd send someone to bust windows out of my car, someone who neither one of us knows, and yet he knows our business? Come on now."

He was right. I couldn't believe Tony would send someone to fuck with Gavin like this. That wasn't going to make me want him any more, and trying to make me fearful sure as hell wasn't going to make me go running into his arms. It wasn't going down like that. For one, he wasn't messing with my man. For two, he wasn't going to disrupt my place of peace and cause trouble for me in my new neighborhood.

"Are you all okay?" my neighbor, Mr. Jim, asked as he came around the corner. "I heard a commotion."

I waved at him. "Some young punk just vandalized my boyfriend's car. I think he was trying to steal it," I lied. He was an older retired serviceman, and I didn't want him to assume we were being rowdy because we were young.

He frowned. "Young punks! We have to have an association meeting now. We've never had an issue with break-ins, but then, Gavin's car is pretty fancy," Mr. Jim commented. "We're not gonna have this kind of activity start up now, though. Do you need me to call the police?"

"No, Mr. Jim. We have it," Gavin answered.

"Okay. Well, let me know the outcome. I'll make sure to send an email to the president of the association so we can get this under control now," he said before he walked back toward his house.

Gavin shook his head and looked at me. "Damn. Now the whole damn neighborhood is gonna know," he said angrily.

"I know," I said, hitting my forehead. "Let me grab the phone to call the police. I told you men bring drama."

He looked at me. "And like I said, women start it."

I disappeared into the house to grab the phone. What an ending to such a beautiful moment.

Chapter 7

Aldris

For the past two hours, I'd been at work, staring at my computer screen. What I hoped to get accomplished, I didn't know. My eyes felt like hot sauce was in them. I was so exhausted. When I looked at myself in the mirrored edge of the picture frame on my desk, I saw that I looked like certified hell. My eyes had dark circles around them, my beard had grown out, and my tie in no way matched the damn suit I had on. I felt like I had been hit by a Mack truck and my life was literally in shambles. I was behind on my workload, and I didn't even give a shit. I felt like shit. My life was shit.

My supervisor knocked on my door.

"Come in, Emory," I said and spilled my remaining coffee on my pant leg. *Great*.

"Man, what's going on with you? Are you okay?" Emory asked, shutting the door and rushing to give me napkins.

"Yeah, I'm fine. I'm just making a mess." I stood up, wiped my pant leg, and threw the napkins in the trash. Emory sat down in the chair in front of my desk.

"You look a mess too. Do you have the report I asked you for yesterday?"

I looked over at him and shook my head. "No. I'm sorry, man."

He exhaled. "I know this isn't you, so I'm going to give you a pass, but I need you to be straight with me. What's going on? I can't have your back if I don't know why you're looking and slacking off like this."

I sat down. "It's personal, man."

"Problems with the soon-to-be wifey?"

I rubbed my face. "Yeah, man."

"Then take some time off to do what you need to do. You have it. I'd rather you leave and come back refreshed than sit here, depressed and aggravated, while costing the company money and risking your job."

"The job is the only thing keeping my mind off of it," I confessed.

"Apparently not, because your performance is below mediocre," he replied, slapping me with the hard truth. After a beat, he stood and rested a hand on my shoulder as a show of compassion. "Listen, Aldris, you're using your job to hide from handling the issue. Do us both a favor and take the time. Now, I'm not suggesting it. I'm demanding it. You're my man, a hundred grand, but I will not let you ruin yourself like this. Lucinda is a great woman. She'll understand, and you'll work it out. Take a week, and then if you need more time, holler at me," he said. Then he turned and left the room.

As he exited my office, my eyes darted from the door to the family photo of Nadia, Lucinda, and me on my desk. I picked up the frame and held it to my chest, and a lump of emotion formed in my throat. "What did you do, Aldris?" I said aloud to myself.

Swiping a lone tear, I put the picture down. I brought my computer to life to set up my out-of-office manager message on my office email. Then I emailed Emory, confirming that I'd be out for a week and detailing what work I hadn't completed. Once I had set my voicemail for my leave of absence, I left the building and headed home.

My drive home was unpleasant. I took the scenic route, since the last place I wanted to be was at the house. Home was supposed to be the neutral zone, the comfort zone, the heart zone. But not for me. Not anymore. When I got home, I changed clothes and lay down on my sofa, trying to force my mind not to remember, but my eyes filled with tears. The dam finally broke, and I wailed from my pain. I still smelled her scent on the throw pillows. I hugged them. My mind refused to forget. It floated back to three days ago, the day Lucinda left me. . . .

I sat up in bed and looked around at the unfamiliar surroundings, and then I began rubbing my eyes, as if this would change what I was seeing. My head was banging.

"Where the fuck am I?" I groaned.

"At my house," Jennifer said plainly.

Startled, I jumped and looked at her. A blanket was over me, but I was stark naked. "Wait. Did we? Did I? Oh, shit! Tell me we didn't," I said, feeling frantic.

With her arms folded, she shook her head. "I knew I shouldn't have confessed my feelings to you. That's what I get for confiding in a drunk!"

"What?" I screamed. "What the fuck are you telling me?"

"I thought you were feeling something for me, Aldris, so I did what I had vowed not to do. I told you how I felt, and we had sex. Only, I told you I loved you, and you told me you loved Lucinda," she yelled, throwing a pillow at me.

"Can you please stop yelling?" I asked, holding my head. "This shit is thumping."

She sat in the chair across from me, with her coffee in her hand and her robe wrapped around her. "Aldris, you need to make up your mind. Do you want me or Lucinda?"

"Wait a minute! Gawd damn it. I was drunk, Jenn. How the fuck you gonna call me out on some drunken shit? I love Lucinda."

"Apparently not," she said condescendingly.

"Shit," I said, hitting my forehead. "Ouch."

"So, what was last night?" she asked with an attitude.

"Last night I was drunk." Scooting forward, I focused my attention on her so that she could fully grasp what I was saying. "Listen, I care about you Jennifer, yes. A part of me will always love you, true. But I love Lucinda. I'm in love with her. That's my fiancée, and she's going to be my wife."

She stood up and let her robe fall open. "So you can give this up?"

No lie. For a moment, I was mesmerized. "Oh, shit." I shook my head to clear the impure thoughts that quickly tried to invade my head-space. "I can't believe this shit."

"Well, can you?"

I stood up and retrieved my clothing. "Jennifer, you're fine as hell. No man could resist having all of that, but I'm not even supposed to be seeing that to try to resist it. I have an obligation to Lu because I love her. Please, stop."

Her face contorted as she fell back into her seat. The befuddled look on her face spoke volumes, but her next words took me by surprise. "You finally made a choice. Wow. You chose her." She lifted sad eyes to me. "I never came into this trying to hook back up with you. I just thought after last night . . ." She paused and swallowed. "You've made your choice."

After slipping on my clothes, I walked over to her. "Jenn, I'm sorry. I've been unfair to you, and I know that you may have residual feelings for me. I didn't mean to bring up old feelings. I can't apologize enough to you."

She absorbed my words and then threw her hands up in concession. "I can't even be mad at that. I'm woman and adult enough to know the rules of the game. At least it's more than I got when we were first together. I'm sorry that I crossed the line, knowing you were engaged to Lucinda. She deserves better."

With my hands steepled, I closed my eyes in humble appreciation. "Thank you."

"You're welcome."

I was walking over to her mirror to fix my clothes when it hit me. "What time is it?"

"Seven thirty."

"At night?" I asked, buckling my pants.

Her eyes pierced me. "Uh, no, Aldris. In the morning."

I felt as if the blood drained from my body, and I fell back a few steps as her words settled in. "In . . . the . . . the . . . m-morning," I stuttered. "You're lying."

"Afraid not. I just got up ten minutes ago."

"Oh, shit." I hit my forehead with my fist. "Please don't tell Lu that I was here. Please. She's gonna kill me," I yelled, grabbing my cell phone and keys. "Please let this whole thing stay between us. Please."

"No worries. I won't tell if you don't."

"Thank you."

Without wasting another second, I ran out of her house like a bat out of hell and headed to mine. A million and one thoughts ran through my head as I looked at the ten missed phone calls I had from Lucinda. Shit! I couldn't even tell her that I was at my mom's or Mike's house, because she'd probably already checked with them. Knowing that I'd pissed both of them off and that they were both in Lucinda's corner, I realized they wouldn't hesitate to announce that they hadn't seen me. I also thought of telling her I was with Rod, but she knew Alize personally. I couldn't guarantee that Alize would stand behind a lie for me even if Rod asked her to, so I went with the half-truth plan: I got drunk at the bar—truth. And I fell asleep in the car—half-truth.

I did fall asleep in the car. I just wasn't there all night. I prayed that I could keep a straight enough face to pass this off as the truth, because I already knew that this was going to be the battle to end all battles. I still was in the middle of

Hurricane Lucinda, and now I had this on top of it. By now, she had to have been upgraded to a damn category five.

"Lord, if you're real, please let me live through this," I prayed as I got out of my car and walked into the house through the garage. "No gunshots or baseball bats. Good so far," I mumbled aloud as I checked our bedroom, which was untouched.

I walked into Nadia's room, which was also untouched. Then I headed into the living room. I paused when I saw Lucinda's back. She was sitting up on the sofa, waiting. Waiting for me.

"You're home," she said, without turning around.

I slowly walked farther into the living room and around the sofa to stand directly in front of her. "Hey," I said sheepishly.

She looked up. Her face was marred by tiredness. "Hey," she barely mumbled. "So you decided to come home, huh?"

I nodded. "Yeah. I didn't know if . . . uh . . . I could or not."

"Fair enough. I did kick you out."

Stunned, I could only stare at her for a moment. That was not Lucinda. She was too calm. Way too calm. Something was up. "You did, but I know it was for the best at the time."

She looked down and then looked back up at me. "So, did you get my calls?"

"I did. I didn't get them until this morning, though. I . . . uh . . . I was drunk."

"Yeah, I could smell the alcohol on you as you came in."

"Yeah, I was pretty faded," I confirmed. I put in my plea quickly. "But I'm home now, and we can talk as much as you want. I honestly see what you were saying and, Lucinda, I want you to know that I am devoting my all to making our relationship stronger again."

She exhaled deeply. "That's great."

"And I just—"

"Aldris, where were you last night?"

She'd caught me off guard with the sudden question, so I rattled off my answer quickly. "Baby, you wouldn't believe it, but I went to the bar, and I got drunk. Man, I was so faded. The bartender wouldn't even serve me any more drinks. So I actually ended up sleeping in my car."

"Really?" she asked in amazement.

"Yep," I answered confidently.

She stood up. "Aldris, tell me the truth, please. Where were you?"

"Baby, I told you—"

She put her hand up as a single bloated tear formed and slid down her cheek. "No. I mean after the bar. Please, just tell me the truth. I need to know where you were last night, Aldris," she said, clearly trying to keep her voice strong despite the impending tears.

"Baby, I . . . I told you . . . I told you where I was,"
I lied.

She huffed. "Please! Do not patronize me. If you
don't do anything else for me, tell me the truth. I
deserve it. I need to hear it for myself. I'm begging
you," she cried.

"Baby, I can explain—"

"Aldris," she hollered.

With my hands out in front of me, I lifted my
open palms, begging her to listen. "I can explain
it to you. I just need you to listen first." I had to let
her know that I loved her and that what I did was
a mistake.

She threw her hands up. "Last chance. Just tell
me," she pleaded, her tone steady.

We stood there staring at each other. It felt like
I was in General Custer's last stand. My palms
sweated, and I could hear my heart racing in my
ears. My breathing turned shallow as I realized
that I was not going to get away with my half-
truth plan. Looking into Lucinda's face was like
staring directly at pain. I could literally feel all
the pent-up hurt and anguish that I'd brought to
her life over these past few months. I couldn't
hurt her any further by lying. So I gave her what
she needed . . . the whole truth.

I sucked in air, hoping that we could survive
this news. "I was at Jennifer's house," I confessed.

She fell back a couple of steps, as if the truth had knocked the wind out of her. Then she composed herself and calmly asked, "Did you sleep with her?"

Now I was in panic mode. I'd already admitted to more than I'd wanted to, and God only knew how this would end up if I admitted the entire truth to her. I tried to stall. "I slept over there . . . yeah."

She put her hands together, as if she was begging me for the answer. "Aldris, please. Don't do this. Please." She took a deep breath. "Did you have sex with Jennifer last night?" she asked outright. "All I want is the truth."

"Lucinda, let me explain something—"

"No. Aldris. No," she bellowed. Her patience was waning by the second. "No explanations. No excuses. No detours and road maps. It's a simple yes-or-no question. Yes or no?"

With my hands atop my head, I paced back and forth. Indecision flooded me as I considered the ramifications of a confession. "If I tell you, you have to listen to me—"

Her sharp glare halted the words coming out of mouth. "Yes or no, Aldris?"

How could I resist eyes that were pleading with me to tell her the truth? It was weird, because I could tell she honestly wanted to know the real deal, but it was as if her soul was ripping in half.

Mine was too. I had never wanted this to happen to us. As I stared at her, I was scared for my life, for our life together, but I had no choice. I had to tell the truth. I'd never wanted to be that man that lied and hurt Lu, so I admitted my wrongdoings.

With a heart full of sorrow and a soul full of regret, I answered, "Yes."

That one word flicked the light off in her soul. She closed her eyes and held her chest as two tears fell. Then she opened her eyes and stared at me for what felt like eternity. "Thank you," she barely managed to say. "I needed to hear that from you. I needed it for myself. Thank you."

I rushed to close the gap between us. I didn't give a damn if she fought me. I deserved it. As long as she said she'd forgive me, I'd take anything she dished out. She folded her arms.

"Lucinda, I can explain. Baby, I love you so much. I know I fucked up. I fucked up so bad, but I was so drunk and hurt that I did the unthinkable. But, baby, I understand everything you said to me yesterday, and if you just give me a chance, I'll make it right between us. I promise I will do that for you."

Standing on her tiptoes, she reached up and kissed me on the cheek. "I hear you," she said, and I pulled her into my arms and held on as if my life depended on it.

"Lu, I'm so sorry, baby. I love you, and I'm so glad that you forgive me," I said as my emotions welled up. *"So sorry."*

She pulled back and wiped her tears with her hands, and then she asked me to excuse her. When she turned away, I silently thanked God for the reprieve. I was so grateful that we'd survived, and she'd decided to give me another chance, but when she returned, she had two big suitcases in each hand and her purse.

"Wait. Whoa. Baby, what is this? What are you doing?" Panic welled up in me.

"Leaving, Aldris." She attempted to walk past me, but I blocked her.

"Leaving? What? To go where? I thought you'd forgiven me and that we could work on getting our relationship back on target."

"Leaving you, Aldris. I can't fight like this anymore. I'm too tired. I thanked you because I needed to hear the truth so that I could have the strength to walk away. You're not ready for this relationship, and you're not ready for Nadia and me. Aldris, I love you. I swear to God I really do, but I can't take this. I can't be in a relationship with you, and I can't marry you. We're over. I'm leaving you."

My head was spinning, and this time, I knew I wasn't drunk. If ever some shit could sober a nigga up real quick, this was that shit. Did she

*walk out of the room with already packed bags
and tell me she was leaving me? No, this wasn't
happening.*

*I continued to block her path. "No, Lu. You can't
give up on us. You can't give up on me. I need you.
I know that sounds selfish, and that's because it is.
I messed up, but that doesn't mean I'm not ready.
Just give me a chance to prove it to you."*

*"Don't make this harder than what it has to be.
I'm trying really hard to be an adult about this. I
just want to cut my losses and be done. Please let
me go," she begged.*

*I was shocked. I couldn't believe this. "Are you
serious, Lucinda? You can't be serious. We're
getting married. We share this house. It's both of
ours."*

*"I am very serious, Aldris. This house is yours
now. Your name is on the loan, and you can have
mine removed from the deed. I don't want it. I just
want to leave."*

"No."

*She moved to the left, but I blocked her, so she
moved to the right, and I blocked her again. She
sat her luggage down and threw up her hands.
"So you're just going to block me in the hallway?
Really?"*

"Yes! Until you change your fucking mind."

*"So, no piss breaks, shit breaks, and just forget
that fact that I have to get Nadia, and we both
have jobs," she said sarcastically.*

"I'm hoping it won't last that long."

"Do you need a chair? It's gonna be a wait," she said haughtily.

I shrugged. "Fine."

With a hard eye roll, she shoved me. "Move."

"No. I'm not going any fucking where until you change your mind. And neither are you," I said defiantly.

Flames flickered in her eyes, indicating that the calm that she'd amazingly maintained was on the brink of collapsing. With that move, I knew I'd unleashed the winds of the cat 5 hurricane. But fuck it. I was going to have to risk that shit today.

Looking as though she was about to come unhinged, she lit up on me. "Why should I? You didn't change yours. Last night you had a choice. You chose to sleep with Jennifer. You made your decision. You could've brought your ass home last night, but you didn't. That's fine. You did what you had to do for you, and now I'm doing the same. Now move!" The shove that followed felt as if it'd caved my chest in, but still I held firm.

However, since that approach obviously hadn't worked, it was time for Plan B. I'd pretend to concede. "Okay, Lu. You're right. I have no right to hold you here. The last thing I want to do is hinder you. If walking out on us is what you think is best, then I won't stop you. That's your decision." I moved out of the way.

She exhaled and picked up her suitcases. "I'll be back tomorrow for some of Nadia's things. Hopefully, I can get everything cleared out soon." She threw the last part over her shoulder as she headed toward the door.

Time to abort Plan B, because she was really leaving. Hell no. Plan C. I ran after her. "Wait, Lu. Please. You begged me. Now I'm begging you. Please don't leave me, baby. Please."

She stood at the door and took her spare key to my car off her key ring, and then she placed the key and the garage-door opener on the table. She opened the door to leave. "Goodbye, Aldris," she whispered without even turning to look at me. I could hear the tears in her voice. Hurt radiated off her.

Plan D. Desperation. Doomsday. "Damn it all to hell" day. Whatever you wanted to call it, I was there. I could not lose the woman that I loved. I couldn't lose my wifey. I just couldn't. I ran up to her and shut the front door.

With one hand on the door, I used my other to hold her in place by her arm. Nuzzling my nose in the hair on the top of her head, I pleaded with all my might. "No, baby, no! Please! Okay, I'll do whatever you want. Whatever you ask of me. Just don't go." After dropping to my knees, I held her by the waist as I begged, desperation in my voice. She still wouldn't turn around. "Please, Lucinda. What can I do? Just tell me. Consider it done."

By now I was drenched in sweat, and it appeared as if I was about to have real heart attack. My chest felt like it was about to explode, and my eyes danced with pain. The more I tried not to cry, the harder it became. Tears streamed down my face as every good moment we'd ever had flashed before my eyes. I remembered the first time we made love, our first date, the first time I met Nadia and her mom, and our first kiss. I thought of the times we used to chill out together on Sundays, eating her latest baked confection in bed, and having game nights as a family. I remembered the day I proposed to her. I remembered everything. And it hurt . . . like . . . hell.

Finally, she turned to face me. She looked down at me with the most sincere but most serious expression I'd ever seen on her face. "What can you do for me, Aldris? Absolutely nothing. It's over, Aldris. I'm done. Me and you . . . we are over."

With that, she spun on her heels and walked out of the house and my life. The panic that was in the pit of my stomach swelled up in my chest, and my emotions exploded. She had already put the bags in her car and she was about to get in when I made a mad dash toward her.

"Lucinda! Lucinda! No. You can't leave me. Please, I love you. Please."

"Go back in the house, Aldris," Lucinda demanded as she went to open her car door.

"No, come back." I blocked her from getting inside the car.

Just then Mrs. Williams, our neighbor, stepped out of her house. "Is everything all right, Aldris and Lu?" she asked.

"Yes, Mrs. Williams. Go back inside," I said to her.

"No, Mrs. Williams. Go inside, Aldris," Lucinda said loudly.

Mrs. Williams walked over with her hands on her hips. "Aldris, I think you better let her get in the car," she said as Lucinda and I stared each other down.

"I can't. Go home, Mrs. Williams," I yelled, never taking my eyes off Lucinda.

"I don't want to call the police, Aldris." Mrs. Williams walked in front of me and placed a hand on me as she pleaded sorrowfully, "Son, let her go."

I dropped my head, and a flood of tears rushed out. "Lucinda, please. I love you so much. You know you love me. We can work through this. I know we can if you just let me make it right. Please, baby. Let me make it right. I can fix this. I can. I'm begging you, please." I got down on my knees. "I'm not perfect. I wish I were. But I am perfect for you. We're perfect together. Don't do this. Don't give up on us. I'm sorry, Lu."

Lucinda looked down at me. Even with her tears, her face was set, and that told it all. "I can get over many things, Aldris, but not this. Not this. You can't undo what's been done. You can't make it right. You can't fix it. What you can do is let me leave with my dignity and pride—the little that I have left, which I'm fighting so hard to hold on to. We're done."

This time I didn't even have the strength to stop her. She got in her car, and while still down on my knees, I somehow mustered the strength one last time to try to change her mind. "Please, Lu."

The door shut; then she cranked up her car. I stood up, defeat dripping off me. She rolled down the car window and stuck her hand out, never once looking in my direction.

"Here," she said, holding out her engagement ring.

I pushed her hand away, refusing the ring. "No."

"Here," she bellowed, anguish rising from the pit of her soul.

Although I knew I should take the ring to end this fiasco, I couldn't. Hell, I couldn't even move. Taking that ring out of her hand would make our breakup final and official. Taking the ring—that would make it real.

Mrs. Williams walked over and took the ring out of Lucinda's hand. "I'm so sorry, Lucinda," she said, in tears from witnessing our breakup.

"Me too, Mrs. Williams," Lucinda said, wiping her tears. And then she left.

Mrs. Williams turned and opened my hand, placed the ring in my palm, and then closed my fingers around it. Her sad eyes met mine as she patted my hand before walking away. I stood there for God only knows how long, just staring at the ring. I knew it was long after Lucinda drove down the street and out of my pathetic life. When I finally came to the realization that she was truly gone, I walked back in the house with my head hung low, a single man again.

Ever since then, I'd been a mess. I hadn't talked to anyone. I hadn't seen Lucinda, Nadia, Jennifer, or Jessica. I had refused to answer anyone's call, text, or email. I had gone to work and come home. Taking a shower and brushing my teeth had been big enough feats to accomplish. I hadn't eaten anything other than chips and cookies. I'd drunk water to sustain myself. I hadn't slept in days.

My mind kept running over how I had messed everything up. I couldn't even sleep in the bed, because her scent was still in the sheets. I couldn't stand to look at her empty closet. Even the sign I'd made for Nadia that said NADIA'S ROOM was gone. I was depressed, angry at myself, and tired as hell. My job was the only thing that had been holding me up. Now I didn't even have that.

I woke up on the sofa and felt like I was in a crazed daze. *Shit*. I'd managed to cry myself to sleep. I looked at the clock. Six thirty in the evening. Why couldn't I have slept until morning? I thought as I sat up on the sofa. I looked at my cell phone and found that I had twenty-five missed calls, sixteen text messages, and twenty voicemails, all from either my mom, Mike, Rod, Jennifer, my supervisor, or my brothers. None from Lucinda. Not a call, not a text. Nothing. I decided to start with my mom.

"Aldris," she yelled into the phone when she picked up. "I have been worried sick about you. I talked to Lucinda. How could you do this to her? Oh my God. Where have you been? I could kill you."

"Then you'd be doing me a favor," I mumbled. "I'm too much of a coward even to kill myself."

"Don't talk like that. It's not the end of the world. You just have to find a way to get your life back on track and to get Lucinda back."

I huffed. "I can't, Mom. She hates me."

"She doesn't hate you. She's hurt."

"I don't see why she doesn't. I hate myself."

"Come over here, so I can see you. Your brother came up from Savannah tonight. We were going to go to the police and report you missing just to get into your house."

"Tell him I said hello and I'm good. I just wanna be left alone."

"And do what? Fall further into a depression?"

"Sounds like a plan."

"Aldris, where is your faith?"

I huffed. "It left when Lucinda backed out of my driveway."

"Have you lost your mind? You're walking away from God, not Him from you. You messed up, Aldris, not Him. He'll guide you so you can make it right. Don't give up on God because of your mistakes. Ask Him to sustain you so you can learn to live and learn again. Maybe you'll get Lucinda back, and perhaps you won't, but you live on to show others what not to do."

I knew she was right, but at that moment, I didn't want to hear that shit, especially when she said I might not get Lu back. "I gotta go. I love you." I hung up.

I stood up and walked over to pick up the books that were still on the floor from when Lucinda had hurled them at me during our first confrontation about Jennifer. Neither one of us had bothered to straighten up the mess, so I decided to busy myself with the task now. I picked up a small plaque Lucinda had purchased from an art gallery. It read WHEN YOU REALIZE THAT GOD IS ALL YOU'VE GOT, YOU'LL UNDERSTAND THAT GOD IS ALL YOU NEED.

The words touched my soul. God was indeed all I had, because without Lucinda and Nadia, I had nothing.

"God, please. Help me."

Chapter 8

Lucinda

Leaving Aldris was the hardest thing I'd ever done in my life. I'd already known the truth when he came into the house. I just needed him to say the words to me so that I could truly believe them. When I hadn't been able to reach him, I'd gone to his mom's house, Mike's, and even Rod's. He hadn't been there. It had taken me until three o'clock in the morning to muster up the nerve to ride over to Jennifer's house to see if he was there. Lo and behold, whose car had been sitting in her driveway? Aldris's. I couldn't believe it. I had actually got out and peered into the car, hoping he was sitting inside it, but he hadn't been. It didn't take a rocket scientist to figure out where he was and what he was probably doing.

The old Lucinda would've knocked on that door and laid hands on that ass. But the new me? No. I had wanted the truth. I hadn't wanted to be blamed for anything or for it to be turned around on me. This Lucinda had wanted only to hear what she had been thinking for quite some time now and to move on with her life. And I had.

The part of me that truly loved him wanted to forgive him and move past it. Real love fucked you up like that. With everything inside of me, I wanted to say to him, "Baby, it's okay. I forgive you, I love you, and we can make this work." However, that would be a lie, because every time I thought of Aldris touching me, I could see him touching Jennifer the same way, and that thought was enough to rouse so much hatred in me toward Aldris that it scared me.

How could he do this to us? How could he do this to me? What did I ever do to deserve this treatment? Was there not one man on this earth who thought with the head on his shoulders instead of the one between his thighs? Was one night of throwback pussy worth tearing down everything we'd built together? Obviously so.

Now I was happy that I had made the decision to leave, because the bitterness had set in. I'd begun to loathe Aldris, and not just for what he did, but also because of my feelings for him. I hated loving him, and even more so, I hated that I hadn't stopped loving him. The only good things about this entire situation was that neither one of us had reached out to communicate with the other. Nor was I living with him, so I didn't have to see him.

Which brings me to my current living arrangement: I'd been living with my mom, and I'd become fed up with that after only one day. Nadia loved it, of course, because she was playing with her aunties and uncles, but I didn't. I had to witness my mom and Emilio Rojas in love again. With all the things going wrong in my life, my dad had managed to weasel his way right back into my mom's life. It was plain damn sickening.

For instance, one of them would say to the other, "I love you, baby."

And the other would reply, "No, I love you more."

If I'd had another place to go, I would've left on sight. I didn't want to stay with LaMeka, because she already had a full lot, and I didn't trust anybody else enough to live with them. But I declared that I couldn't stand seeing Emilio every day. I was convinced I was in the Ninth Circle of Pure Hell. It was time to get on the hunt for an apartment. I needed my own space for my own sanity. If this situation with Aldris wasn't enough to drive me crazy, this living arrangement with my mom and Emilio damn sure would.

"Good morning, sunshine," my mom sang, just as perky as she could be, as I walked into the kitchen.

I waved. I didn't see shit perky about it. It was only a Saturday just like any other Saturday.

"Wow, Lucinda. I gave you all of that, and all I get is a half wave," my mom said sarcastically. "Today is a brand-new day to thank God for."

"Yeah, well, today is just another day to me," I said, flipping my hair back and reaching to get a coffee cup.

She passed me the coffeepot and glared at me. "Just because you're going through trials with Aldris doesn't mean that you shouldn't be thankful for seeing another day. You're hurting right now, Lucinda, but you'll heal, and maybe you and Aldris can work things out. Sometimes we have to go through the rain to see the sunshine."

Sometimes we have to go through the rain . . . yada yada yada, I mimicked in my head. *What the fuck ever*. Now I was getting in a pissy mood.

"So I guess that's what you and Emilio did, huh? Go through the rain. And now everything is just gumdrops and lollipops between y'all, huh?"

"What the hell is your problem, Lucinda?"

"And what the hell is yours, Mama?" My words matched her same level of intensity. "I can't believe you accepted Emilio back into your life."

She drummed her fingers on the counter. "First off, stop disrespecting your father by calling him Emilio. I didn't raise you that way. Secondly, your father and I found each other again. What is the problem with that? I'm happy. We're happy with each other, Lucinda. Can you not just be happy for me?"

I damn near spilled the entire pot of coffee at that declaration. "Do you hear yourself right now? Stop disrespecting Emilio? Well, he stopped being my father the day he walked out on you and started taking care of Maria's kids instead of us. And you're right. You raised me. Not him. *You*. Now I have to respect him as my father? Between him and Aldris, I've had it up to my ears with the disrespect, and I refuse to deal with his crap or Aldris's anymore."

"You are going through your own battles, so do not take them out on me and your father. I won't be brought down by your personal problems," my mom spewed.

Was I getting punked? I had to be. Either that or I had woken up in the twilight zone. The twisted turn of events left me truly mind fucked. "Everyone I know is losing their mind. Have you forgotten that not only did this man leave you, but he also left you to fend for yourself and eight children? It's one thing to get a divorce because you no longer love that person, but you're going to honestly forgive him for walking out on his responsibilities? We had nothing to do with the demise of your marriage. Now I'm supposed to respect him and this newfound relationship between you two? You may have fallen for the okey doke, but I'll be damned if I do."

"No, what you're not going to do is curse in my house. That's number one. Secondly, I'm not asking you to like it. I don't care if you do or don't. I'm telling you it is what it is, because it's my life and my decision. You don't know what's been going on over here, because you've been living your life with Aldris in your own home," she said, fuming, before providing further explanation. "I didn't just accept your father back. He had to prove himself. Jose and he are getting very close. He's being a male figure of support to the boys. He helps me around the house. He's taking care of the bills, not me. He pampers me. He even joined the church a couple of Sundays ago. He's changing, Lucinda, and if you stop being hateful toward him because things didn't work out between you and Aldris, you'd see that."

Right after her statement, my dad walked into the kitchen. "Good morning, ladies," he said before walking over to my mom and kissing her on the cheek. "I think."

"Good morning, baby. Do you want some coffee?" my mom asked, smiling at him.

"Sure, baby." He kissed her on the lips. "But you are all the morning fix I need."

"Aw," my mom gushed and hugged him.

My stomach turned at the sight. I picked up the paper to hide my disdain. "Emilio, do you mind if I take the Homes and Apartments section? I have to find a place to stay ASAP."

He turned to face me. "No, I don't, Lucinda. Do you mind if I talk to you in private for a moment?"

"I'm really busy, and I was gonna—"

"It'll only take a moment. Please."

I nodded. "Sure."

He held out his hand, indicating that I should go out on the back porch. I walked outside, with him right behind me. He shut the door to give us privacy.

"Look, Lucinda, I'll get to the point. I know you don't trust me, and you have every reason not to, but I'm still your father. I love you, even though I haven't shown it in recent years. I want to try to make up for that, but at the same time, I want you to respect the decision that your mom and I made to be a couple again. I've realized that everything I thought I had to search for was with me all the time, and I just want to be happy and make your mom happy."

"So, what do you want from me?"

"Your respect and support."

"Whatever, dude."

"Lucinda—"

"Do whatcha like. I have my own issues. Are you done?"

He paused for a beat, but when he saw that I hadn't backed down from my position, he caved. "I guess so."

"Thanks." I walked back in the house. "Mom, are you going anywhere anytime soon?"

"No. I'm just going to be working in the garden."

"Is it okay if I leave Nadia here?"

"She's living here, isn't she?"

"She's still my responsibility."

"Lucinda, I'm here to help you. Me and your father. We have her. Go take care of what you need," my mom said as my father sat down beside her.

I rushed off to jump in the shower. I had to get out of this United States of Hell. Once I was dressed, I left to view a couple of apartments and one house, but none of them were what I really wanted. I was tired and frustrated, and I needed someone to talk to. Just as I had that thought, I passed by a set of condos and turned in. After pulling up to unit E, I eased out of my vehicle and knocked on the door.

"Lucinda?" Mike answered, both surprised and seemingly excited about my impromptu visit.

"Hey. Are you busy?"

"No. I'm here just chillin' out today. Come in." He stepped back, allowing me inside.

While entering his condo, I looked back over my shoulder and said, "Thanks."

Once inside, we sat in the living room.

"I haven't heard from or seen you since you were looking for Aldris. I've been worried as hell. I haven't heard from either one of you, and neither one of you has answered my phone calls. What the hell is going on?" he said, full of concern.

That was when I couldn't take it. Everything inside crashed down, and the dam that I'd tried to hold together finally broke. I fell over in a heap of tears. Mike picked me up and sat me next to him, his powerful arms around me, and I snuggled close. There were no words spoken. He simply held me for what seemed like hours as I purged all my heartache on him.

Once my verbal cries ceased, Mike spoke. "Everything is going to be okay. I'm here." He stroked circles on my back. "I'm here."

With wet eyes, I looked up at him. "He slept with her. He slept with Jennifer."

"What?" Confusion was splayed across his face.

"That night after the birthday party. He was at her house, and they had sex. He admitted it to me. I saw his car there, and he admitted it. We broke up. I hate him," I said around garbled cries.

His embrace tightened. "It's okay. Don't talk. Just let it out."

For the next thirty minutes, I lay on Mike's sofa, with my head in his lap, as he stroked my hair and I cried. I'd gone through half of his box of tissues, and I was completely exhausted.

"Would you like something to drink?" he asked.

"Water," I said meekly and sat up. "And aspirin, if you have it."

He got up and brought me a bottle of water and some Motrin. "Here you go."

I popped three pills and drank half of the water before placing the glass down on the coffee table. I lay back down, and that was the last I remembered before jumping up again.

"What time is it? Where am I?" I asked, looking around.

"It's a little after three," I heard a voice say from across the room, and I jumped.

I looked to my right and saw Mike sitting in his La-Z-Boy, watching basketball on television.

"Oh my God. Did I fall asleep?" I asked, rubbing my eyes. "I must have. I feel relieved."

He laughed. "Yeah, after you drank some water, you were out like a light. I figured you probably needed it, so I got you a pillow and a blanket and let you rest. You were out for only a couple of hours."

I stretched. "Thank you. You don't know how much I appreciate and needed that."

I drank the rest of my water, then reached for my purse and rummaged around until I found some gum and popped a piece in my mouth.

"It's no problem," he said. "I made some tacos if you're hungry."

I shook my head. "Nah. Not really."

"When is the last time you ate, Lucinda?"

"Um." I thought it over. Shrugging, I answered honestly. "I really don't know."

He got up and walked over to me, took me by the hand, and walked me into the kitchen. "You're eating. Sit," he ordered, pointing to his breakfast table, and I did as I was told. He pulled out a plate and started assembling a taco for me. "What do you want on it?"

"Lettuce, tomatoes, cheese, and sour cream. Do you have any Bud Light?"

"You already know," he laughed as he reached in the fridge for a bottle, and then he brought it and the plate of tacos over to me.

"Thank you. I didn't mean to intrude." The food looked and smelled so good that my stomach growled instantly. I bit into one of the tacos and scooped into my mouth a dollop of sour cream that had fallen back onto my plate. "Damn, this is really good."

"Your boy can burn now," he joked as he sat in front of me. "And you're not intruding. I'm happy you stopped by. I was worried about you, like I said."

I put my head down. "Yeah, I know."

He touched my hand. "Don't. Just eat."

With a head nod, I did as he had told me. Afterward, we walked back into his living room, and I called my mom. She told me that Nadia was good and that she had her, so I decided to sit at

Mike's a little while longer. I told him the entire story, from when I found Aldris's car at Jennifer's house at three in the morning to our subsequent breakup later that same morning. I even explained how I was staying with my mom and how her foolishness over accepting my dad back in her life was getting to me.

"I don't know, Mike. Everybody around me is just crazy. My mom is crazy, my daddy has been crazy, and Aldris—he is gonna drive me fucking crazy with his crazy ass."

"No, he's not. He's crazy, yes, but he won't *drive* you crazy. You're resilient. I see it in you. He did the absolute worst thing he could've possibly done, and you're still standing."

"I needed to hear that." I glanced at him and gave him a genuine smile for the first time. Then his condo's décor caught my eye, and I looked around. "Your place is really nice."

"Would you like a tour?"

"Sure."

We stood, and he took me through the dining room, the small playroom, his sons' bedroom, his daughter's bedroom, his bedroom, and then the small backyard. "It's not a whole lot, but it's big enough for me and my kids when they're here."

"It's lovely. You decorated it very well."

"I tried."

"You did good," I complimented. "I was looking for a place near Nadia's school. I didn't realize how spacious these condos are." I turned and admired his place again. When I turned back to face him, he was staring at me with a questionable look on his face.

"What is it?" I asked.

He rubbed his forehead and then stuck his hands in his pockets. "So, you're really not going back to Aldris, huh?"

I shook my head. "He made his choice, Mike. I made mine."

"But you love him."

"What does love have to do with it?"

"Can you just let go like that?"

"No, I can't, but I have to move on."

"Lucinda, maybe you should—"

My hands flailed in the air in my effort to stop him from pressuring me to reunite with his boy. "Mike, I realize that you're Aldris's friend first, but please spare me. He fucked up, not me, and I refuse to go back and be his doormat. I'm not the one singing 'Shoulda, coulda, woulda' here. All I have is my word and my pride, and I do not comprise that for nobody."

"Okay, hot tamale. Don't blaze up on me. I'm just saying. I know that you love Aldris, and I know that he fucked up, but I just don't want you to make a decision in anger now that you'll regret later," he said, offering his full reason behind the questions. "Oh, and I resent that 'Aldris's friend' comment. I'm your friend too."

"Ay, I'm sorry, Mike. I'm just so stressed. I know my decision seems abrupt, but I can't see myself going back. I just can't."

"I understand. And I apologize too. You've been through enough, and whatever you decide should be supported, not questioned."

An awkward silence settled in the room; then I laughed as Mike's comment finally hit me. "Did you just call me a hot tamale?"

He cracked a smile. "Yeah."

"You're stupid. I can't believe you said that shit."

"Well, you know how you Latina girls do. You were about to set my ass on fire, so I had to put up my guard," he teased, furthering my laughter.

After a moment, I turned serious and placed a gentle hand on his arm. "I could never blaze up on you too bad, Bruce Leroy."

He rubbed my hand. "And neither could I."

I looked at my watch and groaned at the time. It was four thirty.

"What?" Mike asked.

"It's nothing. I need to get to my mom's house and see about Nadia. I hate it there. Nadia loves it, but if I don't hurry up and find a place soon, I'm going to go straight postal. I can't stand living there almost as much as I can't stand Aldris," I said before preparing to head to the door. "That will teach me to live with a man and give up my place."

Mike cleared his throat and opened his mouth as if he was going to propose something, but instead, he said, "Well . . . never mind."

"What?" I asked him as I grabbed my purse.

"You'd say no."

"Say no to what?"

Mike glanced at me with an unsure expression as he rubbed the back of his neck. "I was kinda thinking after you told me about that living arrangement, I mean . . . if . . . you know . . . you needed . . . you know . . . someplace to stay and all, you could . . . I mean . . . if you wanted to . . . you could . . . stay here with me," he offered, stammering nervously.

My mouth fell agape at his offer. "Are you serious?"

"Yes. Since it's temporary, you and Nadia could stay here. I'm a bachelor living by myself, and my kids are here only twice a month, on the weekends. You two would just have to share the room with my daughter during those times, but if you wanted to, you could stay. No charge."

"Mike, I really couldn't intrude on you like that—"

"See, I told you, you'd say no," he interrupted.

"But even if I took your offer, there's no way I wouldn't let you charge me."

"Well, if you did take my offer, if you agreed to bake me a chocolate cake and keep my fridge full of Bud Light, then that would be payment enough."

"What's a case of Bud Light between friends?" I shrugged, then sat back down for a moment to ponder his suggestion. "Listen—and please don't take offense at this—but if I agree to this, I don't want Nadia to come with me."

"Okay, but why?"

"I'm not used to having my daughter around different guys. I know we're friends, and she knows that too, but when I lived with Aldris, she knew and respected him as her dad. I don't want to convey the wrong message to her."

He smiled. "I think that is very admirable. You're a great mom, Lu."

"And you're a great friend." I stood up to go. "I'm going to talk to my mom about Nadia staying with her until I find a spot, and if she's cool with it, you just found yourself a roommate."

"Cool. Anything I can do to help."

"I better go. The sooner I can find out if I can get from over there, the better."

He walked me outside and then retrieved a key from underneath a potted plant. "Here is my spare. Just in case you want to go ahead and move and I'm not here. Or even if you just want to chill out and get away. I'm cool with that," he told me, holding the key out to me.

"You ain't gon' never get a girl with me hanging around like that," I joked.

He waved off my joke with a chuckle. "It doesn't matter. Friends are forever. Besides, Gucci Mane already said, 'Girls are like buses. Miss one, next fifteen one comin'.'"

I cracked up laughing. "Ay, *chico*. You're a mess."

"Besides, I'm not looking for a girl. When the time is right, God will show me the woman who is supposed to be my wifey."

Mike had really matured over the past year, and I admired him so much. I was so happy that we could work through our differences and become friends. Without him, I didn't know what I would do.

I took the key; then I leaned forward and kissed his cheek. "You are so sweet and amazing. I don't know how I could make it without your friendship." I wiped my lip gloss from his cheek.

Mike rubbed my cheek. "You're pretty amazing too."

We said our goodbyes; then I hopped in my car and headed back to my mom's house. When I got there, Nadia and my brother Peter were sitting at the table, eating spaghetti, and my mom was cleaning up the kitchen.

"Thanks, Mom, for watching Nadia."

She smiled at me. "Don't thank me. Thank your father. He did the majority of the babysitting while

I tended to my garden. He even cooked," she said with a smirk.

"That's good." I didn't even feel like going there with her at the moment.

"Mami," Nadia said excitedly as I walked up and hugged her. "You've been gone all day. Where have you been?"

"Looking for places that we can live."

"Well, why don't we go back and live with Daddy? Are you that mad with him?"

My mom and I exchanged glances. There was no time like the present to break it down for Nadia. She understood that I was upset with Aldris and that was why we had moved out, but she didn't fully understand that he was no longer going to be in our lives.

"Peter, let's go in the other room," my mom said to my brother.

"I never get to hear the good stuff," he whined as he and my mom walked out.

I sat in the seat Peter had occupied. "Don't you like staying at your *abuela*'s house?"

She met my gaze with a toothy grin. "I love *abuela*'s house. And with *mi abuelo* here, it's so much fun. He is funny." She giggled, and I had to laugh. I remember being her age and feeling the same way about my father. Times had damn sure changed. "But I want to go home, to my room, and see my daddy. I miss him and Jessica."

Tears sprang into my eyes. I knew that she would take our breakup hard, but I had had no clue that it would truly affect her this much. "I know you do, sweetie. Maybe one day I can arrange for you to see Jessica, but Mommy and Daddy have a few things that we can't work out together, so that's why we moved."

Nadia put her head down. "We're not going back, are we?" she asked sadly.

I shook my head. "No, kiddo. We're not. Daddy loves you, and I love you too, but Daddy and I just can't be together anymore."

"It's because he missed my party, isn't it?"

That broke my heart. With everything else that had happened, I'd completely forgotten that this course of events had happened on her birthday. All she understood was that we had ended our relationship because of her party, and that both hurt me to the core and pissed me off to the core. "No, sweetie. He would've been there if he could, but he had a true emergency that came up. This is about something different." After turning her chair to face me, I cupped her face in my hands so that my next words resonated with her. "I need you to be good and to support Mommy."

She sighed and then got up and hugged me. "Okay, Mami. Everything will be okay."

I kissed her on the forehead and then walked out in a hurry. She made me want to break down,

and I could barely make it out of the kitchen without a few tears escaping. I went outside to get some
fresh air, and lo and behold, Emilio and my mom
were out there. This was getting a little out of hand.

"How'd she take it?" my dad asked.

"Better than I would have. She's mature beyond
her years."

"Kids are resilient like that," my mom said.

Since they were both there, I figured there was
no time like the present to talk to them about
Mike's proposition. I sat down. "I don't mean to
intrude on your private moment, but I do have a
question to ask."

An unsure glance passed between them. "What
is it?" my mom asked.

"I think that with all our differences, it may be
better if I live somewhere else until I find a place to
stay. I'm going through a lot with Aldris, and to be
honest, your new relationship bothers me. I can't
change what you both want, because you're adults.
Hell, you're my parents. At any rate, rather than
drag Nadia around the world, I would appreciate
if I could let her stay here. I could really focus on
finding a place and getting my head in the right
space."

My dad gazed at my mom for approval, and she
nodded. "It's your call. I don't have a problem with
it."

"Who are you going to be staying with?" my dad asked.

"My friend Mike."

He eyed me suspiciously. "Jumping into another relationship to replace one is not healthy—"

Putting my hand up, I cut him off. "I said *friend*. Not boyfriend. He is only my friend." Like he was one who could talk about jumping into relationships.

"If you feel that is best. I don't mind. I know you have to go back to work soon, and the noise level in the house will probably distract you," he said, giving up on his argument. Not that I was really asking him for permission anyway.

"Thank you," I said and stood up. "Let me go explain this to Nadia. Hopefully, I'll have a place to stay quickly."

"I told you. We've got you," my mom said. "Regardless of how you feel about our relationship, we love you, Lucinda. You and Nadia. That won't ever change."

"I love you too." I hugged my mom and intentionally left out Emilio. He hadn't earned the privilege from me yet.

Walking inside, I felt such an amazing sense of relief. I was shocked that my mom had agreed to the living arrangement, but I thought they were thankful that I and my negativity toward their relationship were leaving, so they'd agree to anything. It was all to the good, though. I didn't want to be around them any more than they cared to be around me, so it worked out.

Nadia was a little upset by the news, though, but after I explained that she'd see me every day, she was cool with it. Hell, truth be told, I was missing her already, but I needed this time to myself. I needed to heal so that I could continue to be beneficial to her and myself.

The arrangement worked out for my job as well. I'd taken a personal leave when all the shit with Aldris went down, and I'd have to be back to work soon. I had to set up my laptop at Mike's house so that I could begin work in the next couple of days, but that was no biggie since he was an IT guru.

I couldn't believe what close friends Mike and I had become. It was weird that just a few months ago, I could've spit on the ground he walked on, and now I could kiss the very feet he used to walk on the ground. I also wondered how my living arrangement was going to affect his friendship with Aldris. Even though I hated Aldris, Mike didn't have to hate him, and he was putting his lifelong friendship on the line for me. I could never forget that. I wasn't going to tell Aldris about my temporary stay if Mike didn't, but that was not because of Aldris. That was for Mike. I couldn't and wouldn't come between them and mar their friendship.

When I got to Mike's place, we made sure to set up my workstation first, and then I moved into his daughter's room. I felt ten again with the Nickelodeon posters and the décor, but the comfortable full-size bed, my own bathroom, and the television made it worthwhile.

I heard a knock at the bedroom door as I was unpacking my clothes. "Come in."

"Getting settled?" Mike asked.

"Yes. I can't thank you enough. This is a breath of fresh air to me."

"You've already thanked me enough. I saw the new case of Bud Light in the fridge," he laughed.

"A deal is a deal, right?"

"Yep. Well, I ordered some Pizza Hut. If you want some, you're welcome to it. And there are some UFC bouts coming on if you want to watch them with me."

I put down the items I was arranging on the dresser. "Pizza, beer, and UFC. I'm in." I hightailed it past him as he laughed.

We were sitting there analyzing the fights and eating when I noticed Mike shaking his head. "What?" I laughed. "You're amazed at how much I'm into this, huh?"

He drank a swig of his beer. "No, I'm amazed at how Aldris fucked up. I don't know what he thought he was missing. A part of me keeps trying to find something wrong, but I can't," he admitted.

"I guess he was missing Jennifer rather than it being something about me."

He quickly changed the subject back to the UFC, and I was glad. No talk of Aldris for at least one night was all I wanted. We watched a couple more bouts, until I decided it was time to hit the sack. I showered, brushed my teeth, and put on my black silk pajama pants and tank top.

By the time I'd hopped in the bed, rain was pelting the window, lightning was streaking across the sky, and rolling thunder was rumbling. As I lay there listening to the ferocity of the storm grow, I became nervous. I'd been on my own all these years, but it was the first time in forever I'd been without Nadia and Aldris. I felt scared and lonely. I wanted to call Nadia, but I knew she was asleep, so I lay there, scared out of my mind. After a good ten minutes, I went to the kitchen to grab a bottle of water to calm my nerves and ran smack into Mike.

"Oh, shit," I screamed. "I thought you were asleep."

"I thought you were too. What are you doing up?"

"What are you doing up?" I asked him right back.

"I was checking the house to make sure I locked up."

"I was just—" The flash of lightning, followed by a clap of thunder, caused me to jump out of my skin. "Scared," I added, finishing my sentence hurriedly.

He laughed. "Of God's weather?"

I put my hands on my hips. "Ha ha. Very funny. It may sound crazy, but I haven't slept alone in seven years. If it wasn't me and Nadia, it was me and Aldris. So I'm a little scared and lonely right now."

"I understand. Well, stay up as long as you like. *Mi casa es su casa*," he said and then went into his bedroom.

I sat in the kitchen for a minute, but that didn't help, either, so I tiptoed to Mike's room and knocked on the door. "Are you up?"

"Yes. Come in."

"I don't mean to be a bother to you, but can you stay up with me until the weather stops?"

He sat up. "Lucinda, why don't you just lie in here? I don't bite."

"I couldn't." Just then, there was a clap of thunder so loud, I damn near dove for Mike's bed. "Okay, maybe for a little bit," I said with the covers pulled up to my eyeballs.

He got a kick out of my fear, then scooted away from me. "Good night, Lucinda."

"Good night."

Lightning flickered through his curtains, and I instantly snuggled against him as I used to do with Aldris, but then I quickly moved back. "I'm sorry. That was inappropriate. It's just a habit I had with Aldris."

"No harm," he said, lying on his back, stiff as a board.

"I'm making you uncomfortable. I should get up."

His warm hand on my waist stopped me from moving. "No, it's just a little odd. I'm cool."

I inched away from him, and as I was listening to the rise and fall of his breathing, sleep found its way into my eyes. I was so used to being snuggled under Aldris that I moved under Mike again.

"What are you doing?" he whispered sleepily.

"I'm sorry. I'm just used to—"

He covered my lips with his index finger. "It's okay. Go back to sleep," he whispered, encircling me with his arms. A minute later he drifted to sleep.

But now, I was wide awake. The heat between my legs told me so. *What the hell?* I loved Aldris, but something about being here with Mike like this was turning me on. Biting my lip, I gazed up at him as he slept so peacefully. He was absolutely gorgeous. His build, his smell, his goatee. I had to get away from this man.

His eyes popped open. "Lu? What are you—"

"I'm sorry. I don't mean to stare. I'm sorry. I really need to go."

We lay there staring at each other, unsure of what to say or do. My mind said, *Get out*, but as I went to move, I felt Mike's hand on top of my mine. I looked back at him, and my body betrayed my thoughts. Slowly, I leaned toward him. Hesitantly, he met my movement. Breathing deeply, we allowed our lips to meet after a pregnant pause, and we lightly brushed each other with a kiss. Unable to resist, he pulled me to him, and we kissed passionately.

"Mmm, Mike," I moaned, straddling him. He kissed my neck, and his hands found their way inside my pants to rub on my ass. "Ay, Papi."

"Oh, baby," he moaned as he caressed my backside and his manhood rose to life underneath me. And, damn, did it have a long rise to the top.

Suddenly, Mike pushed me off him and scrambled to sit upright. "Shit, Aldris!"

"What? What about Aldris?" I knew it was wrong, but my body was on fire for him, and I wanted that comfort.

"He's my friend, Lu. I can't do this to him," he said, taking deep breaths. "I can't do this to you."

I sat up behind him and began massaging his shoulders. "Do you want me?"

"Lu, that's not fair." He looked back at me. "You're fine as all hell, and lying in my bed with that sexy shit on and smelling good, and it's raining, and you can kiss—"

"Do you want me, Mike?"

"Aldris is my friend. It doesn't matter what I want."

"So you do," I whispered in his ear.

"Do you want me, Lu?"

I looked at him seductively and smiled. "Yes." I ran my hands down his back. Yes, I wanted Mike, but for all the wrong reasons. I wanted him because I knew he cared, and I needed to feel loved. I needed the pain of losing Aldris to go away. I wanted to hurt him like he'd hurt me.

"Is that because of me or because you're pissed at Aldris?" he asked. "Don't do something you'll regret later. You still love him, Lucinda. That doesn't just go away."

He was right. I was vulnerable, and I was confusing my lust for him with my loss of Aldris. I was attracted to Mike, yes, but if I did this, it'd be out of selfish revenge and not because I truly wanted to be with Mike.

"You're right," I said, relenting, and stood up, struggling to fight back tears. "I don't know what came over me. I'm so confused and hurt right now." Light tears began to flow down my cheeks. "Now that I've made a complete idiot of myself, I really better go to Michaela's room."

He stood up and walked over to me. He held my face between the palms of his hands. "I know you're hurting, Lucinda. I realize that you just want to be loved. I'm not gonna flex and say I didn't want to, because, woman, you did something to me. I can admit that. A part of me would love to explore where things could go between us, but you and Aldris are my friends first. I abstain for the benefit of both of those friendships and for the relationship that may still exist between you and Aldris. Just know that if I knew tonight was going down for all the right reasons, I wouldn't hesitate . . . one . . . second," he explained, and with that, he kissed my forehead and opened his bedroom door. "Good night, Lu."

I walked out and turned around. "Thanks for being a good friend. Good night, Mike."

Damn, I was wrong. There was one man left who thought with the head on his shoulders instead of the one between his thighs, and that thought did the exact opposite of what I wanted. It made me want Mike that much more. I fell asleep with thoughts of Mike running through my mind. But for the sake of our friendship, I had to fight this thing . . . this thing . . . growing . . . between Mike and me.

Chapter 9

Lincoln

Ryan managed to weasel his way out one more time. This slimy bastard was so good, he could sense his downfall in the air. Sometimes I wondered if he had a damn GPS system on both my car and Charice's, because I could not believe I was so close to blowing the lid off that muthafucka without anything intentional on my behalf and I still didn't succeed. By the hair on his balls, he managed to dodge his own bullet again. I was almost positive that the shit Ryan wanted was nowhere near an emergency, but he needed an excuse to try to save his marriage, and he knew that if he cried wolf, Charice would coming running. Well, Little Bo-Peep better keep watching his sheep, because if I ever got the opportunity to tell Charice what she wanted to know, I was gonna sing like a fucking canary.

The thing that really bothered me, though, was the fact that I hadn't heard from Charice. I knew that she was okay, because I saw her carrying grocery bags into her house the day before, but she was so adamant about hearing my story that it was almost unreal that she hadn't tried to communicate with me. I wanted to call or text her, but the last thing I needed was for Ryan to catch wind of that. Charice would be in a worse position than she already was with Ryan, and I wasn't going to be the cause of that. Therefore, I was stuck in limbo, wondering what the fuck was going on in the Westmore residence.

"Dad," London yelled.

"*What*?" I said. I panicked and slammed on the brakes of my Mercedes G-wagon.

"There's a dance studio over there. *Look*. Can we check it out? Please?" London begged.

"Don't scare me like that. The way you yelled, I thought I was about to hit a car or something. *Jeez*."

"Well . . ." She folded her arms and gave me the side-eye as if she were the parent. "If you stopped daydreaming about Ms. Charice, then you would know that the car in front of you had already turned. Can we go before you miss the turn?"

Smart ass. I turned on the blinker to make the left turn instead. "And I wasn't daydreaming about Ms. Charice. What would give you that impression, London?"

She sat back in her seat and looked over at me sympathetically. "The other night when you fell asleep across the bed, you kept saying her name in your sleep. If you miss her, Dad, why don't you tell her?"

Even my child knew I had it bad. Damn. I thought that I'd managed to purge my feelings for Charice, but that impromptu meetup had stirred all the feelings that I'd tried to quell. I hated that my daughter had to witness my heartache, and it was definitely a subject that I could not delve into with her, although I knew she told me the truth out of concern for me and due to the fact that she loved Charice.

"It's not that simple, London. She's married."

"Well, why did you all break up in the first place? I liked Ms. Charice," she said, with a pout spread over her face.

"That's a story that you are too young to know about," I said, pulling up in the parking lot.

She pursed her lips. "I am ten. Not five."

"And you ain't twenty-five, either."

"Kids today are more mature than when you were growing up," she said matter-of-factly.

"And that's you all's problem today. You want to be grown in the wrong situations. Be mature when it comes to doing your schoolwork and learning, to listening to music that educates rather than discusses killin' and drug abusin', and be mature enough to know that no matter how mature you think you are, you ain't grown yet."

"Well, Dad, you listen to Rick Ross, and he talks about killin' and drug dealin'," London so graciously pointed out.

"True. However, I am a mature adult. I have the mature adult sense to know that is just music. That's not life or the life I want to live. You kids get so caught up and gassed up on what these rappers are saying, without thinking that if they were truly doing everything in those songs, they wouldn't have time to be writing the songs, rapping, making money, and performing at concerts. I realize that's not their lifestyle, but you kids don't. Then there are some knuckleheaded sixteen-year-olds running around, thinking they're Big Meech and not knowing who in the hell Big Meech really is, not knowing that he's in prison because of the things that Rick Ross raps about."

Her eyes grew wide with surprise. "For real?"

"Yes, London. For real," I confirmed, realizing that I'd just dropped some knowledge on her.

"Wow. I never knew that. I guess you are right, Daddy," she told me, relenting.

Inside, I smiled. *Score one for the parents!* "Yes, London. I am. I probably shouldn't be listening to Rick Ross in your presence anyway, so I'm going to stop doing that and lead by example. So no hard-core gangsta rap while we're together."

"This is gonna be funny. You love rap," she teased behind a fit of giggles.

After laughing at her joke, I admitted, "Yes, I do. But I will sacrifice to show you a better way. As parents, we don't always get it right, because we're human too. What I can give you is the knowledge that I've been ten and any other age that you will get to, so I know what pressures and consequences lie ahead for certain things. If it wasn't for my dad, I don't know where me and my brother would be. I certainly wouldn't be an athlete, that's for sure. It's my duty to look out for you in the same way."

We finally got out of the SUV, and once I went around the car and met her, she hugged me. "Thanks, Daddy. I love you."

Damn. My grown ass wanted to cry. It was the first real bonding moment we'd had since she'd moved to New York. I bear-hugged her in return. "I love you too, little lady," I said as we walked toward the building.

"But sometimes I wish you weren't an athlete, though."

"Why?" I looked down at her. "Am I not around enough?"

She giggled. "No, it's not that. I love being at Grandma's anyway."

"Well, what is it? It's a respectable career, and not to toot my own horn here, but even though I'm not Rick Ross or Jay-Z, I'm well known too, you know."

She giggled. "Oh, *I know*. To me, you're just Dad, but to my classmates and a couple of my teachers, you're *the Lincoln Harper*. I get tired of them asking about you all . . . the . . . time. And I overheard my assistant principal, Ms. Lewis, talking to one of the third-grade teachers, Mrs. Bowman, saying that you were fine as wine. Yuck! I'm, like, ew, that's my dad."

I burst out laughing. I was used to the reactions and the comments from women, but it was hilarious to see how London reacted to my fame. So I had to mess with her a bit. "Hey, where do you think you get your looks from?"

She laughed. "OMG. That's gross. TMI."

"Okay, kiddo, you've got to stop speaking in text lingo," I said as we reached the building. I read the sign posted on the door. "They just opened, London. They are still hiring staff," I said, relaying the message on the sign, before I opened the door for her.

"The Art of Dance," London said aloud as she read the name of the building.

The receptionist greeted us brightly when we walked inside. "Hello. My name is Kira. How may I help you?"

"Yes, I wanted to check out your facility. My daughter is a dance student, and we just moved here, so I am trying to find her a new studio."

"You've come to the right place. We have only a few classes right now, but new classes will be added as we bring on more instructors. We just opened up so it's a work in progress, but I can take you on a tour. I'm sure you'll find that this is the place for your daughter," Kira said. She looked over at London and offered her hand. "And your name, sweetie?"

"I'm London," she answered, shaking Kira's hand.

I shook my head at my own rudeness. "Excuse me for being rude. I'm her dad, Lincoln."

"No worries, Lincoln. Right this way."

As we walked through the facility, I could tell that it was state of the art. It was spacious and had different classrooms for different age groups, advancement levels, and genres of dance. London was in awe. It even had a cafeteria area and a high-tech waiting area, complete with flat-screens and computers. I had to admit I was impressed too.

During the final stretch of the tour, Kira gave me a brochure. "We also have tuition assistance and grants to help with the financial needs—"

"Oh, my dad doesn't need money help," London interrupted. "He's *the* Lincoln Harper," she added, joshing me from earlier.

Kira's mouth dropped. "*Oh my God.* I thought you looked familiar. You're him—the guy from the billboard."

"Gee, thanks, London," I said, faking sarcasm. "Yes, that's me."

"*Oh my God*. I have to introduce you to the owner. You'll probably know her. Her husband plays football too," Kira said as she motioned for us to follow her.

We walked down the hall and stepped inside the owner's office, and before the receptionists could even speak, I did.

"Charice?" I asked as she stood up from her desk, in shock.

"*Ms. Charice*," London screamed and ran to hug her.

"London? Lincoln?" Charice asked, puzzled, as she hugged London.

"I'm sorry, Charice. When they brought it to my attention that he was the guy from the billboard, I had to bring him back. I take it you two know each other, so I'll leave you," Kira said. She walked out and shut the door behind her.

Charice looked as if she'd seen a ghost or some shit. "What are you doing here?" she asked nervously.

London spoke before I could even part my lips. "I was looking for a dance studio. Please tell me you'll teach me. Please!"

This must've been the reason why I hadn't heard back from Charice. Ryan had to have sprung this dance-studio crap on her to make up with her. He knew this was her dream, and if he could provide that for her, then she'd be too joyous to stay pissed with him. That nigga had always been one slick-ass playboy, and I just couldn't believe Charice had fallen for his shit yet again.

"So he suckered you in with the studio, huh?" I shook my head.

"Lincoln, don't. He's my husband," she said, defending him. "How about we go out front, to the lobby area?" Charice suggested.

I picked up on that hint. She wanted us to go. "London, we'd better find another studio. I don't think this one will be a good idea."

"Why?" London whined. "I want Ms. Charice to teach me."

"Because I said so," I boomed in frustration. "Didn't we just talk about maturity?"

I didn't feel like discussing it anymore. Charice was already trying to get rid of us, probably before Ryan brought his raggedy ass in there, and I'd had enough of them and all their fucking drama.

"But, Daddy," London said, pouting. "Just because you and Ms. Charice aren't dating doesn't mean she can't teach me to dance. You're so unfair," she whined.

"Little girl, I do not have time for this. There are things you don't understand, and Charice will not do it," I snapped, my anger unnecessarily directed at my daughter.

Charice looked back and forth between us and blurted, "*I'll do it*. I mean, the studio is open to anyone. Can we just head to the lobby?"

Now I knew something was up. There was no way she'd willingly agree to teach London to dance, especially knowing how Ryan would feel about it. Something was up with her.

"Why are you so jumpy, and why would you agree to do that, given the circumstances?" I asked.

She looked as if she were sweating bullets. "Nothing. I just would rather—"

Suddenly, we heard a wail. A cry almost. A baby's cry.

"You have a *baby*?" I asked her.

"Um . . . ," she mumbled, stalling.

A thought overcame me, and I prayed to God I was wrong. She hadn't been with Ryan long enough to have a baby. All of a sudden, I thought about Ryan's behavior, Charice's behavior, and her insistence on getting us out of this building. I knew damn well . . .

Anger brimmed inside of me. "How old, Charice?"

"Um . . ."

"London, go sit in the lobby," I instructed, never taking my eyes off Charice.

London must've sensed the seriousness in my voice, because she left without an argument. Charice and I stared at each other for a few moments, until the baby started to cry again.

She went into the room on the other side of her office and came back with a small bundle all wrapped up. I couldn't see the baby, but I could see that Charice was shaking like a leaf.

"Whose baby is that?"

"Mine," she said nervously.

"And Ryan's? You and Ryan had a baby to-gether?" I had to know. I could be wrong. I had to be wrong. Right?

Instead of answering me, she closed her eyes, and tears fell down her cheeks.

"Wait a minute, Charice. *Who is the father*?"

Instantly, all my senses were out of control. I felt nauseous and angry, defeated yet elated, nervous yet duped all at the same time. I just knew that she wasn't going to tell me what was running through my mind. It couldn't be. It . . . just . . . could . . . not . . . be.

She walked over to me and removed the blanket shielding the baby's face, and I swore I was looking at an image of myself when I was a baby. I gasped. My closed fist covered my mouth as I fell back about two or three steps.

"This is Lexi McKenzie Westmore, and she is your daughter—our daughter," she admitted through her tears.

That admission knocked the rest of the wind out of me, and I fell backward into one of her chairs. I had a daughter—with Charice. I couldn't move. I couldn't think. I wanted to hug Charice and kill her at the same time. Then I looked up at her, and I got mad. M-a-d. A rage swelled up inside me that was so intense that I knew if I didn't get out of there soon, they'd have to call the police on me. I stood up and turned to walk to the door.

"Lincoln, please don't be upset. I can explain."

She walked up on me with the baby in her arms. I turned around and put my hand up to block her. "*No*. Back the fuck away from me, Charice. Seriously. You don't want it with me right now. I'm so fucking pissed off right now. I can't even think straight," I said, then turned to leave.

"But, Lincoln—"

"But, Lincoln, what? Huh? *What*?" I snapped. "You're gonna explain to me how you were pregnant with my daughter and didn't tell me? Or how you had the audacity to have the baby and didn't tell me that I was a father? Or better yet— and you're gonna love this one—why you named my fucking baby after your damned husband? *Westmore*? Really? Are you shitting me? You gave *my* seed Ryan's last name? Believe me, you don't want it with me right now, damn it. I'm so gawd-damned mad, it ain't even fucking funny."

I slung the door open, stormed out to the lobby, and motioned for London to follow me. "Let's go. *Now*," I said with such finality in my voice that London jumped up quickly and hightailed it with me.

"Mr. Harper, did you like the facility?" Kira asked as we approached the receptionist's desk.

"It was fine," I said and walked out the door, with London fast on my heels. "Get in the car and do not say a word. You will not be coming here for dance, and that's final," I hollered as we got in my car.

I dialed my mother's number.

"Hey, baby," she answered.

"Ma, I need to drop London off. I have some things to work out. Can you keep her for a day or so?"

"What's going on?" my mom asked.

"Nothing. Well, something, but nothing I need to discuss right now. Can you do it?"

"Yes, of course."

"Good. We'll be there in, like, twenty minutes." I disconnected the line. "You're staying over there for a day. Grandma will take you to school."

"Dad, what's wrong?" London asked, filled with concern.

"Everything and nothing all at the same time. Trust me, be a kid for as long as you can, because being an adult is a bitch."

We rode the rest of the way in silence.

Chapter 10

Charice

Once Lincoln left, I sat in my office, trembling like the nervous wreck I was. I didn't know what to say or do. All kinds of shit was running through my mind. Would he try to retaliate and hurt Ryan and me? Would he sue me for custody of Lexi? Would he fight for his parental rights? Did he hate me? He had left so abruptly that I hadn't been able talk to him. Of course, I had known I wouldn't be able to get a word in edgewise once he found out. Now I regretted not listening to my mom, LaMeka, and even Lucinda, who had told me it was better to tell Lincoln and let the chips fall where they may than to keep it from him. My hardheaded decision was definitely making for a soft ass.

The more I thought about it, the angrier I became with myself. I couldn't believe I'd hidden Lexi from Lincoln all this time. She was four months old now. What the hell had I been thinking? No matter what Lincoln had done to me, he didn't deserve not to know about his child or not to have the opportunity to develop a relationship with her. Now I knew how Aldris felt. Hell, at the time it had made sense, Lincoln had been an ass, and we hadn't been together. It had seemed like the perfect solution. But with one look into Lincoln's eyes, I had known that it was the worst decision I'd ever made in my life. He had looked at me as if he hated me.

I decided the best thing for me to do now was to take Lexi back home to Johanna so that I could be by myself and figure out what to do. I definitely couldn't tell Ryan what had happened, at least not until I figured out what to do to get the situation under control.

"You're back early, Mrs. Westmore," Johanna said, surprised, when I walked in the house. "Mr. Westmore just left to go to a meeting with his agent."

"Yeah, he told me he had a meeting today. I just needed to drop Lexi off with you. I have some errands to run."

"Are you okay, Mrs. Westmore? You seem very troubled," she commented, taking Lexi out of my arms.

I rubbed my forehead. "I just have a lot on my mind."

She put her hand on my shoulder. "Let the Lord guide you. He will. Just trust Him."

Even that little bit of comfort was enough to calm me down. I sure was going to need every bit of the good Lord to help me figure out how to handle this situation. I kissed Lexi, left the house, and got back in the car.

"Lord, I need you now." Just as I said that, my cell phone rang. I knew before I even looked at the screen that it was Lincoln.

"I'm coming back to the studio, and we are gonna have a long muthafucking discussion when I get there. But I'm letting you know right fucking now that I want to be a part of my daughter's life, and I want her name changed to Harper," he seethed as soon as I answered.

"I'm not at the studio—"

"Well, I'm bringing this discussion wherever the fuck you're at," he retorted.

I deserved his anger and his harshness, but I still had to try to contain this situation. As mad as Lincoln was, if his fury was compounded by Ryan's anger and *if* Ryan found out that Lincoln knew about Lexi, I couldn't even imagine the outcome.

"I will talk to you about everything. That is a promise. Can we just not do it at our homes? The nanny is at my house, and you know what happened the last time Ryan caught me at your house."

He huffed, his frustration evident. "The only reason I'm giving you any kind of sympathy is that my mom calmed me down a little bit and that if I see your bitch-ass husband, I'ma put his ass in a box," he screamed. "Meet me at my parents' old house in Queens."

"Queens?" I said, more to myself than to him. Traffic was a bitch when you went over the Hutchinson River Parkway Bridge to get to Queens, and the trip there could easily run anywhere from forty minutes—on a good day—to an hour.

"Or we can make it two-forty Murray Hill. It's your choice," he said, his tone threatening.

"No. I'm just thinking of the traffic, but I will be there. Are you leaving now?"

"As soon as I pull over and get some gas."

"Okay, I'm leaving my house now." I pulled out of my garage and checked the fuel gauge to make sure my tank was full.

"A'ight. See you then," he acknowledged and hung up.

The ride to Queens was a somber one. I played all kinds of inspirational gospel music to help keep my stomach from lurching out of my body. My nerves were all over the place because I didn't know what to expect. Would Lincoln flip out and beat the hell out of me? How the hell did you have a decent discussion about keeping a child away from a parent? I had to pull over to get some Pepto

Bismol just to make the rest of the trip. I called Johanna and asked her to get the boys from school and told her to tell Ryan that I had an important meeting, so I wouldn't be home until later that night.

As I suspected, when I pulled up in the driveway, Lincoln was already there. Let's just say I had taken the scenic route to his parents' house. He'd already called me twice, and I hadn't been able to bring myself to answer the phone. He came out of the house as soon as I pulled up, and stopped short when he saw my car. He stood with his arms folded across his chest.

"I started to drive back to Scarsdale and go to your house," he said as soon as I stepped foot outside my vehicle.

"I couldn't exactly remember the way," I lied.

"That's why I called you. You shoulda answered. But I'm sure you enjoyed the extra time to avoid me," he said as we walked into his parents' old house.

Stepping over the threshold, I said, "I can't avoid the unavoidable, Lincoln."

"But you sure as hell was gonna try."

Trying to calm him, I pleaded for a smooth conversation. "Lincoln, let's try to be adult about this. I know that what I did was messed up, but let's just deal with the here and now."

Lincoln looked at me as if I'd lost my mind. "Woman, you have some nerve. I swear, you've been around Ryan too long now. How do you skip over the fact that you've lied to me for a year? You were pregnant and never even told me, and then you had the nerve to have my baby and pass her off as Ryan's, and I'm supposed to be calm now? You and that fuck nigga husband of yours are fucking crazy," he spewed angrily.

"Well, what do you want me to say, Lincoln? What do you want to do about it, huh? Do you want to beat me up? Cuss me out? Kill me? Is that it? Go ahead. If it makes you feel better, then do what you gotta do. It doesn't change the fact that Lexi is here, and she is yours. And it damn sure doesn't change the fact that Ryan and I were wrong, but what can we do about it now?"

Lincoln took a step back; then he turned, walked into the living room, and sat on the sofa. I sent up a "Thank you, Lord" as I walked into the room behind him, happy that he hadn't done any of the things I suggested. At least now I knew I was safe. I just didn't know what else was going to go down with regard to Lexi. There was no way he was going to take her away from me. If that was his plan, he could go ahead and do me in, because that was the only way I was giving up my child.

Lincoln held his head in his hands, and I sat down on the other end of the sofa, just waiting for him to say something. Anything.

The next thing I heard was weeping. "How could you do that to me, Charice? *How*? And from you—*you*. I've gone through so much shit, so much shit that hurts, and you did this . . . this . . . this horrible, despicable thing to me. How could you?"

It was the first time I'd ever seen Lincoln truly break down. I felt so horrible. I had to be the worst person on the face of the earth to him and myself at this moment. His pain made me tear up, and I couldn't believe that I actually had been heartless enough to keep Lexi from him. Especially after he had told me the story about how he had to fight for London. I should've come clean then, but it just hadn't seemed as devastating at the time. Now I realized that it was. He had every right to hate me and Ryan. We deserved that and so much more.

I had to tell him the entire story. I owed him that much. I also needed to air it out for myself so I could let go of all the pain. I wiped my tears. Then I forced him to remove his hands from his face. I wiped his tears with my hands, and then I held his hands in mine as I began to confess to him.

"I don't even have the words to say as to why I did what I did, Lincoln. All I know is that I was hurting. You'd left me, and I loved you so much. So damn much. The night you broke things off, Ryan came over, and he was there for me. That's how we got close again. Ryan was the first person I told I was pregnant. He wanted to get back together then, but I couldn't. I wasn't over you.

"Then, when my baby girl Charity got sick, it nearly tore me down. After she was hospitalized, I got so angry with you. I mean, I was so furious with you for leaving me, and it was compounded by Charity's illness and subsequent death. I won't lie to you. I wanted to hurt you. I wanted to get back at you for leaving me and our family, so I took all my feelings and emotions for you and I bottled them up into keeping Lexi from you. I forgave Ryan and decided that I should marry him and be with him. And I did." The floodgates opened, and I allowed every tear that I'd held in over the past year to pour down my face. Those were the realest, rawest, and sincerest emotions I'd ever shown him.

Lincoln looked at me as I put my head down and cried a river. The next thing I felt was him pulling me up to hold me in his arms. For the next few minutes all that could be heard were sniffles and cries as we both let out our emotions on each other.

"So if you're going to hate me, hate me. You have every right to hate me. Hell, *I* hate me. You didn't deserve that, no matter what happened between us, and neither does Lexi. And even though it's not worth shit now, I'm so sorry," I added after our tears had somewhat subsided.

He exhaled slowly, and I could feel his tension and anger easing away. "I want to hate you, but I can't, because I failed you too, Charice. As your man and your soon-to-be husband, I failed you so badly."

Something about what he'd just said drew fear inside of me. I didn't want to hear what he was about to say. Don't get me wrong. My heart wanted to hear it. More than likely, I needed to hear it. There were so many doors left open in our relationship, ones that we had never bothered to close, so I had made my closure, or so I thought. Until that moment. This ball of conflict tore me apart. My head screamed, *No, don't listen*, but my heart . . . my heart said yes.

In a last-ditch attempt to leave the past in the past, I pleaded, "Let's just focus on what we're going to do about Lexi."

"No, I'm gonna say what I should've said over a year ago." He turned my face to him and cradled my cheek. "You need to know the truth, Charice, and I'm gonna give it to you."

"I can't, Lincoln, because it will—"

"It will *what*? Change things? Make you look into places and feelings you thought you'd closed and overcome? I face that shit every day, every time I see you with Ryan," he explained with conviction.

I stood up and turned away. I was ready to jet out of that house. This moment of reckoning had become too much to bear. "If this isn't going to be about Lexi, I don't need or want to hear it. Ryan is my husband."

He grabbed my hand. "And don't you think you need to hear about the kind of man your husband really is?" he asked, turning me around. "Look, I will admit that I came to New York to be a thorn in Ryan's side. I wanted to ruin your marriage. But I have a new outlook. I have a daughter to raise, and now another one to love and raise as well. It's time-out for the bullshit. Whether you stay with Ryan or not doesn't matter to me anymore. Lexi and London are who matter to me. I just want you to know the truth. I want you to know that I didn't just leave you—I was forced to."

My mouth flew open, and I shook my head in disbelief. "Huh? What?"

Lincoln took my hands and gently pulled me back down onto the sofa. Then he pulled over the ottoman from the La-Z-Boy and sat in front of me. "The truth is your husband is the king of deceit. After he found out about me and you, he threatened me all the time, him and his little clique on the Cowboys team. At first, it was just physical shit—you know the altercations that we got into—but then that shit got real. During his unrestricted free-agent status, he worked out a scheme and told the Cowboys' administration he would reject the contract the Giants had offered him and would stay on the team if they traded me. At the time, he was the best running back they had, and I was the best linebacker, but the team had two other good linebackers and a decent backup, so I was expendable, and Ryan knew that.

"The only problem was my salary. Nobody in the league was willing to foot the cost of my contract at the time, and Ryan knew that too. That meant they could just waive me, and I'd be stuck searching for a team. He issued me his ultimatum—either leave you or have my contract waived. The sneaky shit, which no one took into account, was that whether or not I gave up on you, he was leaving the team anyway. His goal in all of it was just to break us up, and either way, I'd be on the losing end." He took a deep breath.

He went on. "That shit hurt me so bad, Charice. We were newly engaged, and I couldn't be in limbo with my money and career, not with having you, the boys, Charity, and London to support. In the NFL, your only lifelines are your practice and game stats. I couldn't take the risk of having to sit out a season or mulling about teams that weren't the best fit for me. That's when you and I began arguing and having problems. I couldn't bring myself to tell you what I was considering."

Talk about being floored. I couldn't believe what I was hearing, and to what lengths Ryan had gone just to get me away from Lincoln.

"Oh my God. Lincoln, why didn't you just tell me?"

"Why? I'll tell you why. After we started arguing, I started drinking a lot. Ryan convinced me that he wanted to call a truce. He said that he understood that I wasn't going to leave you, and he'd learn to live with it. He said we both could just squash the shit and keep playing for the Cowboys. No hard feelings. I thought he was being straight up with me, nawimean? I guess a part of me wanted to believe him because I didn't want to give up on what we had.

"But that grimy, dirty, reckless bastard took me out with him to go drinking, and he brought some laced cigars for a fellas' night out. While we were out, he told me this elaborate lie about how you two were cool now, and how you'd confided in him that you were pregnant, but since we weren't married, you didn't want to have another child out of wedlock, so you had an abortion. I was so upset with you. I lit up a cigar to relax my nerves. Being a little tipsy already, I didn't realize weed was inside the cigar, nor that he was capturing it all on video. Then he told me that if I confronted you about the pregnancy, he'd report me to the team, which, of course, would've led to a suspension and made it easier for the team to release me.

"This bastard even went so far as to send the video to Lauren, which he knew would also cause issues for me about London. Of course, Lauren threatened to take London completely away from me and actually had my visitation restricted to supervised visitation. That started an all-out battle between her and me. Your husband tried to ruin my career, forced us apart, and tried to take my child away from me."

My ears were burning. This could not be the same man I had married. It absolutely could not. The person Lincoln had described was a villain to the umpteenth degree. Only the devil could mastermind something this extravagant. This was not my Ryan. Not now. Not ever. It couldn't be.

I jumped up, as if a fire had been lit underneath me. "You're a liar. Ryan would never do that to you or me."

Lincoln's fiery gaze met mine. "Oh, yeah? Well, call Rosalyn, then. Why the hell do you think I had to fight so hard to get London after her mom's breakdown, huh? Come on. Not only am I her father, but I have plenty of money and a sound environment too. There's no way in hell the judge could even deny me. I had my parental rights, but my custody rights were stripped with the whole 'drug abuse' issue. Hell, you can call my mother. She knows what Ryan did to me. Why do you think I came home and broke up with you that night? Wasn't I drunk and high then? And I bet Ryan ran over to your hotel room, swearing he was clueless about anything just to be your fucking knight in shining armor.

"Then this bastard signed his contract with the Giants anyway. Why do you think I came all the way to Atlanta to whip his ass the day Charity passed out in the yard? I gave you up . . . for what? Nothing. He left the team anyway, had me tied up in all kind of nonsense legal bullshit over my little girl, and we still ended up not being together. So, if you want to blame somebody for losing me and our family, blame your husband. If you don't believe me, ask him. He schemed to take you away from me."

My body shook with such intensity that I thought I'd begun convulsing. I felt like my chest was about to explode. This couldn't be, could it? I had always known there was a reason Ryan was so secretive about leaving Dallas, but this? But how could it not be true? If I look at just the things that had happened that I knew about, they coincided perfectly with what Lincoln had said. We had begun to argue a lot. He had developed trust issues with me and had pulled away from me. He had drunk a lot. He had had problems with London, and more importantly, he'd always alluded to the fact that Ryan was the cause of his troubles and mine too.

Where did that leave me with this information? I was hurt, devastated, and pissed. When Ryan had done what he did, he'd known I'd turn to him for solace, and with Charity passing, I naturally had flocked to him. No wonder he'd asked if Charity's death was God's way of punishing him. I had never known why he'd think that, especially since he'd made up for his wrongdoings with the kids and me. I guess now I knew.

Despite being damn near hysterical about everything Lincoln had told me, for some reason, the one thing that pissed me off more than anything was the fact that Lincoln had felt I'd ever kill our child. "How could you think that I would kill our baby without even mentioning it to you?" I managed to choke out, hitting his chest with my fists.

He absorbed the hits until I grew tired and I fell into him. I was distraught over everything that had taken place. I felt hurt, betrayed and, most of all, like a damn fool.

"I don't know, Charice. I was so messed up in the head during that time, I didn't know which way was up or out. I knew you and Ryan talked, and I've always felt he had the advantage over me, because you two had children. I also knew how much you used to love him. When he sprung that on me, he made sure I had plenty on my plate to deal with so that I couldn't even fully focus on you," he explained before he pulled away from me, stood, and started pacing the floor. "What about you, huh?" he continued. "You ran to him, as if I was nothing. As if I meant nothing to you. Then you married him so fast, I wondered if you had even loved me at all. Now I find out you're passing my seed off as his."

"Are you kidding me right now?" I stared at him in disbelief. "*You* left *me*. I begged you like a fool to stay, to trust in us. But you gave up. You gave up, and I was the one left holding on to my feelings for you. Hell, I still loved you even after I married Ryan. I prayed and asked God to take those feelings away, because I couldn't let go," I blurted out. I gasped, covering my mouth.

Shocked, he looked back at me. "You what?"

With my hand still over my mouth, I shook my head, refusing to repeat my innermost secrets. "Nothing."

Calmly, Lincoln approached me with determination. His demeanor begged for my honesty. "Charice, don't lie to me. For the first time in a very long time, we have the opportunity to be totally honest. Are you telling me that when you first married Ryan, you were still in love with me?"

And there it was. My truth. As bad as Lincoln had hurt me, as angry as I was with him, as much as I wanted to hate him, none of that mattered, because to my core, I had loved him. And to my core, a part of me still did. Very much so.

Wiping my tears, I confessed, "Yes."

"Is that why you lied to Ryan and didn't tell him about the kiss? Did it stir up feelings for me that you didn't want to admit you still had?" he asked as he closed the space between us.

I couldn't say it. I couldn't let the words fall from my lips. I began trembling and backed away from him. "I lied to protect him."

He eyed me with a half smile on his face. "Come on now. Be truthful."

"That's the truth." We both knew I was lying.

A hint of mischief flashed in Lincoln's eyes as he rubbed his hands together. "You know, the funny thing about the truth is that it always has a way of getting out."

A beat passed before he licked those LL Cool J lips of his and then invaded my personal space, cornering me in a world I'd fought so hard to escape. Lincoln's land. In the land of Lincoln, I was a captive, a willing one. In that land, love, lust, and longing dwelled, and when I was trapped in that land, it was euphoric. Fuck that. Utopia. As I backed away, he inched forward, determined to make me linger there just long enough to apply for an all-season pass.

"I told you and Ryan, New York is *my* state. And your husband should never tell his personal business to his business partners who happen to be really good friends with me." He pulled me close to him. There was nowhere for me to go, and I was dangerously close to giving up the fight. "I know what you said to Ryan in the shower, Charice. Just be real with me."

My knees buckled, but Lincoln caught me and held me upright. "You . . . you . . . know," I stammered.

"When it comes to you, there isn't much I don't know, except about the baby. That you kept hidden pretty good."

"It was a mistake."

"Was it?"

"Ye-yes."

"Not that," he said, lifting my face to match his gaze and confirming that he was no longer referring to the baby.

"I'm married."

"I love you."

"Even though—"

"No matter what," he interrupted.

"I can't—"

"Hush." He placed his thumb to my lips and then replaced it with his lips and kissed me passionately.

My mind said, *Resist*—I promise it did—but my heart and my body gave way instantly. I kissed him with such fervor and frenzy that it scared me. I knew I'd crossed a line with Lincoln, and I pushed back from him immediately.

"Oh my God." I touched my lips in disbelief and glanced at my ring finger. "I'm married."

Lincoln grabbed my hands and caressed them. "Are you married in your heart, mind, and soul or on paper?"

I snatched my hands away from him. "Married is married. Unless I'm not married, I'm not going there with you."

"So, what you're saying is you want to go there with me, but you can't, because you're married?" he asked, eyeing me.

Shit, that was exactly what I just said to him. Would I? Did I? I didn't know. My mind was swirling off this new information about Ryan, which I just didn't want to believe. I was angry at both of them and myself. Not to mention, I was confused and jacked up on old feelings and new feelings, so I couldn't trust what I was feeling at the time.

"Lincoln, I don't know what to think or feel. If you're truthful, you've just told me that I lost you because of Ryan, whom I probably would've never married if he hadn't manipulated you and me. However, I did marry him, and I married him for a reason—"

"It sure as hell wasn't love," he cut in.

"But I love him *now*. My anger toward him doesn't turn that off. Just like it didn't turn it off for you."

He rubbed his neck in frustration. "So you'd really be with him, knowing what you know?"

"I don't know. I have to sort it all out for myself. You've known for a year. I've known for all of ten minutes, and my position is different than yours. I can't change the fact that I love him, that we have kids, and that we are married at this very moment." I walked over to the window and leaned my head against the cool pane of glass. My life was such a mess.

I heard him walking toward me. He stood behind me and rubbed my shoulders, then whispered, "You're right, Ma. You can't. I'm sorry for trying to force you to choose. I was wrong for that. I love you so much, Charice, and I want you back so badly that I overstepped my boundaries. I know you need time to work through this, and whatever you decide, I will support. I give you my word that if you choose Ryan, I won't interfere ever again. The only thing I ask is to be a part of Lexi's life and that she bears my last name. I'll pay child support, do visitation, and anything else, according to your terms, but Lexi is my daughter, and I want her in my life. Having her mother also would be an added bonus, though."

I smiled. "You just had to add that in, didn't you?"

"You know I had to get it in. You know, do my campaign plea, like the politicians," he said as I laughed.

I turned to face him. "I hear you. Loud and clear. I have to go and break this down to Ryan and get some answers from him. But I will contact my attorney in the morning to get the process started on the name change. As for visitation and child support, I can discuss that after I've talked to Ryan. Fair enough?"

"Fair enough . . . for now . . . but I trust you."

I reached up and hugged him. "Thank you for forgiving me and being patient and understanding. I promise you I'll make it right. And I thank you for the information."

He looked down at me. "I know you can't accept it now, but when you do, I'll be there. As for my forgiving you, I can never stay angry at you for long. Real love doesn't allow that. I just hope you forgive me for allowing our relationship to end the way it did."

I nodded. "Yes, I do."

"Thank you."

"I better go home. Ryan is probably livid."

Lincoln lifted my face to his. "If I never get this opportunity again, I want you to know that I love you. I always have, and I always will."

My eyes misted. It took everything inside of me to keep from getting choked up. "I gotta go, man."

He bent down and kissed me softly, sweetly, and gently. I was so lost in that kiss that my eyes were still closed even after he pulled back. "Open your eyes, baby. I'm done. Go home and get your answers. I'll be waiting."

My eyes slowly fluttered open as I came out of my Lincoln land trance. "I . . . I . . . am. I'm going."

I picked up my keys and purse and headed to the front door. Lincoln walked me to the door and then stood back. As I gripped the handle, I noticed he wasn't leaving.

"I have to lock up," he said, as if he was reading my mind.

I nodded and turned the handle to leave. I swore, a part of me wanted to shut the door and stay, but I forced myself out, because staying was not the solution.

When I got in my car, I picked up my cell phone. It'd been three hours. Ryan had called me twenty times and had left six voice messages.

Great, I thought. *Now I have to deal with his attitude, but he's got another thing coming.*

He was giving me truthful answers tonight, 'cause I could promise him, he didn't want it with me.

Chapter 11

Ryan

"Are you sure she said she had a meeting to go to?" I asked Johanna, holding the phone between my chin and shoulder as I tried to warm Lexi's bottle.

"Yes, Mr. Westmore. That's what she told me. Do you need me to come back to the house to help? Or perhaps try to call her? I'm sure she should've been home by now," Johanna offered.

"No. It's okay. I'm sure she'll show up. If she's not here in thirty minutes, I'm calling the police."

Johnna offered her apologies again before we disconnected the line.

"Dad, can you check my homework?" Ray asked.

"And I need my clothes ironed for tomorrow," Junior chimed in.

"Okay, just give me a second." I dropped Lexi's bottle as I was trying to dial Charice's number, and it hit the floor with a loud thud, waking Lexi up.

"*Wanhh*," Lexi wailed.

"Shit!" My frustration only made her wail louder.

"Dad, do you—"

"Everybody, shut the hell up!" I hollered, causing Lexi to scream harder and the boys to stare at me in disbelief. Taking a breather, I looked at my kids. "Okay, I'm sorry, boys, and I'm sorry, baby girl," I said, apologizing, as I put her on my shoulder and patted her back. "Where the fuck is your mother?"

Not only was I worried about her well-being, but I also needed rescuing. How she did this every day, I did not know. I was here by myself feeding the kids hot dogs and chips, because I couldn't cook, and trying my best to do the things that Charice normally did for the kids.

Ray picked up the bottle and washed it off, and Junior retrieved Lexi's pacifier. "You need help, Dad," they said in unison.

Leave it to my sons to bring a smile to my upset face. It was a soothing balm to my soul. "Thanks, you guys. I'm sorry for yelling. I'm a little tired and frustrated. Ray, leave your homework on the table, and I will check it later. Go ahead and take your bath and put your pajamas on. Junior, I'll take care of your clothes in the morning. Go ahead and put your pajamas on too."

The boys scurried off, and I put Lexi in her bouncer with her pacifier so that I could test her bottle. Too hot. I filled a pot with cold water and placed the bottle inside it. Leaning against the counter, I shook my head with worry. Where the hell could Ricey be? She wasn't with Lincoln, because he wasn't at home. What if she was off somewhere with him, though? *No, Ryan. No. Don't think like that. Ricey would not do that to you. Never.*

The only problem was no one was at her studio, and I could've shot myself for not getting Kira's number. She had to know who Ricey was with or where she had gone. I had no idea who she had this supposed meeting with. Her building was paid for, and I knew all the contractors, attorneys, and real estate agents involved with the sale. In fact, if any problems arose, they'd contact me before her. I'd assumed maybe she was meeting with a potential teacher, but I had let that theory go three hours ago.

I prayed nothing had happened to her, since she hadn't answered or returned any of my calls. In my gut, I knew something wasn't right. I just hoped it had nothing to do with the one and only Lincoln Harper. I wasn't crazy by any means. As much as I hated to admit this, deep down, I knew a part of Charice would always love Lincoln—probably a little more than she should, and especially since Lexi was born.

That fucker was a thorn in my side. Sometimes I swore I should've reported his ass to the team during his night out getting blazed. True enough, I had been the cause for it, but he'd been a grown-ass man. Just like Smokey told Craig in the movie *Friday*, "I didn't put that joint to your lip and make you smoke it." In the same way, I had only encouraged Lincoln to get blazed with a few bullshit lies. *What's a lie when you're fighting for the woman you want? Nothing.*

I'd stop at nothing to keep Charice. If that meant stripping Lincoln of everything he'd worked hard for and anyone he loved, I'd do it. *Go hard or go home. Always.* Lincoln didn't get that. He had too much heart. I had heart only for the things I wanted, and anything else be damned. That was why I was who I was today. Ryan Westmore, number one running back in the league, highest-paid running back in the league. And while he had been busy having a heart, I had been busy stealing his woman—who was my high school sweetheart anyway— making her my wife, and raising his daughter as my own, along with our two boys. Hopefully, with the way I'd been putting it down on Ricey lately, I could do what was next on my list—get her pregnant again.

If we had another daughter, then she wouldn't leave. Her feelings for Charity would take over, and although Lexi was Lincoln's, it wouldn't matter, because by then, I would have given her everything she wanted: a husband, a family, and a career—the life she had dreamed of. With any luck, I could knock her up with twins or triplets again. Money was no object, so if I had to hire a whole team of nannies and maids to help her, I would. There'd be so many damn Westmores running around there, she wouldn't give a good hot damn about the one child being a Harper. And, well, as long as Lexi's name was Westmore, we could just pretend that she had come from me anyway.

I smiled to myself, thinking about how I could even raise Lexi to hate Lincoln. Plant all kinds of shit in her head about him not wanting her, so he left Charice, and I took them in. Damn. By the time she would be old enough to want to know him, she'd hate him so much, she wouldn't care to know a thing about him. A flash of Lexi calling me Dad in front of Lincoln's face was enough to bring me to laughter. *Fuck with me and get fucked up. Period.*

I pulled off my dress shirt, laid it on the back of the stool at the kitchen island, and checked Lexi's bottle. She was so cute as she sat there smiling at me. I rubbed my finger across her cheek, and she reached for the Rolex on my wrist. "Don't worry, little mama. You'll have your own one day. Daddy will make sure of it." I picked her up and strolled into the hallway.

"I could get used to this," I said aloud as I looked at myself in the hallway mirror and laughed.

Damn. I kinda look like Pooch, I thought as I looked at my reflection. I was wearing a wifebeater, dress slacks, and gators. Nah, that nigga was way too hood for a stunna like me. But we had the same mindset, though. We protected what was ours at all cost, and for that, I respected him like a muthafucka. Locked up or not.

I went back into the kitchen and began to feed Lexi. I'd almost finished feeding her when I heard the garage door lift. Charice. I willed myself to stay calm, since I needed Charice to see that I wasn't always ready to act a fool, even though I always was. I didn't want to come off as the abusive type. I was never that. My mama would kill me for hitting a woman, but I was definitely going to regain control over Charice, though. Back in the day, I'd kept her ass on a short leash. Now, with this newfound love I had for her, I'd given her some rope, but if she'd been with Lincoln, I was going to tighten that muthafucka with a vengeance. Watch me.

She jumped when she came in and spotted me. "Ryan."

"Charice." I gave her an inquisitive glare. "You do realize the hour, don't you?"

She nodded. "Yes. I had a—"

"Meeting?" I raised an eyebrow.

"Yes," she said, sitting her purse down. "I can get Lexi."

"No, I have her." I took the bottle out of her mouth. "She just fell asleep anyway." I put her up on my shoulder and patted her back. She burped and went right back to sleep. "Put the bottle in the refrigerator while I lay her down," I instructed Charice before I went to put Lexi in her nursery.

When I came back, Charice was leaning against the kitchen counter.

"She'll be out for a while."

She looked up at me. "Are the boys asleep?"

"Yes. I just put Junior in his room. He fell asleep playing with Ray."

"Okay. Sorry I was so late tonight."

"Uh-huh. Did you get my phone calls?" I asked, trying to control my temper.

"Yeah, I did. I was really busy," she said nervously and turned around to grab a coffee cup.

I walked up behind her and kissed her neck so I could sniff her. She smelled just like Lincoln's cologne. I shook my head. *Muthafucka. I got your ass*, I thought. I stepped back, and she tensed up. Then she slowly turned to face me.

I folded my arms across my chest. "Interesting fragrance you have on. It smells a lot like a very familiar cologne."

She swallowed hard. "Ryan, can we talk in the sunroom?"

"Sure. Ladies first," I said, sweeping my arm away from my body and allowing her to lead the way.

We walked into the sunroom, and I sat down on the wicker sofa as Charice began to pace. *Stay calm, Ryan.* Leaning forward, with my arms on my knees, I asked, "What's up?"

"Ryan, I don't know how to say this, but I have to. There are just some things I'm so confused about, and I need to get them straight in my mind—"

I tapped the table. "Ricey, let's cut the crap," I interrupted her. "Get to the point. Who were you with?"

She stopped pacing, turned to me, and folded her arms. "Fine. Lincoln showed up at the studio today, looking for a place to enroll London."

I shrugged. "Okay. Did you sign her up? We'll take his money. That's never been an issue for me."

She huffed. "Wow. You hate him that much?"

"No, I dislike him, and last I checked, you did too, right?" I eyed her questionably.

"That's not the point."

"What is?"

"He saw Lexi. He knows."

Shit. Fuck me. My plan was for him to find out years later, not now. I had to think quickly. What could I do? Nothing was coming up. *Shit. Fuck. Damn. Shit.* I stood up. "Okay, so what does he want?"

She rolled her eyes. "What do you think? To be a part of her life and have her named changed to Harper."

"Over my dead body."

"How can you stop him?"

"The same way I . . ." I paused. "We can think of something." *Damn*. I almost fucked up.

"What were you going to say, Ryan? The same way you did what?"

"Nothing. We need to concentrate on—"

"The same way you stopped him from telling me about your Cowboys-Giants scheme with your free-agent contracts?" she blurted.

"You know? I mean, I don't know what you're talking about."

Charice approached me, her arms folded and her gaze stern. "Even when you're caught, you refuse to stop lying. Just admit it, Ryan. I know everything."

I stood up from the wicker sofa and started pacing. I rubbed my head, trying to figure out my next move. I had known that if that bastard ever found out Lexi was his daughter, he'd do exactly what he'd just done. He'd tell Charice everything that I had done. Sue me for wanting my woman back. So what? I'd take the hit. Finally, I had deduced that Ricey loved me, so it didn't matter what Lincoln told her.

Stopping my pacing, I turned and faced Charice and gave her the cold, hard truth. "Yeah, I did. I lied to the Cowboys administration to get them to release Lincoln. Yes, I was gonna leave anyway.

The Giants were paying more. What loyalty did I have to a team who couldn't pay me my worth? And to see the man who claimed to be my best friend go down was an added bonus."

There, I'd said it. I'd finally admitted my dark secret to Charice. Since she now knew anyway, perhaps I'd score more brownie points with my honesty. Then we could hash this bullshit out and move on with our lives. I was sick of Lincoln holding this blimp of a secret over my head anyway. Now he had no power and no woman. It was a win-win for me.

What caught me off guard, though, was that when Charice glanced up at my face, she had tears in her eyes.

"And you'd take London and Lexi away from him just to split us up?" she said, shaking her head.

Now I was mad. "I wasn't in that decision alone, Ricey. You had your hand in not telling Lincoln about Lexi. You could've told him before you agreed to be my wife, but you didn't. And as far as London goes, well, he didn't lose her, obviously."

She pointed at herself. "I did what I did because I was hurt. Not out of revenge. You knew that, and you had no problem capitalizing on it because it went so perfectly with your scheme. And to lie and say that I'd killed his baby, when you knew the emotional scars I had from the baby I had to abort when you cared more about the league than you did me or our kids was heartless."

I threw my hands up. "Okay, sue me. I lied a little bit. Did I do some shady shit? Okay, yes. But if I didn't, I wouldn't have you, and we wouldn't have the family that we have now. So, what are you saying, Charice? Huh? That you regret marrying me? You regret our family?"

"No," she said weakly. "I don't regret my family, but—"

I stood back and put my hand up. "Oh, wait. I know what this is. I get it. I finally get it."

She looked confused. "What?"

"You just regret marrying me," I said, pointing to myself.

"No, Ryan—"

I nodded. "Yes, that's exactly it. You want to be with Lincoln. My scheme interrupted your hopes of being with the great Mr. Harper. Isn't that it? I mean, why else would you be so upset over what I did? What I did wasn't fair or right, but everything I did, I did for you—for us. Now I'm being ridiculed for it by you, of all people. So what? You don't want to be married to me no more, Charice? Is that it? You want to be back with Lincoln?" My questions were harsh and intense as I closed the gap of personal space between us.

"I just need to think," she cried. "I just want to know that you're not this monster of a man. I want to be able to trust and believe in you, Ryan. I want to be able to stand by my decision, knowing that I mean more to you than the chase to get me did. Is that too much to ask?"

Her words stung me. I hadn't expected this outpouring of her heart. I thought she'd go into a tantrum or defend Lincoln's honor, because she was so noble. Then I'd feel justified in my actions and my response. However, this conflict had more to do with me. She believed in me. She believed in us. She loved me. That melted the ice block caging my heart. I loved Charice, I honestly did, but I wouldn't pretend that a part of my love was fueled by my incessant need to prove that I wasn't the man she wanted and loved. I hated to admit it, but my love for her and my feud with Lincoln over her heart ran neck and neck in terms of importance to me. The chase was just as thrilling as the capture. It was who I was.

I pulled her to me and held her face in my hands, wiping her tears away with my thumbs. "I'm trying so hard, Ricey. I am not a monster. Not to you. I just love you so much that it clouds my judgment. I saw my opportunity to have you back, and I took it. Can you really blame me for that? I just wanted my family back."

"But, Ryan, at any cost? If we were meant to be, couldn't you trust me enough to let me make my own decisions?"

Everybody with these fucking soft-ass hearts. She wanted me to feel sorry for what I'd done to Lincoln. I didn't. Hell, I couldn't. The nigga was my best friend, and he had stolen my babies' mother from under my nose and had been about to wife her. Ain't a man alive who'd feel sorry for the man who'd done that to him, especially not me. However, I had to show human decency to keep my wife. I figured I'd just steal a page out of Casanova's playbook. He had got my Ricey with his charm and sincerity, so that was what I would keep her with.

Sighing and kissing her forehead, I managed to conjure some fake tears. "You're right. Hindsight is twenty-twenty. I didn't realize how badly I truly affected you or Lincoln with my actions, and looking back, I was wrong for what I did to both of you. All I ask is that you please give me a chance to make it right. If it would make you happy, I will agree to let Lincoln change Lexi's name and be a part of her life. We can get with our attorney and have an amicable agreement set up with visitation, child support, and the name change. And I will personally apologize to him for all the ill things I've done. It's time to let bygones be bygones for the sake of the children. I love Lexi too much to risk her growing up to hate me, and I love you too much to lose you over past mistakes," I said, playing to her sensitive and loyal sides.

Lincoln wasn't the only one who knew Charice. I was the king, damn it. I'd had her head and pussy wrapped in a cloud since tenth grade, and it was time to reclaim that fucking throne permanently. I was done playing games with that muthafucka.

Charice smiled demurely. "You'd do that? For Lexi and me?"

"Yes, I'd do anything for you and Lexi." I stared into her eyes with sincerity. "I love you and my family with my whole heart. Your happiness always comes first."

She smiled brightly, then lifted herself up on her tiptoes and hugged me tightly. "Aw, baby. I knew you couldn't be as terrible as it sounded."

"Never." I kissed her. "I just don't want to lose you as my wife. We took vows in front of God and our children, right?"

She looked at me and confirmed, "Right."

"That means you're my wife, and I'm your husband. Forsaking all others until death do us part, right?"

She paused for a few moments and then finally conceded. "Yes, those were our vows."

I pulled back and looked her in her eyes. "And I'm keeping them. Are you?"

She swallowed hard, and I could practically see the turmoil churning inside of her from the seeds that nigga Lincoln had planted in her head when he told her all I'd done. But I knew Charice. Whatever inner demons she was fighting, she'd overcome them. She was loyal, and her sense of right and wrong won out every time, just like it would this time. No matter how she was feeling about what I had done or what she felt about Pretty Boy Floyd, one thing guaranteed that it wouldn't matter—the vows. No matter why she had married me or what I had had to do to get that ring on her finger, she was my wife now. Period.

She finally closed her eyes, exhaled, and nodded. "Yes, I'm keeping them."

I smiled and kissed her forehead, then hugged her.

Checkmate. Game over.

Chapter 12

LaMeka

After the entire thirty minutes the police spent at my house, taking statements and pictures of Gavin's car, they informed us that since the perp never identified who had told him to come over and vandalize the car, they couldn't do anything to Tony. Well, *I* sure as hell could, so I hauled ass to his house. Tony and his parents thought they were slick. His mom played me to the left with some old bullshit lie, talking about Tony was gone with his dad. Now, I might have believed that if I hadn't just seen his dad up the street at his neighbor's house, and Tony wasn't with him. I didn't argue with her, though, but now I knew what time it was on her ass.

I thought that maybe his dad would be different, so I called him, and he had the nerve to tell me that Tony was at the hospital. I went there, thinking he could be telling me the truth, but Tony's physical therapist said he wasn't scheduled until the next day. Slick bastards. They knew he'd done something, or they knew exactly what he had done. After all the time, love, and care I had put into nursing their son back to health, they did me that way? It was all right. I had my time for all of them.

So guess what? When they called in the future and asked about the boys, those boys would always be gone somewhere with Misha, my mama, Lucinda—any and everybody—because neither they nor Tony was going to see them, not while they caused drama in my life or for my man. Not at all. Hell, none of them were supporting the boys anyway, so I didn't owe them shit. I was tired of people taking advantage of my kindness and mistaking it for weakness. I had sacrificed myself and my happiness for so many people, and now that it was time for me to be happy, the world wanted to be against me. Fine. I had no problem with it being Gavin and me against the world. If Tony thought his little bitch move was going to draw me and Gavin apart, he had another thing coming. If anything, it had drawn us closer together, because now I was riding hard for my Gavin. Now go run and tell that.

I'd been so stressed out that my mom suggested that Gavin and I go out and have a little fun, and she even volunteered to watch the boys for us. I was all for it. It'd been forever and a moon since

I'd gone out, and as an added bonus, I convinced Lucinda to go out with us. She definitely needed the breather too, with her recent breakup with Aldris and everything else going on in her life. We decided to go out clubbing together at the Velvet Room, one of our favorite old hot spots. We decided to meet up at Mike's house so we could all ride in his SUV.

"You are sexier than a muthafucka," Gavin said, walking into the bathroom. "You are working the hell outta them shorts and heels."

A blush reddened my cheeks as I finished putting on my earrings. "Thank you, baby. You look hot too." I cut my eye at him and admired his light tan slacks, which matched his peach-colored button-down shirt perfectly.

He walked up and grabbed me by my ass, then pulled me into him. "It's a good thing we are taking this back to my house after the club, because I got some thangs I need to handle," he whispered in my ear and then kissed it.

My knees buckled. That man knew he had an effect on me. "Don't make me skip this club altogether."

Giving me a nonchalant glance, he shrugged. "I don't care if we do or not. It's your choice."

Biting my lip, I turned and wrapped my arms around his neck. "Lucinda better be glad I love her and that I haven't hung out with her in a long time. Let's go before I change my mind."

After checking on the boys, I grabbed my ID, and we jumped in Gavin's corvette, headed to Mike's. When we got there, Mike answered the door.

"'Sup, y'all?" Mike greeted us, hugging me and one-arm hugging Gavin.

"Hey, Mike," I said, walking inside.

"Ooh, pimpin'!" Gavin said, admiring Mike's outfit. "I ain't got nothing on you pimpin'."

Mike laughed.

"Okay, where is my girl, since y'all doing this male bonding?" I said.

"I'm in the back," Lucinda yelled.

"Once you reach the back, hook a left," Mike said, directing me.

I walked into what was clearly a little girl's room. "I love what you've done with the place," I teased as Lucinda rushed over to me and hugged me.

"Shut up, fool," she said as we giggled. She stepped back and admired my outfit. "Girl, work that shit. Gavin got that nose wide open now. You ain't never been so free with showing your body."

"That's what happens when you have a man who loves and takes care of it the way that Gavin does."

"I hear that," she said, high-fiving me.

"You talking about me? Look at you." I admired her ensemble, in awe. Her black, one-shoulder minidress and platform stilettos had her looking smoking hot. "That dress barely covers your ass, and you know you ain't lacking in that area, either."

"Ay, that's right, Mami," she said, doing a shimmy while she pinned up her curly hair. "But you know how we do it when we do it."

I leaned close to her. "But my question is, who are you doing it for? Be real with me. Are you and Mike . . . you know . . . kicking it?"

"No, Meka. Mike and I are just friends. In fact, I have a condo a few blocks from here, and I'll be moving shortly."

"So, why did you stay here in the first place?"

"I told you about my mom and Emilio," she said, spraying her perfume.

"Mm-hmm. I feel you on that, I do, but . . . Never mind," I said, not wanting to start an argument.

"No. What? Say it. He's Aldris's friend?" she asked, cutting her eyes back at me.

"That and the fact that you two seem really close lately, and you don't seem to mind all too much. I don't want to see you jump into something else when your heart isn't healed, especially with Aldris's homeboy. That's just not right."

Lucinda spun around, with her hands on her hips. "I told you. We're *friends*. That's it. We're close because he's been a really good friend to me, and he understands best, because he's friends with both me and Aldris. Now, I really don't want to go out to have to talk about Aldris all night. Besides, you need to worry about your situation with Gavin. Tony is not done with you all, and I'm not one to play the race card, especially being the only Hispanic chick in the group, but this is the South, baby girl. He ain't the only one who's gonna take issue with you being with the 'Cablanasian,' as you call him."

That was Lucinda. A hotheaded Latina. I was used to this behavior from my friend, so I didn't take offense. I knew that I'd overstepped, so I pulled back. I didn't even take offense at what she'd said about Tony and Gavin, because she was right. My situation was real and present. Hers was just speculation. If she said they were friends, who was I to question it? Therefore, I left it alone and focused on my issues.

"If you say so, it's all good. I won't pressure you," I conceded. "As for the race thing, we've dealt with that a little bit already. You know I get the stares from the brothers when I'm out with Gavin, but my heart can't help who it loves. Besides, not one of those niggas giving me the evil eye would be worth my time or energy, so I don't know why they trippin'. As for Tony, I have my time for his ass. Believe that."

She lifted my hand and held it in hers for comfort. "They trip for the same reasons sistas trip on me about being with black men. I ain't black, and neither is Gavin."

"Hell, you're blacker than most sistas."

"Maybe." She shrugged. "But on that issue, personality doesn't matter. Color does." She turned to apply her lipstick.

"You've got a point. You ready?"

"Yep," she said before popping her lips and turning to face me again. "Well, you know I'm in your corner, because if anybody understands, it's damn sure going to be moi."

"Thanks, hon."

We hugged and then walked out to the front to join the fellas. Mike's eyes widened when he saw Lucinda.

Friends, my ass.

"Damn, Mami—" he blurted, then cut himself off. "You look real nice, Lu." He stood and shook it off.

"You do too." She smiled coyly at him.

Gavin and I looked at each other. *Mm-hmm.*

"Come on, Mike. Let's step back and let the red-carpet couple go first. They doing it celebrity style," Lucinda said, breaking up the moment between them.

The entire ride to Velvet, we were straight turned up. We laughed, joked, and rapped with songs on the radio, getting pumped to go in the club and have a good time. We knew a couple of bouncers, so we managed to get in for free, and we even managed to grab a couch.

"What are you ladies drinking?" Mike asked us.

We looked at each other and said in unison, "Cîroc and lemonade."

Once Gavin and Mike were on their way to grab our drinks and were out of earshot, I addressed the issue of Mike with Lucinda. "Girl, you can say what you want. Mike is feeling him a little Spanish fly. I saw how he looked at you."

She giggled and hit me. "Stop, girl. No, he isn't. I have on a minidress, and I have a butt. What man ain't gonna look at that?"

"True. But it was the way he looked."

"What other way is there to look at a fine-ass woman with a big ass?" she asked, rolling her eyes at me. "Trust me. Mike is not interested."

I eyed her suspiciously. "Is he gay or some shit? Spill it."

She nudged me playfully. "Hell no." She sighed, realizing I wasn't dropping the subject. "Let's just say he had ample opportunity to go for it, and he didn't, because of our friendship and my ex."

I gasped. "You ho," I whispered jokingly. "I knew you were trying to seduce that boy."

"No, I wasn't. I swear it. We only kissed, and he immediately backed me up. It was a moment where I was vulnerable and weak, and he was there like he always is. Girl, I won't lie. It's so hard not to be attracted to the man he's become. I'm fighting it hard, Meka, because when I think about Aldris, my heart breaks, and that's how I know I'm not over him."

"Honey, any man on their grown-man tip is attractive. Believe that. Most of these fools in the world ain't worth the time it took to print out their birth certificates. I'm telling you, birth control needs to be the hottest commodity on Earth."

"You are a mess. But the sad part is that you are so right."

Just then, this guy approached us. "Hey, ladies," he said, smiling at me. "Miss Lady, I've watched you since you came in, and I was just wondering if you'd like to dance with me."

"Naw, I'm good."

"Aw, come on now—"

"We're here with our men," I interrupted him.

He looked around. "So where they at?"

"Minding their business, Casanova. Look, Papi. My friend is here with her man, and she turned you down real easy. You may have missed it, but it did happen. Please move along, because you surely interrupted our very private conversation," Lucinda interjected, annoyance written all over her face.

"She's *back*," I teased, referring to how Lu used to act a fool.

"I could've sworn I was talking to your friend," the dude said with an attitude.

I nodded. "You were, but my friend pointed out what you obviously missed. That little n-o ended the conversation. Keep it pushin'. Thank you."

He rolled his eyes and walked off. Lu and I looked at each other.

"Dude, was relentless, wasn't he?" I groused.

"He was about to get his feelings hurt is what he was," Lucinda said, rolling her neck. "Talking about he saw you when you got here. Well, if he did, he saw you had a man. Ol' loser-ass fucker."

Just then, the fellas walked up with the drinks. "What's going on?" Gavin asked.

Taking my drink from his hand, I waved off the incident. "Some dude tried to holla at me, and he wasn't taking no for an answer at first."

"Who?" Gavin asked, looking around.

"We're here to have fun. Let that mess go," I insisted.

"These nigg . . . I mean dudes, be trippin' up in here sometimes," Mike said.

Gavin laughed. "It's cool, man. Don't change the way you speak around me because I'm white. I'm not here to offend you, and I don't get easily offended."

Mike chuckled before drinking a sip of his Hennessy. "You just can't say what I can say."

We all laughed as Gavin nodded and gave Mike pound.

We all sat there until we finished our drinks,

enjoying one another. I noticed that the more comfortable Mike and Lucinda got with the drinks, the more comfortable they got with each other. I'd catch them leaning on each other as they bobbed their heads to the music and joking with each other in their own little world. As a friend, I wanted to step in and pull my girl, but the devilish side of me—which was pissed off, along with her, about the men who pissed on us—was like, "Go 'head, girl, and get your flirt on." Ain't nothing wrong with browsing if she ain't buying.

Once our glasses were empty, Gavin and I left them on the couch and descended onto the dance floor. I swore God dipped him in the wrong gene pool, because he could boogie too. I'd made up in my mind that Gavin was just bright skinned. Ain't no way he was white, with all those qualities. Once we were breathless from dancing, we eased over to the bar so that we could sit and rest a bit and so that Gavin could order another Hennessy. As we sat there, I gazed out at the dance floor and saw Lucinda and Mike dancing together. I could tell by their eyes that the liquor was saying what they didn't have the heart to say to each other. They were good and tipsy, and that action on the floor surely proved that. It became apparent that I was going to have to do a little intervention before the night was over.

"Your girl is gonna do what she wants," Gavin whispered in my ear, breaking my thoughts.

"Huh?" I refocused my attention on him.

"I know you, baby. You're looking over there at Mike and Lucinda and wanting to pull her from jumping into a messy situation. I feel you. That's what friends are for, but tonight is for you to relax. Don't take on that problem, because Lucinda is clearly going to do what she likes. And if they like it, you love it," he said, then kissed my ear.

I turned to face him. "I know. I'm so protective of everyone. I know this ain't her, and she needs to slow it down, because she's taking herself to a place that she's not serious about going. Mike is a good dude and shouldn't be played. He truly cares about her. I see it."

He nodded. "True. He does care about her. I can tell how he treats her and responds to her. He wants your girl, but he's holding on to his loyalty to his friendship with Aldris. You have to stay out of it because they need to work through that on their own. I'm sure you've said your piece to her already. She's grown, Meka."

He knew me too well. Begrudgingly, I relented. "I'm focused. Me and you." I wrapped my arms around his neck and kissed him.

"That's what I'm talking about." He kissed me again.

"Wow. That slave mentality is taking over our black women now. This broad dissed me for a white boy," I heard someone say beside me.

Gavin and I turned to see the dude who had approached me earlier talking to some dudes about me, close enough to us that we could obviously hear him.

"Yo, my man. Are you talking about my lady?" Gavin quickly defended me with an attitude.

"Oh, man, and he's a token white guy too. Not secure enough to be white and not black at all to be acting black," the dude joked to his boys, who laughed at his antics.

"Aye, yo, pah'ner," Gavin called out. "You can say whatever you like to your little boys, but you better not disrespect my lady. For real." Gavin pointed at him.

"Gavin, baby, don't trip. Let's just go dance or go back to the booth. We don't want no problems."

"And I ain't bringing none, and I ain't lettin' nobody else bring none, either," he said. "Muthafuckas just can't take no."

"Baby, let it go," I pleaded and tried to pull him away.

Mike and Lucinda walked over just then. "Is there a problem, Gavin?" Mike asked.

"Now the field nigger and the house nigger done ran over to check on the boss," the guy sneered, and his boys doubled over in laughter.

Mike looked at them crazily. "Yo, what the fuck is your problem, man?"

Lucinda put her hand up. "That is that fucker who approached LaMeka. Obviously, he's giving all of us a hard time since he found out her man is white," she explained. "Y'all, let's just go sit down."

"That's what I told Gavin," I agreed.

"You cool?" Mike asked Gavin.

He blew out a ragged breath and gave Mike pound. "I'm straight, dawg. Let's go sit down." We all began leaving the bar.

The guy continued his harassment as we walked away. "That's right. Massa said leave. Run, niggers, run."

Ignoring them, we found a couch. Once we sat, I looked at all three of them, and they all looked pissed. "Fuck them, you guys. Let's have fun," I said, encouraging them to let it go.

Lucinda relented first and high-fived me. "You're right. *Putos* was tryin'a blow my damn buzz." She flagged down a waitress. "Excuse me. Can I get a Cîroc and lemonade?"

The waitress nodded and walked away.

"There we go. Like I said, fuck them," I said, looking at Gavin.

When the waitress came back, Mike paid for Lucinda's drink, and Gavin ordered a Patrón on the rocks. Oh yeah. He was super pissed. That was the only time he even fucked with tequila.

Lucinda downed her drink quickly. Then she and Mike got up, held hands as they went to the dance floor, and stayed on the floor for at least another hour, grinding and winding to every fast and slow song that came on. I sat beside Gavin in silence, watching everybody else as he sulked. He wasn't even good for conversation. As I talked, he nodded his head, as if he was a million miles away. I was so hurt that he'd let some lame ass spoil our night.

"Baby, come on. Let's dance for a little while. I'm getting tired of sitting here watching Lu and Mike have all the fun."

"A'ight. I'ma try this again. Just for you." He stood up, and we walked to the dance floor.

"Glad you could join us, but my heels just said to me, 'Sit down,'" Lucinda slurred.

"Yes, *mamacita*, you need to sit down," I replied.

She shot me the finger right before she and Mike left to go back to the couch.

As Gavin and I danced, I felt his tension subside, and soon we were having a good time again. On the last song, when I backed it up to him, he got aroused, and I knew the night at the club was over.

"Let me see if Mike is ready to go. I can't wait no longer to tackle that," he whispered in my ear.

The effects of the alcohol had kicked in on me, so I was ready myself. We walked back to the couch, where Mike had his arm wrapped around

Lucinda's shoulders and she had leaned her head on his chest.

"Are you two ready to dip?" I asked.

"Yeah," they said in unison.

As we left, we continued living up our good time with each other. Even though that fool had tried to spoil the night, it had gone well. That was until we saw the dude and one of his boys as we were walking to Mike's SUV.

"Massa and the slave hoes leaving," the dude said, loud enough for us to hear.

"Real men speak the fuck up to the person they're really talking to," Gavin shouted.

"Gavin," I pleaded, his name slipping off my lips. Since he was buzzed, I knew he was feeling right for a fight.

The dude turned around and said, "Yeah, bitch, I'm talking to you and your fuck-ass friends."

"Trust me, nigga. This ain't what you want," Mike said smoothly.

"Such language in front of your massa," the guy said, only this time there was no laughter, as he and his friend sensed the tension.

"Let's just go to the car," I pleaded.

Lucinda and I forced our men across the parking lot, but this dumb fool and his friend followed us. Was he looking to get his ass beat tonight? Seriously? Why couldn't grown-ass people go out and not have to deal with these types of people? So what if I didn't want to dance with his whack ass? Just 'cause his ass needed some pussy in his life, he wanted to be pissed off and hating on us. Why couldn't this nigga just leave us alone and get off his ol' Louis Farrakhan shit?

Before we could get to the SUV, this fool actually rushed up to fight Gavin. Before anyone knew what fully happened, the shit was over and done with. Gavin dropped him so fast that he went lights out instantly, and before his friend could even jump in, Mike knocked him out in one cold, hard punch. Both of the dudes were laid out on the side of the street in what had to be the quickest fight, or non-fight, of my life.

We quickly got in the car before the cops pulled up on us, and then we drove off, leaving the fool and his friend lying on the ground, taking an asphalt nap. When we turned the corner, Mike laughed and looked in the rearview at Gavin.

"My man. You are all right wit' me. I don't give a damn what nobody says. You my nigga," he joshed, and we all laughed.

Gavin reached forward and gave him pound. "I appreciate you having my back too."

"Anytime, man. Besides, I wanted in on that, calling me a fucking field nigger," Mike said.

Lucinda giggled, looking back at Gavin. "You know what you should've told them, right?"

Gavin and I looked at each other and quipped in unison, "You got knocked the fuck out!"

After our laughter subsided, I reflected on our wild time. "There's nothing like drinks and fights to bring couples together. Damn. What a fucking night."

When we got back to Mike's house, we said our goodbyes, and I drove to Gavin's. After the night we'd had, we were ready to handle some business, but when we walked inside, something seemed off, and an eerie feeling came over me. It must've hit Gavin too, because he asked me to wait in the foyer while he checked the house.

When he reached the living room, he yelled out, "Oh, hell naw," which caused me to go running to him. His place had been completely ransacked.

"Oh my God," I gasped as I gazed around the living room.

"*Son of a bitch.* Look at my shit."

I walked into the kitchen and looked around. "Baby, come here."

Gavin ran in to the kitchen. "Don't walk around without me. I haven't checked everything out yet," he said. Then he followed my gaze, and we both focused on the note that had been left on the refrigerator.

> Gavin,
> *I know where you stay at, dawg . . . my bad . . . white boy. So I figured I'd stop by*

and say hello. Did you like my hello? Ha. Ha.
Oh well. Just so you know, I helped myself to
one of your beers and a big-ass sandwich. I
didn't take shit else, because there's only one
thing you've got that I truly want. And I ain't
gonna stop until I get it. Besides, I had it first.
   Deuces!

We didn't even have to say a word, because there was only one person who could've written that note. Tony. That was what happened when you tried to be nice. I swore I should've let the chips fall where they did while his ass was in the hospital. It was because of me that he had received top care, which had given him a new lease on life. Now that he was better, he'd been making my life hell. I knew he was my sons' father, but at this moment, I wished to hell I'd never even met Tony Light.

Gavin looked at me and nodded. "Your boy wants to go to war. Okay." He hit the counter with his fist and walked off to check the rest of the house. "Okay."

I put my head down to collect myself; then I called the police.

Couldn't he let me be happy for once?

Chapter 13

Lucinda

Coming into the house, I felt like a tank of alcohol was swirling around in my stomach. It'd been a long time since any of us had hung out, and I was definitely feeling the after effects of my liquid high.

"Party, party, party, let's all get wasted," I sang as I flopped down on Mike's sofa and giggled. "I'm so tipsy."

He sat down beside me. "I see. I'm a little twisted myself." He chuckled.

As I struggled to get my heels off, I said, "I had so much fun, Mike. Thank you so much for showing me a good time."

He laughed at me and said, "Lean back before you fall off the sofa with your wasted ass."

He grabbed my leg and caressed it slightly before he unbuckled my heel. Our eyes met as he aimlessly slid his fingers up and down my leg, from my calf to my ankle. My breathing became labored from the unspoken tension this caused, and I closed my eyes. He slipped my shoe off.

"There you go."

"You . . . you don't have to stop there."

He let out a nervous chortle. "You're tipsy. I'm buzzed. No, it's not going down like that," he said, shaking his head. He stood up.

Confused, I looked at up at him. I couldn't have misread the sign. Tipsy or not, I wanted to feel alive again. I wanted Mike to help me feel alive. But despite what I knew I had read, he had rejected me. Suddenly, rage welled up inside of me. "So how can you say no to free ass when you're drunk, and Aldris couldn't?"

"Huh?" he asked, clearly taken off guard.

As I stared up at Mike, all the emotions that I thought were dissipating began to resurface and bubble over. Without warning, tears fell from my eyes as I rocked back and forth in agony. Mike sat beside me and held me. "Why couldn't he say no? What did I do to deserve that, Mike? Wasn't I a good woman? I tried to be. Why wasn't I enough?"

"Shit," he said with exasperation. "I don't know, Lucinda. I don't know." He consoled me. "From what I see and what I know about you, you should've been enough. I know you would be for me."

I looked up at him, shocked that he'd said that, yet happy to hear that someone knew my worth.

"Shit." He closed his eyes and leaned his head back. "Did that really come out of my mouth?"

For a moment, we sat in silence, allowing the moment to be. As I continued to wipe my tears, a warm sensation came over me. Being in Mike's arms felt so comforting during a time when everything in my life was pure chaos. I needed this. I needed him. I snuggled against him, caressing his chest. "So let me be enough for you," I whispered.

He looked down at me, and I could tell he was struggling. "I can't. I so wish . . . I can't. I don't want you like this."

"Like what?" I asked, confused.

"Heartbroken over another man," he blurted. "In love with Aldris and looking for comfort. Damn it, Lucinda. I want you, but I want to matter to you. I want you to love me like I—" He swallowed hard, then jumped up again. "Go to bed," he said as he stalked into the hallway.

I jumped up on wobbly legs and followed him. "Wait a minute." I grabbed his arm. "Mike, don't walk away from me."

He turned to face me. "Look, Lu. I never should've invited you here. There are too many emotions swirling between both of us."

"So you don't want me here?" I teared up again. My drunken haze had my emotions on high, and I leaned against the wall for support.

"No," he said definitively. "I'm starting to want you here too much."

That was when it hit me like a ton of bricks. This was about more than sex for Mike. I had never realized that Mike had feelings for me. His actions made so much sense now, and I felt horrible. I couldn't give him what he was looking for, and outside of temporary gratification, I didn't know if I could offer anything else.

"I shouldn't keep putting you in this position. I'm fucked up right now, Mike, and I'm not just talking about from the liquor. I don't know what it is I really want, besides to make the pain go away, and I can't do you like that. You've been too good to me for that."

He leaned against the opposite wall and brought his hands together. "You love Aldris, and I can't knock that. You were his woman, and you were going to be his wife. You have to work through that. Right now, the timing isn't right for us, but if it ever is, I'm here."

I pushed off the wall, walked up to him, bent his head down with my hand, and kissed his forehead. "You're amazing. Thanks for being man enough to withstand me."

"It's a hard damn job, I'll have you know."

"Well, you don't have to worry about it for long. My condo will be ready in a week, and then I'll be moving out."

"Yeah," he said sadly. "I guess I have to help you move."

"You don't sound enthusiastic."

He rubbed his face. "That's 'cause I'm not. I know what you have to do, and I know what I told you, but that doesn't mean that I don't wish things were different."

Just then, the doorbell rang.

"Who the fuck could this be?" Mike asked, walking up the hallway toward the door, with me on his heels. "Did Meka call you and tell you they made it home?"

I snapped my fingers. "As a matter of fact, no."

"Maybe this is them," he said, swinging the door open. "Yo, Gavin. You forgot—" His words were stopped short when he was met with a punch to the face. "What the fuck?" he roared, falling backward.

"What the hell?" I shrieked, backing up into the hallway and steering clear of the commotion. When I looked into the foyer, I saw that it was Aldris.

"You muthafucka!" Aldris shouted at Mike as he stomped into the living room. "You're supposed to be my boy."

"What the fuck are you doing here?" Mike asked as he followed behind Aldris. "And hitting me and shit?"

"I came over because I couldn't sleep, and I wanted to holla at my boy to get advice. I pull up, and Lucinda's car is over here. You just couldn't wait for me to fuck up so you could stick you a little Spanish fly." Aldris spewed the words like they were venom.

After hearing Aldris's rant, I ran into the living room. "You need to go."

Aldris confronted me. "And what are you doing here?" He glared at me. "So you're gonna go and be with my best friend? And what the fuck do you have on?"

"None of your fucking business, Aldris. I'm not your woman anymore, remember? Where's Jennifer?"

"The fuck if I know." Aldris face contorted as he looked back and forth between Mike and me. Bypassing Mike, he stalked over to me, pleading his case. "Baby, I want to be with you. You're supposed to be my wife. What's going on? Why are you here? Can't you give us a chance?"

Had he lost his mind? I was in disbelief that he had the audacity to stand there and question me and my decisions. "A *chance*? Are you kidding me? I gave you plenty of chances. You lost them all when you decided to fuck your ex."

"So you're gonna fuck my boy to get even?"

"Dri! It ain't even going down like that," Mike interjected.

"Oh, yeah, right. You ain't never been about shit, Mike."

"Well, apparently, neither have you. He's more of a man than you are." The words came out of my mouth before I could stop them.

Aldris looked at Mike and charged at him. "Son of a bitch!"

Mike caught him and pinned him against the wall in the living room. "Look, muthafucka, I'm not banging Lucinda. What you need to focus on is her right now. If you want her back, there she is. Focus on her for once in your selfish-ass life. Maybe, just maybe, you can get her back," he said before he eased up and issued a final warning. "Be cool."

"A'ight, nigga," Aldris said.

Mike slowly backed up and straightened his clothes. Then he looked over at me. "I'm going in the back so you two can talk."

Aldris and I stood there staring at each other for what seemed like forever. It felt so different between us now. Just a little while ago, I was ready to marry this man, and now I literally loathed him. To me, he was worse than Raul. At least Raul didn't hide his trifling behavior. He was the way he was. You either accepted it or not. But Aldris . . . Aldris was that dude that hid behind the exterior of a real man, but when push came to shove, he wasn't shit. Nothing.

"Why are you here?" Aldris inquired again.

"I don't owe you any explanations. Nada. We're not a couple."

He nodded. "Okay, I deserve that."

"Don't get me started on what you deserve."

"Baby." He sighed. "I don't want to see you hurt. I know I did what I did, but Mike is not the man for you—"

Pursing my lips, I sneered. "And you are? Mike has been there for me when you were off playing house with Jennifer."

"Really? You are aware that he has a baby mama and three children? How are you gonna come first?"

"I'm not with Mike." I clapped my hands together for emphasis. "Even so, Latonya and he keep it strictly on the friendship for their kids' sake. I've met her. She's a nice chick. Got a nice man by her side. Nobody is secretly trying to interfere or screw anybody on the sly. Hell, they could've stayed together for that," I said, defending Mike. "We all have a past, Aldris, but the rest of us learned how to move on from it. That's what Jennifer was supposed to be to you, remember?"

For a moment, he looked at me strangely. "How do you know all of this? Are you living with Mike?" he asked angrily.

Damn it. My fury had caused me to overtalk. It was time to end this before Aldris really did pop off on Mike. "You need to leave."

Aldris's eyes widened as the reality of my situation with Mike dawned on him. "I'll be damned," he said, rubbing his face. "Ain't this some shit? You and him ain't kickin' it or nothing, but you're living with him?"

He wanted to go there. Fine. I could too. "And why are you upset? Hasn't Jennifer moved into your place yet? Or maybe you moved into hers?"

Frustrated, he threw his hands up. "I haven't even talked to Jennifer. I'm too fucked up over you." Raking his hand down his face, he released a breath before he closed the space between us. "Lucinda, I want to be with you. I want to work shit out so that we can get married and be a family. I want to have a son, maybe even two, and another daughter with you. I want us to grow old together. I know how I've been acting and what I did was fucked up, but I love you so much, Lu. I can't tell you the hell I've been through without you in my life. I can't breathe, baby. I can't breathe without you."

While I was listening to him, tears found their way into my eyes. My lips trembled as I mulled over what my heart felt and what my mind said. Testing the waters, Aldris pulled me to him, and the tears I had tried to withhold slipped from my eyes.

My voice thick with emotion, I struggled to say, "I can't get over what you did."

With his forehead pressed against mine, he pleaded, "There has to be something we can do to save us. Please tell me how I can help us to move on from this. If I could take it back, I would. Tell me what you want me to do, Lu, and I'll fix it."

I was so weak for him. Even with what had nearly transpired with Mike and me, I loved Aldris. Now I fully understood why Mike wouldn't go there with me. My heart still belonged to Aldris. My mind hated him, but my heart loved him, and I hated that I loved him so much.

"I don't know if I can," I said weakly as Aldris tried to get me to look him in the eyes. "You hurt me so bad and cut me so deep."

"I know I did, baby. I'll spend the rest of my life making it up to you. Just give us a chance again."

We held each other close as we looked into each other's eyes. "I don't know," I said softly, and silent tears rolled down my cheeks.

"Do you love me? Because I love you. I love you so much," Aldris whispered sweetly in my ear. "Tell me you still love me, Lu."

"Yes, but—"

Before I could finish, Aldris brought my face to his and kissed me deeply.

"Come home, baby," he said breathlessly. "Come home with me."

Could this work for us? I loved Aldris, but was love enough? Would I be enough for him this time around? Would he be enough for me? I was so un-sure about everything regarding my relationship with Aldris. I wasn't ready to marry him. I wasn't even ready to be committed to him. All I had was my love for him, and even that was on shaky ground.

"Lu, please. *Please.* I'm begging you. I can't make it without you," he pleaded. "I'm nothing without you. I'm stripped down to nothingness. All I have is God and you. I can't lose you."

I didn't know what else to say or do, so I gave in. "Okay."

He picked me up, hugged me tightly. I could feel the wetness from his tears as they hit my shoulder. "Thank you, Lu. I love you so much."

"We have to see where this goes, Aldris. It's not concrete, nor are we together. I'm trying to find my way back to you."

He nodded happily, wiping the remainder of my tears away. "Okay. Understood."

"Let me go grab some shoes and my purse." I turned to walk back to the bedroom that I had been staying in.

When I opened the door, Mike was sitting on the bed. "Going back to Dri, huh?"

"You heard?"

Downtrodden, he nodded and stood up. "It's all good. I'm happy for you two."

His visible agony shredded me. "I'm sorry—"

He grabbed my hands before I could finish. "It's cool. I hope it works." With that, he let my hands go and left the room.

After slipping on my flip-flops, I grabbed my purse and left the bedroom. When I came back into the living room, Aldris was sitting on the sofa, and Mike was sitting in his favorite chair. They were both quiet and were staring at each other.

"I'm ready," I said softly.

Aldris stood up, walked over and hugged me, then grabbed my hand to lead me out of Mike's house. "Holla at you later, bruh," Aldris said to him.

Mike never looked up at us. He threw up deuces. "Indeed."

I couldn't even look at Mike. I shut the door behind me and followed Aldris to his car.

"We'll get your car and things tomorrow," Aldris said.

I nodded as he opened the passenger's-side door for me. He walked to the driver's side and got in. "I love you," he said and leaned over and kissed my cheek.

As he backed out of the driveway, I could see Mike staring at us through a window. He looked so devastated. And honestly, so was I.

Chapter 14

Trinity

It was truly a blessing to be back in marital bliss again. Terrence and I had overcome so many obstacles in our past, and I was looking forward to a bright future with him. The natural balance of our life was finally being restored.

With Big Cal leaving me alone behind his fallout with Terrence, my Dreads was the carefree, laid-back man I was used to having around the house. It also paid off that Pooch's ass was still locked up because of the bribe money. Truly, for the first time, I felt comfortable.

I worried about Big Cal, though. As his friend, I wanted nothing but the best for him. He'd had my back for so long that it saddened me to think I couldn't give him the same in return. His loyalty to me was without question. I knew it seemed weird at times, but what Dreads didn't understand was that when Pooch was really dogging me out when he was locked up, Big Cal was the one who was there for me. At the time, I had felt like he was doing a lot of it because he was Pooch's right-hand man and he generally felt sorry for me. I believed Big Cal had first started looking out for me because he was a UC and Dread's cousin, but it had developed into our own personal bond. Now that I knew that Big Cal had infiltrated Pooch, rather than being solely his boy and main man, I understood fully why Big Cal had kept his affiliation with me under wraps even from me. At the end of the day, during my Pooch era, he'd been a friend who truly understood when I hadn't had one. No one would ever know all the lengths that Big Cal had actually gone to for me during that time, and for that, I would be forever grateful.

However, if sacrificing my friendship to Big Cal meant saving my marriage, it was a no-brainer. Terrence Kincaid came first and always would. I hadn't learned what happened between Terrence and his cousins until after our amazing night together. Cruising out in my baby's Range Rover, dressed in our designer duds, and eating at one of my favorite five-star restaurants, L2O, then ending the evening at our luxurious condo was the icing on the cake, especially taking into account how that day had started.

It had me in the perfect mood to hear about the American Gangsta story that involved my hubby and Big Cal. Otherwise, I would've gone off, and we would still be at odds. It had nothing to do with protecting Big Cal, but rather it was about turning the corner to a different lifestyle. I understood Dreads was pissed, but damn, that hood mentality and penal system lifestyle had to end. When I'd walked out of Pooch's house for the final time, I'd left that life and I'd left him to rot in fucking prison. I didn't want to relive it. I was finally a certified five-star chick, and that was how shit was staying with me.

Luckily, all had been well, so I decided I was due for another check-in with my girls. I didn't know what the hell was going on except that Lu was supposed to marry Aldris. Outside of that, I was out of the loop. I missed spending time with my girls—my sisters. I longed to see them and know what was going on in their lives. Maybe now that we were secure that Pooch was gonna stay behind bars, I could go and visit them, or at least have them visit me. Even though I loved my life now, I longed for that connection.

As it turned out, we all got together remotely. Lucinda and LaMeka gathered at LaMeka's house so they could be on the webcam together, and Charice linked in from New York. Seeing each other's faces come through on the camera made all of us resort to our teenage years before we dived in to talk about our current lives. We were all giggles and sniggles for at least the first fifteen minutes in. My soul felt quenched. I needed that.

Kicking off with *Lifestyles of the Rich and Famous*, Charice dived in first and shared her drama with Lincoln and Ryan, and the fact that Lincoln now knew about Lexi. My concern at that point was for Charice's feelings. She loved hard and didn't do well with betrayal of that love.

"Are you freakin' serious?" I asked her, tossing my hair.

"Yes," she said. "Honestly, I'm a bit relieved, though. I have it in the open about Lexi, and I know that Lincoln is gonna do his part to take care of her."

"So, is it going to be cool with the three of you interacting on a consistent basis? Clearly, Ryan is not comfortable with the history that you and Lincoln have. Not to mention, he betrayed your trust again with his narcissistic ruses."

"Trinity, what's with the hair tossing and your bourgeois *ruses*?" Lucinda cut in, and they all laughed at her comment.

"Whatever, Lucinda."

"No, seriously. What kind of water do they have in Evanston?" LaMeka asked. "Shit, you've got Ms. Scarsdale beat, and I know she dwells in the land of bourgeoisie," she said in a playful sophisticated tone.

Ignoring their banter, I waved them off. "Anyway, Charice, is it really going to be cool?"

"I don't know, but I have to try for the sake of Lexi."

"But what about the sake of your marriage?" LaMeka asked, taking the words out of my mouth. "Putting Lexi aside, are you okay with being around Lincoln, especially after finding out that he didn't just leave you, and that it was Ryan's fault?"

"I put all of that aside because I'm married now. I took vows with my husband. My loyalty lies with him."

"And where does your heart lie?" Lucinda asked.

"With my family." Charice switched gears. "Now, LaMeka, move on to you and Gavin."

Not missing Charice's effort to get the focus off of her, I decided to halt my interrogation. Besides, I had to know who this mystery man was, so I moved on and didn't delve deeper into Charice's life. "Who is Gavin?"

That was when LaMeka filled us in on the entire story about her getting her own house, going through Tony's fight for his life, and finding her new love, Gavin. I was happy for her until I found out that he was white. It wasn't that I was against interracial relationships, but I thought that minorities could relate to each other on a level that no one else could.

"*White?*" My disdain was apparent in my tone. "Damn, Tony wasn't bright enough that you had to go to other side?"

LaMeka rolled her eyes. "Hater."

"Hatin' on what? The fact that there are some good black men in the world and you give your heart and sex to the token white boy? Girl, stop."

"Ay, I am offended," Lucinda said angrily. "I'm not black, but black men are my preference. I can't believe you said that shit. We've been best friends for how long, and you go there?"

"Lu, don't be upset. It's just that there's a shortage of black love, and LaMeka could at least try to give the few good black men left a chance first," I said.

"So I guess you're saying that I'm taking away from the pool of black men, the same way LaMeka is not making herself available to the pool, right?" Lucinda asked with an attitude.

"No, Lu, please. Hispanics are minorities too."

"And that's supposed to make me feel better? You didn't say for LaMeka to make herself available to the 'minority ethnic groups.' You said to 'black men,'" she said, using those damn air quotes.

"So what you're really saying is he could've been any color other than white and you would be okay with it?" LaMeka asked, diving in behind Lucinda.

"Ugh!" I flung my hand in the air. "This is retarded. I called you all to catch up, not to argue.

And yes, I would feel better about it if he was another minority and wasn't white, but if you like it, sweetie, I love it."

LaMeka turned to look at Lucinda. "So you got your answer. She's not upset about minority groups, just white people—"

"Ladies, come on. Let's get back to the purpose of the call," Charice interrupted. "Meka, don't take offense to what Trinity is saying, because more than just her thinks this way. You have to know that if you're going to be in an interracial relationship, you're gonna run across it. It's not like what Trinity said isn't true. How many times have we—Lucinda, you included—had comments about white girls and black men? Come on now."

"No, I never had ill comments about interracial dating, because I get ragged on too," Lucinda said in her defense. "My only statement was about noticing the type of women black men date outside their race. I hate when I hear a black dude judge a black woman about her appearance, weight, or the way she acts, and he refuses to take care of his kids with her, and then he turns around and goes out in public with an ugly-ass white chick lookin' like and acting like trailer trash, with all her little white unkempt kids in tow. All I'm saying is don't down your own people and then go get another race's sloppy seconds."

We all paused and then burst out laughing and clapping.

"Hell yeah! Now, that's the truth." I agreed.

"You ain't lying," LaMeka said, then high-fived Lucinda.

"You got a point, *mamacita*. I hate that." Charice laughed.

"Well, anyway, I guess I get your point a little bit, Trinity. But all I'm saying is don't knock it until you try it, because Gavin is as black as any black man I've dated, and more importantly, he's a real man. You would love him if you knew him. At the end of the day, I just want to be with someone who is going to hold me down," LaMeka said.

"And trust me, Gavin damn sure ain't sloppy seconds, by no means." Lucinda laughed. "Papi is a hottie," she cheered as she and LaMeka gave each other pound.

"I hear what you guys are saying, and, Lu, your argument is one that we all can agree on—"

"But?" LaMeka and Lucinda said in unison, looking at each other as if I was aggravating them with my opinion.

"But . . . I'm still not comfortable with the fact that Gavin is white. I don't know him, true. He may be a good man, true. But there's something about a strong black man who can relate to you in every way that's just different. Acting black and being around black people don't help a white person truly understand our struggles," I argued. "You're a good woman, Meka. I'm sure there is a good black man just waiting on a woman like you. In all fairness, we can't complain about white girls and black men and then turn around and jump ship on those men."

"And in all fairness, why can't we? The good black men you speak of are going after white women by the busloads and leaving us at the bus stops, so excuse the hell outta me for switching my bus pass," LaMeka countered, defending her point. "I'm taking my blessing in whatever color, shape, or form it comes in."

Seeing that LaMeka was ready to go to war for Gavin, I backed down. Besides, I didn't get the opportunity to talk to my girls often, so I wasn't going to waste my time arguing over something that I could not change and that was not my personal business. Rather than defend my "Black love matters" stance, I opted to revel in the fact that LaMeka had found love.

"I can't argue with God's blessings, LaMeka," I conceded. "So, what's the deal with Tony?"

LaMeka shrugged, then finished her story about all the troubles she'd been having with Tony since she began dating Gavin. Of course, she praised Gavin —who, I had to admit, didn't sound bad at all. In fact, she showed me a picture of him over the webcam, and I had to agree that he was

cute as hell for a white boy. And I knew Lucinda
didn't vouch for nobody unless they were certified
for real, so I felt more comfortable knowing that
LaMeka did seem to have a true stand-up gentleman by her side for once.

"Well, I'm glad you didn't take Tony up on his
offer. That fool is crazy," I said. "Nobody wants to
risk their life for some sex, especially from a man
like him. Nobody told him to go out and act stupid
when you two were together. Everybody makes
mistakes, but some of them we have to learn to live
with." For once in the conversation, I saw everyone
nodding in agreement.

"Speaking of mistakes, Aldris and I aren't getting
married," Lucinda blurted, ripping the Band-Aid
off her news.

"*What*?" I hollered, damn near spitting out my
Fiji Water.

"Yeah, Mami. He cheated on me with his daughter's mom—"

"Hold up, daughter!" I flung my hand up, signaling to her to stop and back up with that explanation. "What the fuck is going on down there in the
ATL? And I thought he didn't have any kids?"

Lucinda tapped her forehead, as if she'd just
remembered something. "Damn. That's right. You
don't know the whole story, so I have to go back to
the beginning."

Lu told me the whole story. She recounted how she had received the petition for paternity and had found out Jessica was Aldris's child, how Aldris had started putting her and Nadia second to Jennifer and Jessica, and how he had engaged in the ultimate betrayal. She went through her friendship and brief stay with Mike and the scene that had unfolded when Aldris found out.

"So back up to Mike. Anything going on with you two for real?" Charice laughed. "That's what I wanna know."

"She says not," LaMeka said, rolling her eyes in disbelief.

Lucinda gave us the middle finger. "There isn't. So you don't have to worry about me taking him from the pool of good black men, Trinity."

I shot her a bird in return. "Don't start."

"Please don't." Charice sighed.

Lucinda relented. "Anyway. Honestly, I don't know what I feel. I won't lie. I feel something for Mike. What exactly, I don't know. All I know is that I love Aldris, but I'm so hurt that it's hard for me to allow him in that space again. I need some time to sort through things on my own. Get my head in the right place, so I'll know what I really want for myself," Lucinda confessed.

"Or *who* you really want," LaMeka added, and we all agreed.

"Enough about me and my situation. When the hell are you coming out of hiding?" Lucinda asked me.

"Hopefully, soon. We took care of Pooch, so maybe now we can live our lives."

"Took care of him?" Charice asked worriedly.

One look at her and I was sure our previous conversation had invaded her thoughts. In an effort to put her at ease and explain to the rest of the girls, I told them how we guaranteed his pleas weren't being heard and I explained about the rift between Terrence and Big Cal over me.

"Oh, well, I'm glad that's secure, because a couple of months ago, Chocolate Flava was asking a whole lot of questions about you and Terrence. That heifer cornered me in the grocery store, talking about she was just wondering. Bullshit and die. She was asking for Pooch," LaMeka said.

I fanned it off. "I'm not worried about that trashy broad. She's always wanted to be with Pooch, and she can have him. He deserves a low-class bottom biotch like her."

For about fifteen more minutes, I spoke to them about how Terrence had taken care of our "Pooch problem," and then I told them about my wonderful "Pooch-free and unbothered" life in Evanston.

Once we had finished our conversation, I shut down my computer and poured myself some wine. It felt good to have time to myself. My mom had picked up the kids for the weekend, and Terrence was out closing a deal on some property. I wasn't heading into the gallery, which gave me the chance to chill. I sat in the sunroom and read *Married on Mondays* by my favorite author, HoneyB, as I sipped my wine while snacking on my cheese loaf and crackers.

My cell rang in the midst of my catching up on this read. I picked up. "Hello?"

"Hey, baby. I was just checking on you. How's my favorite girl in the world?" Terrence said.

"I'm fine. I'm sipping on some wine and reading my book right now. I did a video chat with the girls earlier, and, babe, there is so much going on. Everyone is losing their mind."

"Word?" he asked, intrigued. "I was about to ask you how Senorita, Superstar, and Peaches were doing."

"They would slap your face if they heard you still calling them that." I giggled.

"Whatever, *li'l mama*."

"Okay, *Dreads*. You're interrupting my *me* time."

"Okay, well, I should be home in the next couple of hours. Are you cooking? I really would love some of your smothered pork chops and mac and cheese."

"That is so unhealthy. Besides, I just got my nails done," I said, admiring my hands.

"Babe, you've been on this health-food kick. I'm a man, and I like real man food, like how you used to cook. I mean, hell, we all gotta die from something. At least let me be heart-attack happy." He laughed.

"Okay, that's fine, but I'm still not cooking today. Today is my day. I'm not slaving in the kitchen over a hot stove. If you want a good meal, let's go out to Oceanique tonight."

"Does every dinner have to cost me two hundred dollars? Gawd damn, Trinity. We don't have to ball out of control every day. We can hit up P.F. Chang's or something."

"P.F. Chang's is so three star."

"And it goes down just as easy and good as five stars," he said sarcastically.

"Fine. We can hit up P.F. Chang's. I really don't see what the issue is, though. We're multimillionaires, Terrence."

"And I would like to keep us that way, if you don't mind." The sarcasm dripped from his lips. "We'll hit up P.F. Chang's for dinner, and then we could do a movie night at the house, like we used to. Ya know? Just me and you."

I released an exaggerated huff. "Fine, Terrence."

He released a deep and slow breath. "I love you, Trinity. I have to finish up this meeting so I can come home."

"Okay. I love you too, baby."

That was a trip. When I was broke, I watched every penny, nickel, and dime I had, and now that I had money, my husband thought I was going overboard with my spending. Didn't we make money to live the life we lived? With Pooch out of the picture and my life exactly how I had envisioned it, I had no problems finally living it up to the max.

Ring. My phone went off again. "Christ!" My irritation that I couldn't get back to my book was evident. "Hel-lo."

Big Cal's voice floated through the receiver. "Hey, you."

A gasp escaped me at the voice on the other end. I hadn't looked at the name on my cell's screen. "Big Cal," I said faintly.

"I was just checking up on you."

"I'm good, but you know the deal. I really better go."

He chuckled. "Terrence really has gotten to you. So you're keeping your distance, right?"

"Keeping the peace in my marriage, Big Cal. Come on, Terrence is your cousin, and further-more, he's my husband. You know I'm gonna stand by my husband."

He paused for a long while. "Fair enough. Take care, five-star chick."

"You too." With that, we hung up.

I sat there for a minute staring at the phone. I was saddened by the fact that Big Cal and Terrence were still at odds with each other, and by how it affected all of us. I wished they could get over the beef.

Chapter 15

Pooch

Flava was doing her part helping Skrilla stack that paper so I could front my extra hundred grand. Lisa was still on lock, and my inside clique was pulling in that paper too. So I should've been a happy man. The thing bothering me was my lack of good rest. Yes, I was still sleeping with one eye open, as I had ever since I found Wolf and Cock Diesel together. I hadn't seen them together or heard of them being together since that night, but still, I wasn't trying to wake up with my seeds in Wolf's mouth or, worse yet, his in my mouth.

If that were to happen, they could call everything off, because murder would be the only thing on my menu. I'd shank that bastard in front of the warden myself and have a big-screen TV on instant replay to make sure they knew who exactly had laid that muthafucka down. That ain't on no gangsta shit. That's on some real shit. Ya feel me? Wolf had been tryin' his best to stay close to me and be on my good side after that shit, so I really didn't take him to be the type to fuck up his money flow by tryin' me on that ol' gangsta homo shit. But then, I didn't take him for the type to have his pipe stuck down another dude's throat, either. That just goes to show you, you never knew people.

Everybody on my team was puttin' in good work, even Cock Diesel—you know, aside from his extra-curricular activities and all. But word on the block was that he had those muthafuckas fallin' the fuck out over his package, though, and I wouldn't have believed that shit if I didn't see it with my own two eyes. Those bitches—yes, bitches—was fussin' over who was gon' get wit' him that night. Then those muthafuckas started fist fighting in the yard. Two cellmates in the yard were straight scrappin' like some ol' high school broads over a dick. The whole time Cock Diesel sat back, laughing at those clowns. Now that shit was real must-see TV. From what I had heard, Cock Diesel rewarded both of them for their loyalty to him by giving them both hell that night. But one thing I could say, he was definitely gettin' mo' ass than I got pussy around here, and that was for damn sure.

Anyway, all things considered, it was going well. I was biding my time to get the fuck out of here. In other words, I was being patient about it. Pooch Smalls had actually learned patience. I deserved a pat on the back. Fuck it. I'd pat myself.

As I waited on the CO to take me to the infirmary, I was actually excited. It'd been a while, and I couldn't wait to get my dick rocked by Lisa. I wanted the pussy and all.

"Ready, inmate?" Danielle's voice boomed through the cell.

I jumped up. "CO Brown? What the fuck are you doing here?"

"Filling in," she said plainly. "Are you ready to go?"

I looked at Wolf, and he laughed. "You betta hope that bull don't say shit to Lisa," he whispered.

Fuck. The last thing I needed Lisa to know was that I let this ugly bitch suck me off. She had become real possessive over me lately. She didn't like Flava coming to visit me and shit. One time and she was already addicted. Had to be the money. Still, Big Bull was gay, so I was sure it was cool.

She handcuffed me, and we walked out. "So you're sick, huh?"

I coughed. "Yeah, it's my chest."

"I know what could make that feel better," she said and then leaned over close to me. "Giving me some more bones to suck you off."

"Naw, man." I shook my head. "I'm cool."

That bitch was crazy. Pay her again? I was pissed at myself for doing that shit the first time. I ain't never paid for sex in my life, and I was trying to forget I had paid for it then, especially from Big Bull.

"Come on, Pooch. I know you got the grip. Word around here is that you're the muthafucking man."

"I don't know what you talking about." I didn't trust that bitch.

"Then where you get that money from?"

"None of your fucking business."

"Watch your mouth, inmate."

She gripped the handcuffs on my wrists as we walked. I winced from the pain. That bitch was gon' make me issue a hit on her ass if she didn't calm the hell down. Fake riots were easy to start to bring about real casualties.

"Look, CO Brown. I ain't got no money. Now, I know you got a lady and a job to protect, so be easy."

She was getting frustrated and angry. "Nigga, are you threatening me? You don't know shit—"

"Melissa Chambers, twenty-eight years old. Kindergarten teacher at Teacreek Elementary School who drives a pearl-black Chrysler 300, beige interior. License plate number DB'S BOO, which, since I know your first name now, I assume means Danielle Brown's Boo," I interrupted, intercepting her ideal threat.

Her mouth dropped wide open, and she instantly started sweating. "How'd you—"

After turning to face her, I gave her that real talk. "Don't ever think I'm not always one step ahead of the game. I showed you my wild card for a reason.

You needed to know that this inmate is not to be fucked with. Now, take me to the muthafucking infirmary, before Ms. Chambers finds out about your extracurricular activities or worse. Now, *that* was a threat."

"Okay, Pooch. Be easy. I'm sorry," she said, shaking like a leaf as we walked. "Just please, don't fuck with Melissa."

Laughing to myself, I couldn't help but be glad that I had had Pit's cousin find out about Danielle Brown. Something had told me that bitch might try to cause trouble for me. I had been trying hard not to show my card to her, but she wasn't about to fuck up my playtime with Lisa. I had to do what I had to do. Gloating to myself, I thought about how smart I was and wondered how I had let myself slip up that one time with Trinity. Simple. Love. My head was always clear with anybody and everything else, but the one bitch I loved had managed to get over on me. Or so I thought. I was still confused about whether or not Trinity had really left me or what the fuck was up with her. The limbo was what fucked with me. It made me seem as though I wasn't on my game, and I was always on my game.

"You can wait outside," Lisa told CO Brown when she led me into the infirmary.

"You don't need me to wait here for him?" she asked, confused.

"That's not necessary, Brown. I'm used to this inmate."

CO Brown shrugged. "Okay. Holler when you're ready." She took off my cuffs and walked out.

Rubbing my wrists from the steel bracelets, I said, "I thought that bitch wasn't never gonna leave. How's my baby doing?"

She put her hands on her hips. "What do you want, Pooch?"

"Damn, what you all attitudinal for? You haven't seen me in a week."

"So who else have you been fucking for me not to see you?"

"Lisa, I'm locked up. You act like I can snap my fingers and make shit happen. This shit takes a little finesse. Besides, I ain't got bitches rolling through here like this is my crib or some shit. Who the hell could I really be fucking?"

"You think I don't know Flava came to see you last week?" She sneered. "I wanted you to stop seeing that bitch, and I meant that."

Her crazy ass was losing her damn mind. I appreciated the possessiveness over the dick, but the only person issuing out ultimatums was me. "Flava is doing some thangs on the outside for me. She keeps me connected to my attorney. Come on, Lisa. Unless you wanna step to the plate and do it?"

"I can't—"

"Exactly," I boomed, getting up in her face. "So quit tripping, come and rock this dick, and get this grip." She was wasting time, and I was sick of playing with that bitch.

Tears sprang into her eyes. "I thought I mattered to you, Pooch. I thought maybe when you got out, we could be together. Here I was feeling like I was the only one—"

Frustrated, I stopped her by putting my hand up. "What are you rambling on about?"

"Danielle told me you let her suck you for money," she whispered.

That bitch. I was so stunned, I couldn't even say shit. Now what the fuck would make her tell Lisa, of all people, that shit?

"Melissa and I went to school together and are really good friends. Danielle confided in me because she felt bad about betraying Melissa. I can't believe you."

I was living a fucking nightmare. First, Trinity, and now this shit. That Wolf and Cock Diesel shit had thrown me off my game, and I had fucked up. I had to think fast.

"Baby, you don't know the whole story. I found my cellmate and another inmate fucking in our cell. I was frustrated, and you know when I get frustrated, I need a release. I couldn't jack off in front of them two gay bastards, so I fucked up and paid Danielle, but the entire time I was thinking of you."

"Really? 'Cause she said you called her Trinity. Flava's real name is Sonja. I checked out the sign-in log," she said, upset. "So not only am I not number one, but, hell, me and Sonja are behind some phantom bitch that never comes to see you."

Fuck me! Okay, I really needed to find out where this shit was going, because Lisa knew a lot of shit on me. Shit that could seriously backfire. "Okay, Lisa. Okay. The truth is I did say that name, but I thought I heard Danielle say her name was Trinity. Afterward, she told me it was Danielle. I'm sorry, baby. I am. I'll make it up to you. What can I do?" I said, grabbing her by her waist.

She grabbed a Kleenex. "Nothing. I'm done with you, Pooch. I've seen the writing on the wall, and now I know why they say not to get involved with bad boys. The sex may be great and the money good, but they'll stomp on your heart. All I wanted was for you to give me your heart, because you had mine. As soon as you got out, I was gonna take you in and help you get up on your feet. But now I hope you rot in this muthafucka. We are done," she said, giving me a cough drop. "Time to go. Guard!"

"Wait, Lisa. Wait," I begged her. I still needed to know what information was exchanged between these bitches, but it was too late. Danielle walked in.

"You good?" she asked Lisa.

Lisa nodded. "Yeah."

That confirmed it. That fucking CO knew everything. I looked up at Danielle, who smiled at me as she handcuffed me.

"Nurse Johnson," I called out to Lisa, hoping she'd have some sympathy for me.

"Aw, inmate, don't worry. I already know you know her as Lisa," CO Brown said.

"Take him out of here, CO Brown."

I was so fucking mad, I could've beaten both of their asses. If I weren't handcuffed, I definitely would've gotten at Big Bull. She stood there smirking, as if she had the upper hand on me, and I was pissed because that bitch did. I didn't know what all Lisa had told her, but now I knew it was time for damage control. I wasn't about to take the rap for none of this shit if it ever came out. If these bitches thought they could play me, they had another thing coming. I was Pooch Smalls. I never failed.

"You played yourself." Danielle laughed. "Now, don't fuck with me or my baby, inmate, 'cause trust me, I ain't the one, either," she whispered. "Oh yeah, you have a visitor."

"Just shut up and take me there."

When I walked into the visiting room, I knew there was trouble, because my attorney was in one

chair and Adrienne was in the other. Something
was up with Flava.

"What's up, Stein?" I asked, bracing myself for
the worst, as I took a seat.

"We've got an issue—"

"Somebody ratted on Sonja," Adrienne cried.
"You've got to do something, Pooch. She's locked
up."

My head fell in my hands. This shit could not
be happening. I needed time to think, and I was
already reeling from that damn Lisa and Danielle
shit. I knew there was a reason I couldn't be happy.
I wasn't gonna be happy until I was out of this
muthafucka for good, and now this dumb bitch
had done got locked up for pushing weight. I
knew that Skrilla wasn't even gonna front his half
of the money, because Flava getting locked up
had already brought him heat. He couldn't even
fucking touch her now, and especially not me. If
Flava knew what was good for her, she had better
not say my name or Skrilla's.

Looking at Adrienne, I asked, "Y'all muthafuckas betta have some answers for me. Who the fuck
would rat on Flava?"

She threw her hands up. "How should I know?
But I know they had to be targeting her, or they
would've locked us both up, right along with Skrilla.
She called me the other day and told me somebody

was following her. The next thing I knew, she was calling me from the county lockup."

"And you ain't had nobody watching you?" I questioned her. "Think, Adrienne. This shit is real important."

She remained silent and sat back, then shook her head. "No."

"I spoke with Skrilla myself, Vernon, and no feds have been after him. Like I explained to Adrienne, it sounds like someone specifically targeted Sonja. I spoke with Sonja, and she's nervous and scared to death. It's her first offense, so that goes in her favor, but she had a huge amount in her possession, so it's gonna be hard to get her off without serving any time. Damn hard," Stein explained.

"So she needs your help, Pooch," Adrienne said. "You can't let her go down for this shit. You have to give up Skrilla for us so Sonja can get off."

Whoa! Hold up. I was not about to go to war with a supplier I barely knew. Number one, I wasn't no muthafucking snitch, unless it benefited me. Number two, I didn't know who all his connects were or how deep Skrilla's contacts rolled. Lastly, I had never dealt with Skrilla on my own, so that counted my testimony out as hearsay. At least that was what I was gonna pitch now, because Flava's ass was on her own. She had broken the Eleventh Commandment—"Thou shall not get caught."

I grabbed Adrienne's trembling hands. "You know I'm there for you and Flava, right?"

She nodded. "Pooch, I love her."

These bitches had fallen in love. I'd be damned. "What about Wolf?"

She rolled her eyes. "As if you care about Wolf. He was just a meal ticket for you, and Sonja told me what Wolf did. If I were to ever have a man, I need one like you, a real one. Sonja is my concern. She needs our help."

"Wait a minute. Did you tell Wolf you knew?" I asked, concerned because this shady bastard could've been the one to tell.

She fanned off my comment. "Hell no. Sonja begged me not to tell anyone —especially him. She said you'd string her up. I'm only admitting it now because we have to stick together for her. Truth be told, I've moved in with Sonja, and we're a family. And when you get out, it'll be us three— the family. Fuck Wolf."

That was when it hit me. *That muthafucking Lisa and CO Brown.* Lisa was pissed with me about Danielle, so she had taken it out on Flava, knowing that she'd get locked up because she was running for me. I guessed she figured Flava would rat on me too. Slick bitches. Truth be told, a woman could be far more lethal than ten damn men. That shit was crazy, because the only people I could trust were Stein and Adrienne, and even Adrienne was only at about 75 percent, because clearly her loyalty was more toward Flava. I wasn't getting in the middle of this shit, even if I had caused it.

"Look, Stein, do your best for Flava. But I have never dealt directly with Skrilla. My testimony won't help."

He turned to Adrienne. "He's right. His testimony is hearsay. It's no good in a court of law."

She put her head in her hands. "Is there anything you can do?"

"Let me sleep on it, Adrienne. Everybody's emotions are real high, and I need to be able to gather my thoughts. You just see about Flava and keep her head up. Stein and I will deal with the other stuff, a'ight?" I lied.

She stood up and hugged me. "A'ight. Thanks, Pooch."

"You're welcome. Tell Flava I said to keep her head up. We'll get through this. But in the meantime, keep your mouth shut. Don't talk to nobody. Not even Wolf. Just me and Stein."

"I will tell Sonja, and I won't talk to anybody." The look in her eyes told me she was being honest. Her love for Flava was enough to save my ass. She wasn't gonna do shit to fuck up Flava's case.

Stein asked her to wait outside for a moment, and then he spoke with me in a lowered tone. "Do you really want to be involved with Sonja's case, knowing you're trying to get out?"

"Hell no," I whispered. "That bitch is on her own, but you can't tell Adrienne or her that. Keep me posted on what's happening, but I can't be affiliated with that shit."

He nodded. "All right, Vernon. I have to come back to you next week so we can discuss your appeal."

"Cool," I said as we shook hands.

He called the guard, and CO Brown came back to get me. "See what we can do to you?" she bragged. I knew those bitches had done it. Good thing Danielle's mouth was a faucet. Now I knew who I could and couldn't trust. "You shouldn't have hurt Lisa," she added.

"You forget that you helped with that."

She got quiet. "But Lisa forgave me and not you. That's the difference. I bet you wish you could offer me to suck you off now."

She had me there. As much bad news as I had just received, I wouldn't give a shit if I did have to pay her again to get my rock off. Ugly bitch or not, I needed a release. When she brought me back to my cell, Wolf was gone. *Good.* I needed some alone time. I grabbed my small bottle of lotion, sat in the rear corner of my cell, and got to work. I closed my eyes, thinking of nothing and nobody but Trinity. The way she danced and gave me a show, the way she moved her body in the bed, and the way I used to grip that long, silky-ass hair of hers as I tapped it from the back made tears come to my eyes. I missed her so fucking much. In no time, I exploded. I hurriedly cleaned myself up, then plopped down on my bunk.

I needed Trinity so damn bad. I realized that a lot of the reason why I'd been able to stay on top for so long was because of Trinity. She had had my back and had given me advice, even if it had seemed like I wasn't paying attention. I had been. Making sure she was taken care of had helped me keep my focus. Sitting there, thinking about the life we used to live, fucked with me hard for the first time in my life. Not just in my head, but in my heart. It was the first time I'd let myself feel real emotion. I didn't know if I was ever gonna get out of this bitch, ever see my daughter again, ever see my newborn son at all, or ever see my Trinity again. My chest swelled, and for the first time in my life, I cried.

As I began to wipe my tears, CO Billings came over to the cell. "Smalls," he called out. "What the hell is wrong with you?"

"I got something in my eye."

He chuckled. "Thugs do have emotions. I've been alive for forty-two years. I know tears when I see them. It's all right, son. Sometimes you have to cry to survive. You've got a lot of time to serve. It won't be your last time shedding tears."

He was probably right. I had to face the fact
that there may be a possibility that I wasn't getting
out of this muthafucka. Surprisingly, his words
gave me a little comfort. It was funny how life was.
Unbeknownst to him, we were vying for the same
chick, and even though I'd won, he had still ended
up encouraging me behind some bullshit that
same bitch did.

"Thanks, man," I said, rubbing my head. "I
needed that."

"You're welcome, but I ain't standing here for my
health or because we're friends. You have a visitor."

"I already went to visitation with CO Brown."

"I know. You have another one."

Two visitors in one day? What the fuck now? I
stood up like a dead man walking, and he handcuffed me again and took me back to visitation.
Who the fuck could this be? OMG! Trinity! It had
to be. My baby didn't forget me. She loved me. I
was gonna have to beg CO Billings for a private
room, because I was gonna tear that pussy up and
impregnate her again. I was so happy.

CO Billings led me to a private visitation room,
and when I walked in, I got the shock of my life. It
wasn't Trinity. It was Big Cal. How had that nigga
gotten out of jail? We had all gone down in that
bust. CO Billings left, and we stood there staring at
each other.

"I know you're surprised to see me."

"You're fucking right I am, especially without a white and blue jumpsuit on, with some handcuffs and correctional officers around."

He laughed. "That's funny."

"Fuck funny, Big Cal. What the fuck is the deal? How the hell you get in to see me and you ain't on my visitors' list? And how the fuck did you get out?"

"Nigga, sit down and calm down," Big Cal said boldly.

"Bitch, who you think you talkin' to?" I asked, pointing at him. "You must've forgotten who the hell I am or who you worked for."

He pointed at himself. "And that's why you're locked up and I'm not, right?" I couldn't say shit to that. Something was up. He laughed. "Right. Now sit . . . *the fuck* . . . down."

He pulled out my chair, then walked around the table and sat down across from me. I sat down and interlocked my hands on the table.

"Why are we in a private visitation room instead of in the general public? You ain't my attorney. This visit ain't violating no attorney-client rights," I said.

"You're a smart man. I ain't no attorney."

"The only other people who can meet in here are . . . police," I said slowly as the realization of what Big Cal was really saying to me came crashing down. "You're a fucking cop."

"That's not important. Why I'm here is."

"Bitch, you gon' have a shit storm on your undercover ass when I'm finished with you. My right-hand man a fucking narc agent. I can't believe this shit. Your life in the street is—"

"Don't make threats when you're fucked. I know about your bribes to Judge Watson. I know that Flava is locked up, and you been dealing with Skrilla. I know all about the in-house drug ring you got going on, and your whole fucking crew could get time behind it. Now, do you really want your crew to get additional time behind your ass? Let's see how long you make it in here then. All those years you got is a long time to have to watch your own back."

That nigga had me by the balls. I had no choice but to swallow my pride and my anger and listen to him, 'cause right now, he was one step ahead of my game, and he held all the cards.

"I'm listening. But not for long," I said, playing hard.

"If I told you I knew where Trinity was, how long would you listen?"

That muthafucka knew where my girl was. I bit my bottom lip until I drew blood. My heart danced with emotion. "Where is she? Tell me."

Big Cal's head bobbed up and down. "Mm-hmm. I got your attention now, don't I?"

"What? What do you need? What do you want? I'll do it. I just want Trinity back. I wanna see her and know how she's doing."

"She's cool, and you'll see her in due time. You just have to have my back on something."

"What? Anything."

"Listen close, 'cause I'm only gonna explain this shit one time. Ask no questions. Just help me, and I promise you, you'll be back with Trinity in no time."

"You're gonna help me?"

"If you agree to help me, I'll make sure that none of this shit with these drugs is tied to you at all. I'll tie it to another nigga."

"Deal. It has to be John 'Wolf' McNeil, though."

"Deal."

"Where's Trinity?"

He laughed. "I have a beef with that nigga Terrence."

"Her babies' daddy?"

"Yep." He nodded. "He's also the man she's living with. He's responsible for your lockup. And the word is he's a multimillionaire, living off the millions of dollars he made from hustlin' you."

"I don't believe that."

"Trust me. It's true."

"How did he—"

"No questions. Just know everything I'm saying is real." He pulled out photos. "I knew I'd have to prove it to you, so here," he said, sliding the pictures across the table.

I let out a nervous sigh as I slowly picked up the photos. Each one showed that fuck nigga Terrence around town with my baby, my Trinity. Looking like a real-life celebrity couple. Everything was designer this or that, and that nigga had a fucking Range Rover. The last picture was the one that got me. It more than got me. It infuriated me. It was Terrence with a new baby and my daughter. My son. My son was really his son. He looked just like Terrence. My jaw locked so hard, I thought it'd crack. *That bitch.* The whole fucking time she'd been playing me with Terrence. She'd made a fool outta me. All that time I'd pined away for her while she was being his *li'l mama* with my son. My eyes turned bloodshot red. I wanted his head and hers on a platter.

"So when do we get to get this muthafucka?" I asked, throwing the photos back at him.

"Give me three days. I'll be in touch," he said and stood up.

"You don't plan on snitching afterward, right?"

He shook his head. "Cop work is business. This is personal."

"For me too." We gave each other pound. "For me too."

"But if you cross me—"

"Don't worry, pimpin', 'cause the same shit goes for me."

I was quiet as hell when I walked out. A sense of peace surrounded me after I had accepted that this was where I was gonna spend the rest of my life, because as soon as I got finished with Dreads and his li'l mama, I would have no problem rotting away in this bitch. Yeah, li'l mama had Terrence's baby, and they were a couple. I was damn sure gonna remember that shit for the rest of my fucking life.

Chapter 16

Lucinda

The night I went over to Aldris's was so emotional for me. All I could do the entire time was cry while he begged and pleaded for me to forgive him. I ended up falling asleep at one end of the sofa, and he at the other. The next morning, when I woke up, he took me to get my car, and I didn't even bother Mike. Instead of going back to Aldris's house, I went to my mom's house. For the entire week, I stayed with my parents, while Aldris came over and called to convince me to stay with him. No haps. I needed to find Lucinda again.

Walking into my new condo, I didn't know quite how to feel. While I was proud for getting back on my feet again, I was also dismayed. I should've been getting ready to marry the man of my dreams, go on the most amazing honeymoon, and live my life happily ever after, but instead, I was back to being single. Back on my own.

Nadia was happy to be moving back with me. I believed she enjoyed the serenity of having her own space and not having to share it with a bunch of other people. Grandma's house was only fun for short visits, she'd told me. I had missed her, and I needed her now more than ever because my heart was aching so badly. Nobody could make me feel better than Nadia. The only blessing was that now that I was back on my own, Raul's child support was going back up. He already knew it, since he had received the letter from my attorney. Thanks to him pissing off the judge, my court case was going to be "priority." So here I was again, back at one.

"Lucinda, are you okay?" my mom asked, coming outside on the porch with me.

"Yes, Mama. Just thinking."

"You remind me so much of myself when your father cheated on me with Maria. Always in contemplation and turmoil. Don't let it eat at you. Learn to continue on with your life. At least Aldris wants to be back with you."

"But do I want to be back with him? is the question. I could have my life back right now, but I'm not sure if that's what I want anymore."

Her head nodded gingerly. "I understand. You're hurting."

"How could you take Dad back after all he's done? How could you get over that?"

Leaning forward, she reached for my hand, gently lifted it, and held it. "Because I love him." It was her answer, plain and simple. "I can't explain it. The only thing I know is that this time he had to prove it to me. As much as I love your father, he wasn't going to use me as a rebound for Maria. I set my requirements, and he's followed every one of them to the letter. Things are different this time, and if I even think he's reverting to his old ways . . . Well, he better go shack up with Aldris." She laughed, as did I.

"When did you get gangsta?"

"When your dad left." She laughed. "I'm not the same woman I was when he left, but at the same time, I am still the only woman for him. We both needed it. He needed to become the man I've always needed, and I needed to become the woman I am. We've grown."

"So, what about Eva? Is she staying here?"

"Yes. He was awarded custody, and she should be moving in with us in a few days. It'll be hard to swallow having her around, but I'd rather have her here with us than with Raul and Maria. No child should be exposed to those clowns."

"That's one way to look at it. I guess he'll be hot as hell having to be put back on his higher support for Nadia, but I love pissing him and Maria off."

"Speak of the devil." My mom pointed at Raul's car, which was speeding up to my parents' house.

He flew into the driveway and jumped out, damn near forgetting to put the car in park. "Lucinda! How are you gonna sue me for child support? You know you and that fool gonna get back together, and then what?" he yelled before he could barely get to the porch.

"Then we cross that bridge when we get to it. Right now, I'm single and living by myself. So you have to come up on them payments."

"Is this funny to you?" he asked angrily. "I have to support Maria, and she is such a fucking siddity ho," he said aloud, although I didn't think he meant to.

"Good for you. You wanted that siddity ho," my mom sneered.

Suddenly, he moved closer to me. Fake sadness washed over him. "Come on, Lu. Help me out. I just found out my mother has cancer. I have to help her out."

Shaking my head, I stood up. "I can't believe you'd use that as an excuse not to take care of your child. I've known for months about your mom. You are the only one who just found out because you never cared about anyone but yourself. Had you been more her son than trying to be less of a man, you would've known that. And keep your voice down. She doesn't want Nadia to know. Face the facts. You've got five kids, four babies' mamas, a piece-of-shit job, and your mother's sick. Don't you think you need to focus on getting your shit together? Wake up, Raul. This is real life. You created the hell you're in by yourself."

As Raul paced back and forth, in obvious anguish about my revelation, my dad came out on the porch and patted my shoulder. Raul turned around, and the old Raul resurfaced. "Fuck you, Lucinda—"

My dad put his hand up. "Let me be clear about one thing. You will not speak to my daughter like that again. If you do, I will dig a hole and bury you myself. You made your decision, so live with it. But I know this. You will take care of Nadia, and you will not bother Lucinda. Anything you have to say to her, say it in court. Now, what you are going to do is get off my property and not bother my daughter or granddaughter again. Are we clear?" my dad said sternly, staring him in the eye to let Raul know he meant business.

Raul swallowed hard. "Yeah, we're clear."

"Good," my dad said and folded his arms.

"Tell Nadia I'll come by to see her," Raul said. Then he left.

"Don't hold your breath on that," my dad said.

"Trust me. I wasn't," I agreed, looking over at him. "Thanks, Dad."

A smile of shock spread across his face as he turned to me. "So I'm Dad again?"

Giving him a warm smile in return, I nodded.
"For now."

He shook his head, wrapping his arm around
my mother. "You're always going to be Lucinda—
my special child."

"Every day of my life." I looked at him and my
mom. For the first time, seeing them together
made me feel good on the inside. "Look, I know
I gave you two hell about getting together, but
I want you to know that if you make each other
happy, then I'm happy."

My mom and dad both hugged me. "You don't
know how much this means to us," they said together.

"Trust me, I do. But I can't breathe." They
laughed and let me go. "Can you all do me a favor?"

"We've got Nadia," my dad said.

"Thanks. I have to meet Aldris to talk."

My mom walked inside, grabbed my purse,
came back out, and handed it to me. "Sigue tu
corazón, hija," she said and hugged me. "That's all
you have to do."

I nodded and then patted my dad's shoulder.
"Take care of her." He nodded and winked at me.

My mind raced a mile a minute. I was in so
much turmoil over whether or not I wanted a relationship with Aldris that I had made a split-second

decision to follow through and meet him as we'd planned. He'd been preparing for this night all week. The game plan was for us to have a nice dinner for two at the house, watch a movie on the tube, and then sit and talk about everything. He kept promising me that the night would be excellent and this and that, but on the inside, I asked myself, *Lu, what the fuck are you doing?*

I felt so vulnerable and weak from even dealing with Aldris. The mere fact that I was even entertaining him made me question myself, because it went against everything I'd ever vowed not to do. After how my dad had treated my mom, I had said I'd never take a man back who had cheated. I'd never be a doormat. I'd never give second chances. I'd never be weak. I'd never show emotion. I'd never be vulnerable. I'd never, ever, let love guide me into being taken advantage of. Despite all those nevers, I had decided that I would try, just this once, for love's sake.

"Aye, *pobrecito*. This is not you, Lu." I said aloud as I gave myself the once-over in my rearview mirror before exiting my vehicle. "Here goes nothing."

Aldris answered the front door right away, as if he'd been waiting right beside it. Of course, he looked and smelled so divine.

"Lucinda." He smiled.

I waved sheepishly. "Hey," I said, standing outside the door.

"You know you don't have to wait for me to invite you in."

I shook my head. "I don't live here anymore."

"Come inside, Lu, please."

I slowly walked in, and he guided me to the sofa. I sat down on the edge and placed my purse on the coffee table with my keys. "Sooo," I exhaled, placing my hands on my knees.

He sat down beside me. "Dinner is almost ready. I made all your favorites. I even tried to make a chocolate mousse cake." He chuckled. "I'm sure it doesn't taste as good as yours, but I was trying."

"That's great. I—"

Aldris jumped up. "Oh! And I got us a bottle of rosé," he said excitedly, interrupting me.

"Al—"

"Hold on. I'll be back." He dashed to the kitchen.

"Ugh." I felt so out of place and uncomfortable. I wasn't in the mood for eating, drinking, or watching a movie. I wanted to talk.

He came back in and sat two wineglasses on the coffee table. He popped the cork and poured some rosé into both of the glasses. "Here you go," he said, handing me mine as he sat down beside me. "Let's make a toast to . . . starting over." He lifted his glass, then touched my glass with his, and we both took a sip.

I sat my glass down and looked at him. "Aldris—"

"I got your favorite movies. Chick flicks. *Love Jones. Love & Basketball. Maid in Manhattan*—"

"Aldris—"

"Sit back, Lu. Relax, please," he said, rubbing my shoulders and cutting me off again.

That was it. I shrugged him off and jumped up. "I don't care about dinner. I don't care about the rosé. I don't care about the movies. I want to know if I should even be here or not. I care about you, but I ain't gonna be no man's fool, Aldris."

Rather than immediately address my tirade, he sat there and allowed me the moments I needed to blow off my steam. When I'd calmed down, he slowly rose to his feet and closed the space between us. Though I wasn't sure how I felt about being near him, I didn't pull away when his hands found their way to my face and cupped it. He didn't speak. He simply gazed into my eyes. After a while, I was able to do the same to him. Something about his demeanor had settled me down, and it was only then that he spoke.

"I'm not trying to make a fool of you, Lucinda. I want to make it right. I wanted this night to be special for us."

Feeling vulnerable under his imploring gaze, I allowed my eyes to dart away from him. "Aldris, I don't know if I can do this."

He tilted my chin upward, forcing me to return my eyes to his. "Well, at least have dinner with me, please." I attempted to look away again, but he held my gaze. "Please," he begged.

Reluctantly, I relented. "Okay."

He took my hand, we walked into the dining room, and he pulled out my chair. I sat down and allowed him to serve me all the food and to refill my wineglass. Then he sat down, and we ate. The food was pretty good. The conversation was a bust. Aldris had been my best friend. There had been a time when I could talk to him about anything and have the time of my life, and now I felt so distant from him. He engaged in a lot of small talk that I wasn't interested in, and I guessed in an effort to get me to talk to him outside of one-word answers, he asked about my job and Nadia. Nadia missed him so much, but I didn't offer that to him, because I didn't want him to try to use that to sucker me back into a relationship with him. I kept the conversation focused on her schoolwork and her Girl Scout activities.

"Here you go," Aldris said, cutting a piece of cake and putting it on my plate. Then he urged me to try his concoction. "Go ahead. Taste it."

With a quick prayer to bless it and my stomach, I ate a bite. "Not that bad." I smiled as a crumb fell from my lip. "Oh, shit." I giggled and tried to catch it.

He jumped up, wiped it with his finger, and before I knew it, he grabbed a small piece and mushed it on my lips.

"You ass." I laughed. "Oh, it's like that, huh?" I asked, picking up a piece of cake.

He nodded, preparing to run from me. "Uh-huh." He laughed.

"Oh, payback is a bitch."

I chased him from the dining room to the living room, then around the coffee table. I doubled back and caught him behind the sofa. I mashed the cake on his lips, and he fell over the back of the sofa onto the cushions, pulling me with him.

"You got me." He laughed.

"I did." I giggled.

A silent beat passed as he held me in his arms. Being in his arms like that, the way we used to be, felt like a good familiar feeling. The iciness I'd felt was thawing, and I felt my heart beating the way it used to when I was in his presence. It was as exhilarating as it was scary.

He wet his lips and said, "You've always had me, and you can have me back whenever you want."

Under his intense gaze, I felt conflicted. Love swirled around us, but distrust had created a tear in the fabric of our love. The moment felt too much for me, so I went to pull away from him, but he pulled me back down and held me near.

Those familiar bedroom eyes seared into my soul as he held me captive both in his arms and under his growing trance. "I love you, Lu," he said before pulling me into a deep kiss.

I tried to resist at first, but the more he kissed me, the weaker I felt myself become. Before long, he was on top of me, with his shirt completely unbuttoned and his manhood at full attention. He had taken my ponytail holder out, so he wrapped his hands in my hair and brought me to him for another passionate kiss.

A moan escaped my lips. "Um, Aldris."

"I love you, baby," he said, kissing me on my neck. "I love you so much."

He unbuckled his belt, and that was when it dawned on me. There was no way in the hell I was having unprotected sex with him. I didn't give a hell how badly I wanted it.

"Um, Aldris, wait." I pushed him back gently.

"What? What's wrong, baby?"

"Um, I can't do this without protection. I mean, I know we stopped using condoms after we got engaged, but given all that's happened, I don't feel comfortable not using them right now."

"I understand. I get it." He stood as I sat up. "I don't have any, but I can run to the store. It'll take me ten minutes, tops."

I nodded. "Okay."

He smiled. "Okay?"

"Yes."

"Okay. Don't go anywhere." He bent down and kissed me, happy that I had agreed to continue. "I'll be right back," he said as he finished buttoning his clothes and grabbed his keys.

Smiling, I sat there, feeling anxious and nervous, like it was my first time. I jumped up and ran to the hall bathroom. I washed my face and fluffed out my hair. I sprayed on a little bit of the perfume I'd left behind when I moved out.

"All right, Lucinda. You can do this. Be sexy tonight and make him yours again," I coached myself as I stared at my reflection. "You do want him. You do want this. Just get your head into this."

I won't lie. Despite his ability to resurrect my old feelings, I still had my reservations, for more reasons than one. Should I do this with Aldris, despite the conflicts in my heart? Didn't I owe it to this relationship to try just one more time? Was my love for him strong enough for me to go back again? Was I even in love with him anymore?

Those thoughts took up residence in my mind as I walked back to the living room. Instead of entering that room, though, I turned to the right and headed to our bedroom. His bedroom. I walked up to the door and got nervous as I went to open it. "What's wrong with you, Lu? Open the damn door," I said aloud.

I walked in, and the first thing I noticed was that the sheets, comforter, and pillowcases had all been changed. He never changed those when we lived together, I thought. It was always me who did that. I started looking around . . . scanning . . . scoping. Why would he change sheets? I thought.

Had Jennifer been there? Had they been together, and was he trying to hide the evidence? Thoughts of Jennifer occupying his bed drove my anxiety through the roof. I ran to the closet, jerked the door open, and flipped through his clothes and eyed every empty space, looking for a woman's shoe, shirt, or something. Nothing. I hurriedly closed the closet door and looked frantically under the bed. Nothing. I ran into the master bathroom and opened the cabinet, the hamper. Hell, I even checked the toilet. Nothing. Nothing but those damn sheets. Fresh. Crisp. Clean. Febrezed sheets.

A rage built up in me, and I ripped all the linens off the bed. Tears rolled down my face as images of him hugging, kissing, and screwing Jennifer came into my mind. I cried for a minute, and then I noticed the house phone voice-message indicator blinking. A message. I slowly walked over to it and pressed the PLAY button.

Beep.

"Message sent today at ten forty-five a.m.," the machine said. "Hi, Dri. It's me, Jennifer. I wanted you to know that Jessica's been asking about you. She really misses you and wants to see you. I wanted to set up a day for you two, so please give me a call. Look, I know that you're trying to work things out with Lucinda, and I'm trying to stay away and respect that, but I want you to know that I'm here if you need me. I always have been. I always will be."

Beep.

No truer words had been spoken. *I'm here if you need me. I always have been. I always will be,* I repeated in my head. She was right. No matter what happened with Aldris and me, she'd always be there. She'd be lurking around and waiting. How could he stay away from her? They had a child together. That was what made it real to me. I'd spend the rest of my life looking over my shoulder at Jennifer, and in the back of my mind, I'd know that I played second string to her. I always had; I always would. It was then that I knew I couldn't do this, and not just the sex—the relationship. As I stood there, more thoughts ran through my mind, and I knew then that I had to go. I wiped my tears, ran into the living room, grabbed my purse and keys, and then I left.

All I thought about as I drove was how Mike would never have done to me what Aldris had and how well he would treat me. In fact, a lot of the reasons why I'd been so hesitant to see if I could work things out with Aldris had to do with what things would be like if Mike had given us a chance. I'd never mentioned that to anyone. I internalized a lot of my emotions, but listening to that phone message had helped me decide whom I wanted. Jennifer could have Aldris. I wanted Mike, and that was exactly where my drive took me.

"Lucinda?" Mike said when he answered his door. "What are you doing here?"

I shrugged and bit my lip. "I don't know. Hoping, I guess."

He leaned against his door as I stood outside the doorway. "Hoping what?"

"Hoping . . . that maybe . . . you had changed your mind."

His eyebrows furrowed as an intense gaze graced his face. "Lucinda, the last time I saw you, you left my house with Aldris. What do you mean, me changing my mind?"

"So you're upset that I left with him?"

"No. Hurt and disappointed. But the point was that you were working things out with him—"

"It won't work."

"And why is that?"

"Because I don't want him."

"Who do you want?"

My feet shuffled from the nervous energy that suddenly invaded my body. I looked into his eyes and forced my answer out before I lost the confidence to say it. "You."

Frustration consumed him as he ran his hands down the front of his face. "Lucinda, you're hurt and mad with Aldris. You need—"

I put my hand up, thwarting his words. "No, I'm not. I'm hurt by his actions—yes. But I want to know where things can go between us."

"Lucinda, if things were different—"

It was my turn to be frustrated, and I threw my hands up. "You keep hollerin' about if things were different this, if things were different that. Things *are* different."

He pressed. *"How?"*

"Because . . ." I paused for a beat and then calmed down. "Because I want you, and you matter to me. You matter a whole lot." I uttered these words timidly. "I like you, and I want to know where things could go for us."

We stood there for a few moments, but it felt like an eternity as we stared at each other, not knowing what to say.

When it was clear to me that he had no response, I offered my apologies so that I could leave. "Sorry to bother you. You don't have to worry. I won't bother you again." After turning around, I took a step away from the door.

But before I got another step farther away from him, he grabbed my hand, turned me to face him, and pulled me toward him. "Are you sure this is what you want? If I turn my back on my boy, I have to know that this is real."

My insides exploded. And that was when I knew for sure. I'd loved Aldris with everything, and perhaps, I still did on some level. However, our time apart and my time with Mike had allowed space for something to bloom between us. That blooming had turned into feelings. Feelings that had become too strong to ignore. Feelings that I wanted to explore. Feelings that somehow and in some way had metamorphosed into more than feelings.

Smiling, I wrapped my arms around his neck, then confessed what I'd kept hidden in the crevices of my heart. "Michael George Johnson, *Sigue a mi corazón*. I'm following my heart. I love that we have so much in common. I can have fun with you just sitting back and drinking beer and watching the game or going out and dancing. I love how you make me feel like I am the only girl in the world that matters to you. I love how you know what to say or how to say it or when nothing needs to be said at all. I love how you respect me, even when I'm weak. I love how you take care of me when I'm vulnerable. I love how you stay true to yourself and your manhood, no matter what the situation. I love the pride you take in taking care of Mike Jr., Levar, and Michaela. I love the way you smile, the way you dress, your stride, the rise and fall of chest when you sleep. I love . . . the way you love me . . . even though you keep yourself from admitting to me that you've fallen. And I want . . . I want . . . to be able to fall in love with you too, because you matter so damn much to me."

The fast rate at which his heart pumped indicted that my words had seeped into his being, and his smile revealed the same. He brought his hands to my face and cupped it. "You're the only person in this world who can call me George and live afterward," he joked, and I giggled. Then he turned serious and stared intently in my eyes. "I don't know how or when it happened, but, Lucinda, I love you," he declared, then sealed his words with a kiss.

Instantly, I was mush in his arms. I could've sworn I heard bells, whistles, sirens, firecrackers, and explosions going off in the background. When he kissed me, I knew there was no other place I wanted to be except right there with him. Catching me by surprise, he lifted me into his arms and carried me over the threshold and into his house, and he didn't put me down until we reached his bed. I dropped my purse, cell phone, and keys on the floor as Mike began to undress both of us. My mouth nearly fell off the hinges at what was dangling above me.

Suddenly, Mike stopped in the middle of kissing me. "Shit, Lu. I don't have any—"

Placing my index finger to his lips, I whispered, "Shhh." Then I leaned over and grabbed a box out of my purse. "I stopped at the store down the street."

He looked at the box. "It'll be a stretch, but it'll work."

"Clearly," I said, shaking my head.

"No doubts?" he asked me as he pulled out a silver packet.

I reached up and brought him to me for a kiss. "None at all."

He slipped on the protector and entered me nice and slowly. I'd never felt so filled up in my life. I held on to him as he slowly rocked me back and forth, holding me close. With every stroke, he professed his love for me over and over again. And with every stroke, I allowed him to claim me as his.

"Ooh, baby, let me please you," I moaned.

He looked down at me. "You already do," he said breathlessly. "We'll have plenty of time for everything else, but tonight let me love you, baby."

He was right, and love me down, he did. I needed him to show me that he was serious about the way he felt for me. We needed that connection to tie us together and make us strong. We needed to solidify ourselves as one. He made love to my mind, my body, and my soul. I'd never felt closer to a man in my life, nor had I truly enjoyed the essence of making love until then. Not even when I heard the vibration of my cell phone and saw it light up with Aldris's name did it deter us. I was Mike's now.

"Mike, baby, I'm about to cum," I moaned softly and gripped him tightly.

He huffed breathlessly as he burrowed his face in the nape of my neck. "Me too. Oh God, Lu, I've never felt this way . . . never loved. . . Ooh, shit, this is the best. You're the best," he panted.

Then together we both cried out each other's name in a whirlwind release. I can't even describe it. It was like heaven. Afterward, Mike rolled on his back and pulled me on top of him.

He brushed my wet locks away from my face as I wiped his forehead with the palm of my hand, and then we kissed.

He smiled at me.

"What?" I smiled back.

"I'm admiring what love finally feels like. I'm yours, Lu. Only yours."

"And I am yours. Only yours," I said to him as my phone buzzed again. He picked it up and showed it to me. I shrugged. "I'm with my man. The only place I want to be."

He smiled; then he ended the call and powered off my cell phone. And I didn't care. I was starting a brand-new life with Mike.

Chapter 17

Aldris

Can't I catch one break? I thought as I tried to reach Lucinda again for the twentieth time. I had thought everything had turned out all right, and we were ready to start over. Then I had come back to nothing. Nothing except a ransacked bedroom. The instant I'd laid eyes on the room, I'd known that she had freaked out and had looked for signs of Jennifer. I'd not seen Jennifer since that fateful night, and I didn't understand how to get Lu to understand that Jennifer was only a mistake. I wanted Lu. I loved her. Why couldn't she see that?

I gave up trying to call Lucinda's cell and called her mom, who told me she wasn't there, because she had left to come see me. *Great.* The only beneficial information I did receive from her mother was the address for Lucinda's new condo. Before I disrupted her peace, I wanted to reach out to all possible sources, so after I hung up with her mom,

I reached out to LaMeka, who also hadn't seen or heard from her.

For what felt like hours, I sat on my sofa, dialing her again, and again, to no avail. Eventually, my calls went straight to voicemail. Dismissal. She was dodging my calls. Turning the slip of paper that had her address over in my hands, I sat there pondering whether I should I use the information I'd received from her mom. I needed to talk to her sooner rather than later to reassure her that she was the only one for me, but I didn't want to push too hard. That might force her away when I needed her close. If I could keep her close, I knew I would eventually penetrate her mind and halt those fears.

Her heart was with me. I felt it. I just needed everything else to follow it. However, after her phone went to voicemail two more times, I decided to chance it, but when I arrived at her condo, she wasn't at home. As I sat in my car, the thoughts that I'd been pushing back in my mind were screaming for me to accept them. She was with Mike. I felt it. I knew it.

Just as I started to allow those feelings to overwhelm me, my cell phone rang. I picked up. "Yeah, Mama?"

"How was your night with Lucinda, or is it still going on?" she asked excitedly.

I huffed. "She ran out on me."

She let out a defeated sigh. "Oh no. Why?"

Gripping the phone tighter, I pressed it closer to my ear. "I don't know," I seethed, my attitude evident. "All I know is that everything was going great. We were connecting and conversing. Then I left to go to the store, and when I got back, she was gone. She'd basically turned the bedroom inside out."

"She was probably looking for signs of Jennifer."

"Yeah, I figured that much out," I snapped.

"You know, I've had about as much attitude from you as I will stand, young man. I know that you've been through a lot lately, but I won't stand by and be disrespected by you because of what you're going through. We've had our own differences of late, but at the end of the day, I'm your mother, so better give me the respect that I damn well deserve," she said, chastising me. "Besides, I was only trying to check on you two. I love Lucinda, and anything I can do to help, I will."

She was right. I had been such an ass to her lately because of her new relationship and my failing one. My father was probably turning over in his grave at my actions. I had no right to disrespect her, and I decided that ended right now. Perhaps, it was the reason I couldn't keep my woman in the first place. I needed my actions to realign with my words.

"I know, Ma. And you're right. I'm so sorry for how I've acted lately and treated you. I had no right. Can you ever forgive me?"

I could practically feel her smile radiate through the phone. "Of course, I can. It's already done. You're my son. Every bit your father, but my son. I love you."

"Thanks, Mama. I love you too."

"Listen, I know things may seem bleak right now, but don't beat yourself up. It will all work out in due time."

"I feel you, Mama. It's just I'm so damn frustrated."

"Why? Because she left?"

"No. 'Cause I know where she is," I said between clenched teeth.

"Where?" my mom asked, puzzled.

"Mike's house," I said tensely. "I need to go." I cranked up my car, preparing to head to Mike's.

"Look, Al, I know you don't want to hear this, but if she is over there, you need to keep in mind that you created that doorway."

What a slap in the muthafucking face. How in the hell did I create that doorway? No. The only person creating doorways was Mike, and if he tried to open up Lu's heart or her legs, I was gonna break his. Guaranteed.

My mom had me heated, but I tried to check my burgeoning anger. "How can you say I caused that? I messed up with Jennifer, but I didn't cause that."

"You're the one who gave her the opportunity to run to another man by always following be-

hind Jennifer. If your dad never taught you anything else, he did teach you boys this; while you're
busy running out your front door, another man
is busy sneaking in your back door. So be careful
with your woman. The key to a lasting relationship
is determined on whether or not the back door is
open. If you had paid more attention to Lucinda
instead of Aldris, and even more so Jennifer, then
she wouldn't need comfort elsewhere."

Swallowing hard, I realized that she had a point,
but I'd be damned if I lost the best thing that
had ever happened to me to a nigga like Mike.
That nigga had just stopped sleeping around with
multiple women and was only now standing up as
a man. He didn't deserve a woman like Lucinda,
let alone Lucinda herself. Not on my watch. Yet I
held out hope that Mike was simply being a friend
to Lucinda during our difficult times. He had been
my best friend since grade school. He couldn't
do that to me. He wouldn't. He may have been a
womanizer, but he'd never be a traitor. Would he?

"Well, all I know is that when I turn into these
condominiums, I better not see Lu's car."

"Don't go over there looking for trouble."

"I have to know."

"Aldris, listen to me. Take my advice and go
home."

"I gotta go, Mom. I'll talk to you later." I hung up
before she had a chance to respond.

When I got there, I didn't see her car, and I felt so stupid. *She's probably somewhere clearing her mind*, I thought. This was ridiculous. Ever since I had found out that she'd stayed with Mike for that stint, I had always thought the worst first. I started to turn around, but then I looked across the parking lot. A brand-new black Maxima with the license plate number MSFLY was parked there. I threw my car in reverse, backed up to the Maxima, and made sure I had read the plate correctly. I had. Enraged, I parked and jumped out of my car. He could say what he wanted to say this time, but I knew he'd stepped to Lucinda. I knew it.

"I'm fucking him up on sight." I charged toward his front door and banged on it with my fist. "I promise I'm fucking him up on sight."

Nobody came to the door, but I continued to pound on it. It only enraged me further. *What are you doing with Lucinda in your house that you can't answer the door quickly? Mm-hmm. On sight!*

"Who is it?" Mike finally asked from behind the door.

"Nigga, who you think it is?" I yelled. "Open the door."

"Come back tomorrow, Dri."

Come back tomorrow? Did that muthafucka really tell me to come back tomorrow, with my lady in his house? That bitch had to be crazy. Hell no.

Scratch that. He was stupid. I was the nigga that was crazy. And I was about to go fucking loco on his ass.

"I know Lucinda is in there. So open up," I demanded.

"She doesn't want to see you right now."

"It's not what she thinks . . . Wait a minute . . . Why am I talking to you? Open this fucking door, Mike. I need to talk to Lucinda."

"Like I said, come back tomorrow."

He was tryin' me. He really was. "Mike, if you don't open up this door, I'ma kick the muthafucka in, and then I'ma kick ya ass. There's gonna be a fuckin' situation out here in a few seconds, 'cause you tryin' my fuckin' patience, dawg."

"Lucinda said she'll talk to you tomorrow," he said plainly.

"And who the fuck are you? Lucinda's keeper? Her message boy? Her do-boy? Let her tell me for herself!" I yelled. "Matter fact, I'm done talkin' for real."

The next thing I knew, the door opened partially. Mike stood there with his feet stuck in some tennis shoes, with a pair of basketball shorts on and nothing else. He was half-naked. In front of Lucinda. Hell to the muthafucking no.

"*You muthafucka!*" I yelled, charging at him.

"Son of a bitch!" Mike yelled as we locked up.

Lucinda ran into the living room. "Stop it. *Just stop*!"

Mike pushed me off of him, and I fell back and hit the door, making it slam shut. As Mike slowly stood up and I regained my composure, my heart dropped. Lucinda stood there in one of his basketball jerseys and had nothing else on. No pants, no bra, hell, not even a fucking shoe. Nothing. And if she didn't have those items on, I knew she didn't have on any panties. *Nothing*.

"Lu? What are you . . . What are you doing?" I asked, upset and angry at the same time.

"I can't believe you would chase me over here like a damned maniac," she hollered.

"What was I supposed to do? You left so abruptly, and then you're here with Mike. What the fuck is going on?"

"You were supposed to accept the fact that I left and be an adult about it."

"Really? Be an adult and you're over here at my boy's house in his clothes?" I said, damn near laughing at her statement. "Let me rephrase *that*, 'cause my *boy* wouldn't do this to me."

Mike shook his head. "I was tryin'a stay out of it—"

With a sidelong glance, I yelled, "Oh, muthafucka, you all up in it—in more ways than one, huh?"

He turned and looked at Lucinda. "Before shit gets outta hand, I'ma let you deal with his ass." He began to walk off.

"Don't walk off, dawg," I shouted.

I ran up on him and grabbed his shoulder. He knocked my hand off, and I punched him. He staggered and then charged at me.

"I'ma break ya fuckin' neck," he yelled as we began pounding on each other again.

"Stop it. I'ma call the police," Lucinda screamed.

Disbelief struck me. *The police?* Mike and I got up off the floor, pushing each other. "You're calling the cops on *me*?"

"Get outta my house!" Mike yelled, pointing to the door.

"Get away from my woman!"

"Enough!" Lucinda shouted, standing between us. "Good grief already," she said and turned to me. "You need to leave."

"Not without you. Are you crazy?"

"No. For once, since before I can remember, I know what I want."

"I know you probably think I've been dealing with Jennifer, but I haven't—"

She put her hand up, halting my plea. "I do, but none of those things matter."

"What matters, then?"

"I wanted to sit down and talk to you like adults, but since you're here now, I guess now will do. Aldris, I don't want to be with you. I need for you to move on. If being with Jennifer is what you really want, then do that. I can't be a part of that. Every time I look at you, I see what you did, and I can't deal with that."

Her words were like bricks to the face and a dagger to the heart. My worst nightmare was coming true, unfolding right before my eyes. I couldn't find a way to wake up out of it without it becoming reality. Tears sprang to my eyes, because for the first time, I felt it. I felt Lucinda slipping away from me, and I couldn't handle it. I couldn't handle losing her.

"But I love you, Lucinda. We were getting married." Closing my eyes, with my head leaned back, I pinched the bridge of my nose. "What did Mike say to you?"

Mike just shook his head. "You're unbelievable. You still think I have something to do with Lucinda's decision? This is what I had to do with it. Nothing. You helped her make her decision when you were over there being Jennifer's man and not hers."

My watery eyes pierced him. "So what are you being, huh, Mike? Lucinda's man?"

Lucinda walked over and wrapped her arm around Mike's waist. "As a matter of fact, that's exactly what he's being, Aldris. Mike and I have grown fond of each other. We care about each other, and I've decided that I want to see where things could go between him and me. He didn't push up on me. He gave me the space I needed to make a decision, and he let me go to be with you. But I want to explore what we could be. I want to be with Mike."

My insides went haywire. I didn't know if I was having a heart attack, a nervous breakdown, or turning into the Incredible Hulk. My ears started ringing, my breathing turned erratic, and my body trembled. Did she just tell me that she was dating my boy? Fuck that. *Ex*-boy! Me and this dude had played in sandboxes together, and he had betrayed me for some ass? Okay. I had his fuckin' number.

Focusing my attention on Mike first, I pointed to myself. "This is how you do me? We were boys. All through grade school and even college, we had each other's back. We never let a female come between us. Nothing. No one. You gon' betray me just so you can tap her ass because you saw her stripping at Club Moet?"

Mike shook his head and gripped Lucinda around the shoulders. "I don't expect you to understand. This is not about no damn strip club. I know you've known me to be a playa and a dog, but I've matured. I've changed. I know what and who I want in my life. I'm sorry if that no longer includes you. You're my dawg. I know you won't be my friend anymore, but I'm cool with that. Not because you don't matter to me, but because Lucinda matters more. I love her, Aldris. I never wanted to hurt you, but I can't help how I feel and that I've fallen for her. Nor can I help that she chose me."

The treachery. I didn't know what hurt the most, facing my boy's betrayal or losing Lucinda. At that point, both carried equal weight. Mike and Lucinda were the two people in the world who I'd trusted next to my own parents. Now they were the two people at the source of the worst pain I'd ever felt in my life. Still, I could live without Mike. Fuck him. Niggas came a dime a dozen. But love. Love was once in a lifetime. That was what I had with Lucinda, "once in a lifetime" love. I just needed her to remember that. I had to fight for that. I couldn't lose her. Not like that. Not to Mike.

Turning my attention away from Mike's traitor ass, I put my focus on the only reason I was over here to begin with, Lucinda. Pain erupted inside me, and I wailed, pleading with her as if my life depended on it.

"Don't let him come between us, Lu. *Please.* He's been baiting you ever since I confessed to him that we were having problems. He wanted you to leave me."

"No, he hasn't. He was being a friend when I needed one. Through our friendship, so much more developed. He has always wanted me to work things out with you, but if you had never cheated, we wouldn't have found each other."

My heart dropped as she spoke words that were similar to the ones my mother had spoken to me. "But I never chose Jennifer over you. No matter what I did, I never . . . ever . . . chose her over you, Lu."

She swiped the lone tear that careened down her face. "Only, you did. You chose her over me every time you didn't answer your phone, made a decision without consulting me, picked Jessica over Nadia instead of including her, picked Jennifer over me instead of including me, and the moment you decided that sleeping with her behind my back and lying about it was okay. You chose her. You left me a long time ago, Aldris. I just had the courage to face it."

I stood there, pleading with my eyes. "Please, Lucinda *please*. I want you. I love you. Don't do this to us. *Please*. I'm begging you."

Turning her tear-stained face away from me, she denied me. "Please just go." She buried her face in Mike's chest, and he wrapped his arms around her. She nestled in his embrace.

That gesture between them spoke volumes, and witnessing it made me understand something that I hadn't realized before. Mike had more than pushed up on my woman; he'd taken her. She was Mike's now.

I knew at that point that Lucinda was serious. There was no changing her mind when it was made up. I had liked shit better when I was speculating whether or not Mike and Lucinda were together. If I'd just kept guessing, I guessed I wouldn't feel like my soul had been plunged into the pits of hell.

Squaring up, I cleared my eyes of the tears, and I looked at Mike. I shot a searing glare at him, with a stern finger point. "This ain't over. Trust me. I've got my time for you, muthafucka."

With that, I walked up to Lucinda, kissed the side of her head, stroked her hair, then turned and left.

Sitting in my car, I could do nothing but cry. I'd lost Lucinda. I'd lost everything. The only person I had in this world now was Jessica. I willed myself to go home so that I could try to get myself together for her sake. When I arrived home, Jennifer was in my driveway.

"What are you doing here?" I asked, walking past her as she got out of the car.

"I don't know. I felt it in my heart that I needed to come by."

"Well, feel it in your heart to leave."

She put her hand on my arm as I went to unlock the door. "You don't have to be mean. I'm so sorry about what I caused to happen, and I wanted to check on you."

"I'm fine," I hollered. "I just want to be left alone."

Jennifer sighed, folding her arms. "She won't come back, will she?"

Her words were another reminder of what I'd endured at Mike's, and I began to cry again. After I opened my door, Jennifer followed me inside. Leaning against the inside of my front door, I continued to weep, unable to move.

Jennifer hugged me. "It's okay."

The next thing I knew, she reached up and kissed my tears as they ran down my cheeks, my forehead, my nose, and finally my lips.

"Jennifer, no."

She stood back from me. A few minutes passed before I looked up, and when I did, I saw that she'd stripped down to nothing. "Let me help you to make it better," she said, gliding up to me.

I stood there looking at her and then decided, *Fuck it*. Lucinda didn't want me, and since I couldn't get back the woman I loved, I thought, *What the hell? If you can't be with the one you love, love the one you're with*. Jennifer took my hand, laced her fingers with mine, and I allowed her. As she guided me through my house, I picked up the bottle of rosé. Then I allowed her to lead me to my bedroom.

Chapter 18

LaMeka

Ever since Tony, or whoever he had ordered, had torn up Gavin's place, I'd begged Gavin to stay with me. He hadn't wanted to at first. He had felt like he was being a bitch and running scared. He had felt like no man should run him away from his house. Typical dude. To me, it wasn't about feeling like a bitch or protecting his manhood. It was about me having the security of knowing he was safe, so he moved in with me for a while to appease me.

Now our issue was, How in the hell were we going to tie all this activity to Tony? When the police did a sweep, they didn't find any fingerprints—of course not, not when the perp had gloves on—and since nobody around saw anybody break in, they had no suspects. But we all knew who was behind this foolishness. I'd talked to Tony's parents, and they felt like it was absurd that I believed Tony would do something like that. However, I had kindly reminded them that they didn't figure their handsome, straight As–having track-star son would end up with nothing more than a high school diploma and turn out to be an ex-junkie with HIV, either.

I hadn't said that to dog him out, but the truth was the truth. Tony Light's life hadn't amounted to shit, and the only good thing that had come from his existence was Tony Jr. and LaMichael. Of course, after I'd said that, they had asked me to leave their house and had told me that I wasn't welcome back. Fine with me. I'd been on my own with the boys without any of their help for so long that it didn't faze me if they were around or not. I knew one thing: Tony wasn't gonna keep bothering Gavin. Sooner or later, his lucky streak was gonna run out.

Despite Tony and his antics, things between Gavin and me were still amazing. The kids and my mom loved him, and he had stepped into the family-man role rather nicely. He always spent time with the boys and made me happy, both in the bedroom and outside of it. I'd never known love like this before. Gavin was my heart and soul, and my only regret was not realizing it sooner. Aside from Tony, everything in my life was perfect.

I hit the alarm clock, sat up, and stretched. I'd had the most amazing dream. I'd dreamt that

Gavin was lying next to me in bed and that we'd made passionate love until the wee hours of the night. Then I looked to my right and realized it was true. He was curled up on his side of the bed, with only his boxers on. Leaning over, I kissed his cheek.

"Good morning, sleepyhead," I said to him.

He stretched and smiled. "Good morning, baby."

"The alarm went off a few minutes ago. We have to get up," I reminded him, begrudgingly getting out of the bed.

He sat up. "Can I lie here a few more—" he was asking when suddenly I heard both of his feet hit the floor, and he dashed into the bathroom behind me.

Turning around, I laughed. "Damn. That was a change of heart."

"I saw all that luscious booty going in here, so I wanted to go wherever it was going," he joked.

I playfully nudged him. "Damn clown!"

Gavin went into my closet and grabbed two towels and washcloths while I turned on the shower. "A set for you," he said, handing a towel and washcloth to me, before we both stepped in the shower.

Gavin eyed me like a puppy waiting on his treat. He tried his best to behave, so I gave him the permission he so desperately wanted. "My mom got the boys ready for school, and she's taking them to school today."

No further words were needed. Gavin backed me up to the wall of the shower. "Good," he said as we began to kiss.

This man was certified hell when it came to love-making. You'd think that we didn't make love until two in the morning. I didn't mind, though. With loving like that, how could anyone resist? I held on to Gavin for dear life as he slowly rocked me back and forth against the shower wall. With every thrust, he brought us both closer to a completion that could only be described as electrifying.

As my completion neared, my moans got louder and I bellowed out, "Gavin! Baby! I swear, I've never felt like this." When I exploded, my release was so intense, it felt as if a bomb had detonated.

Laser-focused eyes were trained on me as Gavin dove deeper, chasing the finish line. "Meka, baby, ooh," he moaned. "*I love you*," he groaned as he came.

I was so shocked that afterward words eluded me. Realizing what he'd confessed, he turned his face away from me, but I turned his face back toward me.

"Did you mean it? Do you love me, Gavin?"

Gavin's head leaned forward, and we touched forehead to forehead. Holding me in his arms, he drew circles behind my neck with one hand as he held me tightly about my waist, pressing me against him. His labored breathing returned to normal before I felt his head gesture up and down. When his eyes focused back on me, they revealed his innermost secrets. "Yes, Meka. I do. I love you so much."

Cloud nine transported me to euphoria at his admission. I leaned forward and kissed him on the lips. All my pearly whites showed as I admitted my innermost secret to him as well. "I love you too."

For a few moments, we held each other as the water continued to cascade down our bodies. Standing there, holding my man, I knew that our relationship had come full circle. He was mine, and I was his, and I knew without any more doubts that Gavin and I were meant to be together.

After a few more minutes of bonding, we actually showered and dressed. When we finally walked into the kitchen, Misha was sitting at the island, eating a bowl of cereal.

"Good morning, Misha," we both said in unison.

"I'm sure it was for you two." She laughed. "Just in case you didn't know, your shower has a tendency to echo and carry. You know for future reference."

I gasped. "Oh God! Was Mom—"

"Her and the boys left before your festivities began."

My hand covered my heart. "Oh, thank goodness!"

Gavin laughed. "My bad, Misha. I'm sorry."

She put her hand up. "Don't apologize to me. It's her house. She can do what she wants. I'm asking to maybe not hear so much of it next time, 'cause y'all two jiggas was gettin' it in."

"Well, there won't be too many mornings like this, I guess. You know I'll be moving back into my house soon," Gavin said to Misha.

"Aw, bro-in-law, we like having you around. You should consider staying."

"That's what I said," I threw out, cutting my eye at him. "He feels like he's mooching off of me if he stays," I whispered to Misha, loud enough for Gavin to hear me.

"Exactly," Gavin said. "Misha, please don't start her up on that topic."

Misha lifted her hands in surrender. "I ain't in it."

I turned to him. I felt the need to state once more my position on him staying with us versus moving back to his house. "Gavin, I don't see the issue with—"

"Look at the time," Gavin interrupted. "Time to get to work. I don't want to have to write you up for tardiness," he said and kissed me on the forehead. "Let's go."

He was lucky that it actually was time to go and that we were driving in two separate vehicles since he had to work extended hours and I didn't. Lucky ass. Gavin was so traditional about certain things.

If it wasn't for the fact that he was actually staying with me, we probably still wouldn't have had sex while the kids were in the house. While he was there, he footed all my bills, along with the bills at his place. He had a serious complex about feeling like a woman was taking care of him. I tried to be understanding about that traditional side of his, because in essence, he was right. I'd rather a man want to be the provider than sit on his ass, acting like a bitch. But it was hard to convince him that I didn't mind, because I knew he was good man, without sounding hypocritical at the same time. He felt like I shouldn't be so gung ho about taking care of a man, especially after everything I went through with Tony, but for me, it was more about enjoying having Gavin around so we could be a real family.

An hour later, Gavin walked up to the nurses' station, breaking me out of my thoughts. "Good morning, ladies."

"Good morning, Gavin," we said in unison.

"Tracy, can you refill the main supply room for me?" he asked.

"Sure thing," Tracy said and left.

"Okay," he said, looking at the board. "Let's see what our patient load looks like this morning." He looked over everything and assigned us our particular duties for the day. "Brianne, I want you to partner with Jeanine. LaMeka, you partner with Sara. And, Alison, you're with me," Gavin ordered.

My face turned up, and I peered at him strangely. He had put the white chick with him. When he was chasing me, he always put us together. Now he was with the white girl. What the hell?

"Any questions?" he asked.

I spoke up. "Um, I have one."

He motioned for me to follow him. "Sara, wait here for LaMeka. Alison, I'll be right back. LaMeka, walk and talk with me." He walked away from the nurses' station, and I followed.

"So, what happened to us partnering?"

"We're a couple, LaMeka. Not to mention, I'm staying with you. I don't want there to be any confusion and conflict. I don't need anybody saying that either one of us was being unethical," he explained with a straight face.

"So you choose the white girl?"

He chuckled. "Would you rather I had chosen Brianne?"

Brianne was black, and black women were his preference. He had a point. Still, who cared about what they thought? Most of their nosey asses knew about us or speculated anyway. "No, it's just that most of them know we're dating, and they haven't said anything."

Taking a deep breath, Gavin leaned close to me to limit the ear hustling of passersby. "I have to devote my time between the three of you. Don't you think it will look unethical if my attention is constantly on my girlfriend?" he asked in a whisper.

He had a point, but I still felt slighted. At least he could've told me his intentions beforehand. Since he had put it that way, I backed down. Although I felt slightly defeated. "Okay."

"Baby, I'm not trying to *not* be with you, but I have to balance my time. I can't let our relationship affect the fact that you're also a student."

I guessed he was right. Well, I knew he was right, but he was still my man now, so hell yeah, I was jealous that another female got to spend the time with him, even if it was job related. Before I could speak, one of the doctors called him.

"Tell Alison I'll be right back. We cool?" he said to me.

"Yeah." I turned and walked back to the nurses' station. "Dr. Wilson called Gavin. He told me to tell you he'd be right back, Alison."

She laughed. "Don't worry. I'll take good care of him for you."

The other nurses giggled at her comment.

"What's that supposed to mean?" I asked, catching an attitude.

Jeanine looked at me. "Girl, you know we know you ran over there to ask him about why he didn't choose you. We all know Gavin is tapping that ass."

I was offended. "He's not *tapping this ass*, as you say."

Brianne fanned me off. "Just tell us. Can the white boy really jump?" She laughed.

"Go ahead and let them know, Meka. There are some white guys who can put it down just like a black man," Alison said, hitting my arm. "And the way Gavin looks . . . mm-hmm . . . I know he can definitely put it down." She high-fived Sara as they all agreed.

"Well, she doesn't have to tell us anything. We already heard that Gavin is the shit," Jeanine said to Sara.

Sara laughed. "What's his nickname again, Jeanine?"

"King *Dingalang*," Jeanine said with emphasis. "They said the boy so good, he needs his own slogan."

"Go see the king and get crowned with the best service," Sara announced, making up a slogan.

"That was pretty good." Jeanine laughed, as did the others.

Were those hoes serious? The only reason I didn't go and chin check any one of them was that it would impact my enrollment and my employment. I couldn't believe they had the audacity to disrespect me in my face, discussing my man as if he were solely there for their entertainment. True or not, the only person discussing my man's dick size and stroke was me to him. Nasty hoes.

"I don't feel comfortable discussing my private life with any of you. Let's drop the subject, because I'm not disrespecting my relationship."

Jeanine and Sara looked at each other. "She really thinks she has a relationship with Gavin," Sara said to her.

"What do you mean?" I asked.

Jeanine leaned in close to me. "Let's just say Gavin is the 'love 'em and leave 'em' type."

"No, he's not."

Sara eyed me skeptically. "Okay. Whatever you say. We know what we've witnessed," Sara said, looking at Jeanine.

"What's that?" Brianne asked, stirring the pot.

She and Alison waited anxiously to listen. Nosey bitches.

Jeanine explained, "Let's just say that Gavin has a thing for big-booty black women. It's all good at first, but after a couple of months of loving . . ."

"He leaves them," Sara said, finishing for her. "So your time is probably winding down in a few weeks."

"Say what you want. Gavin is not like that with me. I know him," I said with confidence.

Jeanine and Sara laughed. "You haven't met his brother or father, have you?" Sara asked.

What the hell did his brother or father have to do with anything? I'd wondered why I'd never seen him around his brother or been introduced, especially since they had been raised together, but I had had no idea Gavin interacted with his dad. I had assumed he didn't know him or didn't talk to him, since he had never mentioned him. As for his brother, I figured that would come up sooner or later.

"No. Why?"

Sara and Jeanine looked at each other and laughed. "Uh-huh."

"Come on, Brianne. Let's go," Jeanine said. Then she patted my shoulder. "Poor thing."

We all dispersed, and I followed Sara. "What were you and Jeanine talking about?" I asked.

Sara turned to face me. "Just don't get comfortable being his woman. Gavin means well, but your relationship is not gonna last. Believe me when I tell you that. Anything else you wanna know, ask your man," she said as she handed me a chart. "Time to get to work, Meka. Gossip time is over."

All day I went about my work, with what Jeanine and Sara had told me on my mind. I'd managed to keep my thoughts contained so that I could remain focused on the patients, but I was bothered by their comments. They'd worked with Gavin for years, so I was sure they had seen and heard a lot more than I had. Part of me was unsure if I should believe them, because I knew a lot of women liked Gavin and wanted him for themselves, but still, there was truth in a lot of what they had said.

Gavin did like black women with big butts, he could put it down in the bedroom, the nickname King Dingalang was well deserved, and he did tell me he'd dated a couple of women in the hospital. The way Jeanine and Sara had put it, it was like he'd run up in every black woman who was willing and able to get down. I wanted to brush that off, but that bothered me. If they were on point about all the rest of the stuff, couldn't they be telling the truth about that? And one thing they'd said was most definitely the truth: I'd never met Gavin's family. The fact that they were so positive that I hadn't damn sure made me put more stock into what they'd said, instead of chalking it up to water-cooler gossip.

"Hey, you," Gavin said, walking up behind me as I sat outside, eating spaghetti. He sat down beside me on the bench and turned to face me. "Can I get a bite?"

"I made you some. Did you bring it?" I asked, not looking up from my bowl.

"Yeah, babe. I don't have the time to eat. I have some paperwork to do. I saw you out here and decided to come and speak to my baby," he said before leaning over and kissing my cheek.

"Humph."

He put his hand on top of mine. "Baby, what's wrong?"

"Nothing."

He leaned back. "Uh-oh. That means it's definitely something."

"It's nothing."

"Are you still upset with me about choosing Alison?" he asked curiously.

"No. It's not that."

"So it *is* something."

Giving in, I looked at him for the first time and inhaled sharply. I didn't want to jump into asking him about his sex life at work, because he would've known it came from Sara and Jeanine. So I chose the safer route and the more feasible question.

"When am I going to meet your brother?" I asked abruptly.

He looked shocked. "Where did *that* come from?"

"I'm just wondering. I mean, you're staying with me, and you're practically my family. My mom, sister, and boys love and adore you, and I haven't even met your brother. You don't talk to him or talk about him. Don't you find that odd?"

The pleasant demeanor that he had had when he first came outside faded and was replaced with looks of curiosity and confusion. "Really, Meka? Where is this coming from?"

"Really, Gavin? Why haven't you answered my question?"

He rubbed his hands across his mouth and then knocked on the table. "Can we talk about this later? You're eating, and I have work—"

My head tilted, and I gave him a sidelong glance. "Why? It's a simple question."

Our stare down lasted a few minutes, before Gavin grunted and said what was on his mind. "Okay. Spill it. Somebody said something to you."

Feigning ignorance, I asked, "Why would you say that?"

He bit his bottom lip. "Now we're playing games, huh?" he asked, tight lipped.

I pointed to myself. "I'm not playing a game. In fact, all I want is the truth."

His work cell sounded, indicating that he was needed back on duty. Well, I guessed he could thank God for small favors. He looked at it.

"I have to go, baby."

"I'll bet you do," I said smartly.

He shook his head. "I promise we'll talk later." He leaned over to kiss me, but I turned my face so that his lips landed on my cheek. "Okay, Meka. All right. I'll see you later, baby," he said with frustration.

"Later, Gavin," I said nastily.

Aggravated, he shook his head and walked off. Sitting there, I couldn't even finish my food. Here I was, thinking I had the man of my dreams, and now it seemed that I was being made a fool of again. Something wasn't right about Gavin's family, and I wondered if I should even bother to stick around to find out what.

"Trouble in paradise?" I heard from behind me. It was none other than Tony.

I turned to face him. "Wouldn't you like to know."

He chuckled. "When am I going to see my boys?"

"When you stop harassing my man."

"I don't have a clue what you mean."

Scoffing, I sneered, "Sure, you don't."

He let out a slight huff and pursed his lips. "I came over because you looked a little stressed out. I thought I'd try to be of some comfort to you. Don't let the white boy get up under your skin."

With my face turned up, I said, "His name is Gavin."

"I really don't care," he said nonchalantly.

"I do." My attitude was already on go, so he had better tread lightly.

Tony frowned. "What do you and that dude have in common, Meka? So what if he listens to some black music and he knows some slang? For real, what can he really do for you?" Tony asked, clearly frustrated.

"None of your business. What goes on between Gavin and me has nothing to do with you. In fact, you should leave us alone." I gathered my food and got up to walk inside. "Don't you have an appointment or something to get to?"

"I miss you, Meka," he said, walking up behind me. "He may have you now, but I gave you the boys. I was your first everything."

"Get away from me." I turned to face him. "You disgust me."

He licked his lips. "You turn me on."

I stepped back. "I thought Kwanzie did," I sneered.

The comeback took the wind out of him, and a sad expression took over his face. "That was below the belt."

"So is all the shit you've pulled lately. Look, I just want to be happy."

"He'll never make you happy. Just wait and see," he said to me as I walked off. "Oh, and Meka, Heinekens are for bitches," he called out and laughed. I knew Tony was behind that shit.

When I walked inside, I walked right past Gavin. "Didn't you two look close," he said with an attitude.

"It's not what you're thinking," I said, shaking my head. "You're one to talk. You still haven't answered my question."

"We'll talk later," he said, then walked away with an attitude.

"Indeed, we will."

Chapter 19

Charice

Knowing the truth about what Ryan had done was a hard pill to swallow, but I did. For the sake of my marriage, I pushed back everything he'd done. Despite my feelings, I'd made the decision to marry Ryan, instead of giving my heart time to heal and grieve, so I had to take responsibility for my actions. Despite what Ryan had done to win me back, I was still his wife. I had vowed to remain married even through the worst of events, so I couldn't turn away from that now. I was raised to stick out my marriage, not jump to divorce. So here I was, remaining Mrs. Westmore.

"Don't you look so cute?" I said, admiring Lexi in her sundress and ruffled romper. I hugged her close, and the fresh baby smell melted my heart, as it did every time.

Ryan came into the room. "So what time is he supposed to be here?" he asked with an attitude.

"Lincoln should be here in a few minutes." I sighed. "I really wish you would get in a better mood. What's done is done. Lexi is his daughter, and Lincoln hasn't done anything out of character. All he's done is taken care of his daughter. Besides, you haven't been here for one visitation, and you promised to apologize to him man-to-man."

"This is only his third one, and besides, the other two times I had other obligations. I can't help it if I'm still a little upset about this whole thing. I don't trust him," Ryan complained.

"For what? He's adhered to what we agreed in court," I said in Lincoln's defense. "He gets five in-home visitations first to make sure we're comfortable with him taking Lexi away from home. He gets one week a month with his daughter and a two-week vacation with her, then every other holiday. He's already paid his child support for the next six months, and he doesn't cause any trouble when he comes over. The only thing that has changed is that Lexi's last name is now Harper instead of Westmore. He even agreed with us about keeping the court case and ruling sealed and out of the public record."

"What are you? His attorney?" Ryan asked snidely.

I rolled my eyes. "I'm just saying that the best thing for us to do at this time is to get used to the way things are."

Just then, the doorbell rang. Ryan slowly turned around and headed out. "Let's go downstairs."

He had been so surly since everything had transpired. He had refused even to speak to Lincoln throughout the entire process; however, Lincoln had remained a gentleman. He had refused to stoop to Ryan's level and had always kept Lexi and London first. I was so proud of him for that. He'd also agreed to allow me to be London's dance instructor. We'd had our first dance lesson last week, and she was very talented. She was also very excited that Lexi was her sister, and despite all the hell us adults had brought to the situation, it'd actually turned out to be a positive thing for London. She wanted to be a role model for Lexi, and having her here had brought her and Lincoln closer together.

"Hello," Ryan said plainly after he opened the door.

London waved at us. "Hi, Mr. Westmore. Hi, Mrs. Charice. Hi, Lexi," she said excitedly.

"Hello, Ryan." Lincoln nodded. "What's up, Charice? How's my baby?" he asked, equally as excited, his arms outstretched, as Ryan stepped aside to allow them in.

I handed Lexi to Lincoln. "Here you go."

"Man, I'm still trying to get used to this. It's been years since I've held a small baby," he said as he gently patted Lexi on the back.

"Can I hold her, Daddy, please?" London asked, and Lincoln eyed me for my approval.

"Sure. Let's go to the living room, where you can sit and hold her," I said, and then I led them through the house to the living room.

"Where's Ray and Ryan?" London asked.

"Over one of their friend's house," I answered.

We all sat down in the living room, and Lincoln handed Lexi to London. "Be careful."

"I know. Hold her head and back," London said.

"Exactly," he said to her.

"Lincoln, can we step into the kitchen for a second? Ryan wants to tell you something," I said. Ryan looked at me as if I had said something wrong, but he walked into the kitchen with us.

"What's up?" Lincoln asked, standing face-to-face with Ryan.

Ryan looked over at me, and I gestured for him to go ahead. Squaring his shoulders, he began. "I wanted to tell you that I'm sorry for my part in keeping Lexi away from you and for causing issues with you and London," he said, with his arms folded across his chest.

Lincoln chuckled, picking up on Ryan's resistance. "Are you sure about that, or are you doing what your wife asked you to do?"

Ryan sucked his teeth. "It was my suggestion, but I figured you wouldn't see it that way."

Lincoln folded his arms. "What am I supposed to do with your apology now?"

"Accept it and let it go," Ryan said tensely.

Lincoln's face showed that he didn't buy any of what Ryan had said. "I appreciate that sincere and heartfelt apology. I'm sure that took a lot out of you to come up with."

Ryan was about to say something that I knew was going to be a smart-ass comment, so I intervened. "All right, gentlemen. Our daughters are in the next room," I reminded them, before an argument or fight ensued.

Ryan nodded. "Whatever, man. An apology is an apology."

Lincoln shrugged. "You're right about that," he said and turned to face me. "If you don't mind, I'd like to go back and enjoy my daughter."

"Of course." I held Ryan back by the arm as Lincoln headed back into the living room to be with London and Lexi.

"You apologized to him as if you lied to me about being sorry for what you did," I said after Lincoln had left the kitchen.

He bent down and kissed my forehead. "I am sorry. This entire situation is hard for me. Can we get through this visit?" he said, then turned to leave. Deciding to let it go, I followed him back into the living room.

Ryan was so aggravated that he stayed for only about ten additional minutes before he made up an excuse to leave the house. I was actually glad when he left, because the tension in the air lifted for everybody as soon as he was out the door, and I got to sit back and have fun watching Lincoln, London, and Lexi interact. Lincoln fed Lexi, changed her, and rocked her to sleep as if he was an old pro.

After their visit was up, I called Ryan.

"Are they gone?" Ryan asked as soon as he answered his phone.

"Yes, they are. Where are you?"

"At Jabari's house, shooting pool. I should be home in another hour or so."

"Well, I'm going to the dance studio to get everything set up for next week. I left Lexi with Johanna."

"Cool. Like I said, I should be home in an hour or so."

"A'ight," I said and hung up.

I didn't have time for Ryan's nonchalant attitude, and I certainly wasn't entertaining his foolishness. Lincoln being in Lexi's life was something that never should've been kept from him, and I wasn't going to sit around worrying about Ryan's feelings over the situation. It was what it was, and I wasn't worried about it.

When I walked into the studio, I set the alarm and locked back up. I put the security camera on in my office and made sure the rest were on their designated timers and positions. Then I headed to my office, turned on the radio, and sat my purse and keys on my desk. There was nothing like putting in a little work to relax me from the stress that Ryan brought to the table, I thought as I headed into the side room attached to my office.

"Ready to put in some work?" I asked.

Lincoln's bright smile met mine. "Always." I walked over to him and straddled his lap. "Especially after that lame-ass apology your husband gave me."

I put my index finger to his lips. "I didn't come here to discuss Ryan." I leaned in and kissed him.

"How long do we have?" Lincoln asked.

"An hour," I answered as we undressed.

Lincoln cupped my face and kissed me passionately. "I love you, Charice."

"I love you too."

For the next forty minutes, Lincoln and I made love, as we'd done several times over the past couple of weeks. When I was with him, nothing else mattered. It was he and I, just as it always should've been. Who said I couldn't have my cake and eat it too?

Afterward, Lincoln and I lay cuddled together on my sofa, our fingers interlocked, as he kissed my neck and earlobe.

I giggled. "You know those are my spots."

"Mm-hmm." He kissed my neck again.

"You know I can't get it started again. We have to get clean so that I can make it back home before Ryan gets suspicious."

Disappointment oozed from him. "Why are you with him?"

I pecked his lips first, and then I pulled back and caressed the side of his face. "We've gone over this. I took a vow to stay married to him."

"Yet you're here with me."

"And that's the most important thing. It's so complicated right now. The boys have already lost their sister. I can't take them through a divorce right now. Despite how evil Ryan is, he loves his boys and me."

"But you love me."

I nodded. "Yes, I do, but I'm his wife."

"Do you still love him?"

"I care about him, and I have love for him. He gave me my beautiful triplets, and my dream career, but if you're asking me if am I in love with him or if he has my heart," I said, "you should know that the answer is no. I feel that way only about you, Lincoln. So please let's enjoy our time as it comes, okay?"

Closing his eyes, he took in what I'd said before finally giving in again. "How could I tell you no?"

"You can't." I giggled.

"You're right." He chuckled and then got serious. "You know he's getting frustrated because you're not pregnant yet."

"Yes, I know, but as long as he doesn't know about my birth control, then he can keep on being frustrated with the situation and not me. And your talking-ass friends tell you too much stuff. I can't believe Ryan is still telling his business partners his personal business."

Shrugging, he admitted, "They are looking out for me."

"Yeah, I guess in a way it helps. He'll confess to them his inner thoughts versus telling me. That is one slick bastard. It took a minute for me to see that Ryan could be a totally different person from what he shows, but I get that now."

Lincoln ran his hand through my hair. "I hate that you became his wife before you found that out," he said, then kissed me again. "I want to marry you so badly, Charice." He leaned his forehead against mine. "Damn. I want to make you my wife."

"In my heart, I am," I said as I stood up and wrapped the blanket around my naked body. "You first to the bathroom."

He stood up, his naked body glistening from the sweat of our lovemaking. I couldn't deny that Lincoln's body beat out Ryan's in every department. My man was so fucking fine.

He bent down and kissed me. "We're still on for our getaway this weekend, right?"

I winked at him. "Definitely," I said, and then I smacked his ass as he walked into the bathroom.

Sitting back on the sofa, I reveled in my current situation as Lincoln showered. Ryan may have me as his wife, but Lincoln had my heart. Ryan had been making a fool of me since high school, and I was tired of being a doormat and a fool. It was my turn to hold the puppet strings, so I had made a decision to have everything I wanted—my life with Ryan and my love with Lincoln. Like I said, I had taken a vow to remain married to Ryan, not to be faithful to him. As for the "forsaking all others" part, well, Lincoln never came before my kids and my household. He understood that and accepted it, so for now, I enjoyed the hell out of having my cake and eating it too.

However, in the back of my mind, I knew the inevitable loomed. Sooner or later, I'd have to make a choice. But what would I decide?

Life or love?

Chapter 20

Terrence

"Hey, Aaron. It's me, Terrence, again." I spoke to his voicemail for the umpteenth time. "Man, when are you gonna get over this shit? I've been calling you for weeks, trying to apologize. We're family. I was upset about Trinity, and I reacted with a hot head. But I love you, cuz. You know this. I forgave you when you broke my arm in the third grade, while doing those karate moves, didn't I?" I laughed. "Well, anyway, call me. I need to hear from you. Peace."

I hadn't spoken to Aaron since I shot him in the shoulder, and Thomas had said that every time he brought my name up, Aaron said he didn't want to talk about me or to me. Ain't this a bitch? I got that I had snapped, but I had snapped for good reason. He had tried me on my manhood and every nigga knew you didn't fuck with a man over his manhood, his money, and his cookie. Hell, you

could get over on me about my money, and I would
overlook it, when most niggas wouldn't, but you
couldn't try me on my manhood or fuck with my
lady. Period. Hell, on a good day you may even be
able to get me to overlook the fact that I got tried
on my manhood, especially if my kids were around,
but never . . . ever . . . ever . . . ever on Trinity. Ever.

While most men cheated, degraded, abused,
misused, and disrespected their lady, I was the
complete opposite. My pops had left before I was
even old enough to know what having a dad was.
It had been me, my sister, my moms, and my
grandma, so I had grown up very fond of those
three women. I had been the son, the brother,
the father, the husband, the protector, and the
provider. I had learned early on that women were
to be valued. And with all that my moms and
grandma had done for me . . . Shit, ain't no way I
was gonna dog the woman who had given me my
children, and especially since she also held the title
of my wife. I wanted to be a part of my kids' lives
and have them love me the way I wished I had a
father to love. It killed me how guys could grow
up wishing their mom and dad were together and
wishing their dad was in their life, then mistreat
the chicks they were with and make babies that
they weren't willing to take care of. I just couldn't
see it. I remembered how that shit had felt as a kid,
so there was no way in hell I could put Trinity or

my kids through that. I had vowed to myself to be a better man than those fucking baby getters.

I stayed on the grind for mine every day, just to be sure that I gave them everything I hadn't had. My kids were in the best schools and had the best of everything. Terry was the star of the swim team, and just like his mama, he could draw his ass off. My big girl, Brit, had her thing going on too. She was gonna be the next Alicia Keys on that piano. Besides encouraging them to pursue their own personal interests, I made sure they knew how to defend themselves by enrolling them in martial arts. And they were both straight A students. Princess was already learning to speak in semi-complete sentences, and she even knew some of the alphabet in both English and Spanish. I couldn't wait to see what talents she and Tyson had. It made me proud that I could give them the life they needed and deserved.

It especially made me proud that I'd come up from the D-boy I used to be. My paper was legit, and I could take care of my lady the way she truly deserved. It felt great seeing her achieve her dreams. We'd come a long way since that first tattoo of a lion's head that she'd stenciled for me. I sat back and thought sometimes about how we had started dating from our official meeting at the club. Being four years her senior, who would've thought that I'd be interested in a chick so young? But there was something so genuinely sweet, innocent, and pure about Trinity that had attracted me to her. She was from the hood, but in a soft kinda way. Like a concrete rose. Not to mention she was real and down for me. And, my God, did she develop into a stackhouse. I loved Trinity with my whole heart. She was the only woman I had ever been faithful to from dating to marriage, not only because she was the mother of my kids, but also because I had always known that one day she'd be my wife. I was beside myself that I could give her all her heart's desires.

The ringing of my cell phone brought me out of my random thoughts.

"Hey, Mama Tracy. What's up?" I asked, answering my cell.

"Hey, Terrence. Baby, are you busy?" Trinity's mom asked.

"I'm not working today. I'm just sitting in my office, going over our finances and paying bills, but you know I'll make time for you."

She laughed. "You have always been so sweet. Diane did a good job raising you."

I laughed. "Thank you, Mama."

"But on a serious note, is Trinity at home with you?"

"No, ma'am. I know she was running the kids over to your house so that she could go to the gallery and get some work done. Did you try there?"

"Yes, I talked to the manager, Jalise, and she said that Trinity told her that she'd be back in an hour, but it's been an hour and a half, and she isn't back yet."

"You know Trinity. She's probably out somewhere burning a hole in my Amex or Visa card."

"Yes, Trinity has changed a bit. Lately, she's become so . . . What's the word? Boujee."

Admittedly, I agreed. "Yeah, she has been actin' kinda brand new."

I hoped it was a phase, though. None of us were used to that kind of money, and when you weren't used to things like that, sometimes it could take you out of your element. I felt like eventually the self-proclaimed Barbie of mine would come back down to Earth. I prayed so, anyway, because I couldn't take too much of the Paris Hilton routine. We were from the hood, so I could deal with the Trina routine or the Taraji P. Henson routine, but this tip that she was on was wreckin' even my nerves. Eating salads and tofu and shit. Money or no money, I was black. Always had been and always would be. Give me some fried chicken, pork chops smothered with gravy, and some biscuits and shit.

"But nah, Mama. She ain't here."

"I thought y'all might have been trying to play house," she joked.

"No, ma'am." I laughed, although that would be a good idea. Shit, it'd been three days, and I was fucking hurting. "Why? Is something wrong with the kids?"

"No. I was going to ask her to buy me an extra pack of Pampers to keep over here for Tyson. That son of yours eats and shits all the time."

"That he does." I laughed. "She didn't answer her cell?"

"It went straight to voicemail."

"Hmm." I rubbed my chin. "It may be dead, and she's trying to charge it. Or maybe she mistakenly turned it off. I don't know. I'm sure she'll call you back after she gets out of the store."

"You're probably right. I will try to call her in another ten minutes or so."

"All right, Mama Tracy. Just give me a call if you can't get in touch with her. Kiss the kiddos for me and let them know I'll see them tomorrow afternoon."

"All right, Terrence, I will. See you tomorrow."

I continued looking over the finances and balancing our accounts once I had hung up with Trinity's mom. We were pulling in hella money, and everything was looking real nice, even after paying the bills and Trinity's Visa card bill again. Who in the hell spends five grand just for summer clothes and shoes for kids, especially for a child Princess's age? She still needed to shop for Terry and Tyson. We were gonna have to have a talk about my diamond princess's spending habits.

The way Trinity was going, she was going to have the kids so spoiled that they wouldn't know how to fend for themselves when they became adults. I was not working hard to take care of my grown-ass kids for the rest of their lives. Once they got out of college—and they were going to college—they had better have a plan. I'd guide them, help them, and direct them, but taking care of them was out of the equation. I wanted to retire early, live off the interest of our money in the bank, and travel the world with my wife. Then we'd come back and help our kids raise their kids, not work until it was time to put me in the box. Was that asking too much? I'll answer for you. Hell no. Who didn't want that? Apparently, my wife, if she didn't bring her head and our credit cards out of the clouds long enough to see that she was out of control with the money.

After I finished up with the finances, I poured myself a glass of Cognac and lit one of my Cuban cigars. Now I understood why my Barbie enjoyed having the house to herself. Sometimes you needed that wind-down "me" time. I had been grinding so hard that I hadn't realized I needed a break too. I decided to take this time and enjoy it to the fullest. After I finished off my Cognac, I killed the amber in my cigar and headed to my bedroom to shower up.

My conversation about Trinity's spending habits was gonna have to wait. I needed my wife to come home to handle some business.

I turned on the shower, then watched water cascade furiously from the multiple showerheads. As I waited for the water to heat up, I took out the band holding my dreadlocks together, then eased off my button-down shirt. I never grew tired of admiring Trinity's artwork. The lion's head on my chest was still as fresh as the day I got the tat. On one bicep was the tat that she drew for me with the cross and the rings, and on the other was my grandma's name, with a small set of praying hands underneath it. On my stomach was the kids' names—I had even had Princess's name added. Pooch's or not, she was still my child, and I loved her as such. The last tat that was special to me was the one of Trinity's face over my heart. Wrapped around her face were the words *Trinity's forever*. It meant that she'd forever have my heart.

After I shed the remainder of my clothes, I stepped into the shower and let the warm water run down my head, shoulders, and back, easing the stress out of my muscles. I missed Trinity bad as hell. I could damn near feel her running her fingertips down my six-pack and back muscles. I wished she was right there to wrap her legs around my waist so I could make love to her. Those thoughts brought my manhood to full-attention mode. *Damn it, man.* I had to hurry up and call her to take care of that for real. I stepped out of the shower and finished my routine. I heard my cell ring as I wrapped a towel around my waist. *Trinity. Thank God*, I thought as I ran out of the bathroom into our master suite, but when I looked down at the screen on my phone, I saw it was her mom again.

"Mama Tracy?"

"Terrence, I still can't reach Trinity, and Jalise said she hasn't come back. She's tried to call her too, and she's not answering. It's going straight to voicemail. She's been gone for two and half hours. I'm getting kinda worried now."

"All right, Mama. Let me put on some clothes and see if I can find out what's going on. Are the kids cool?"

"Yes, they're all here with me, and we are fine. So are my other two kids. I just hung up with Jalise. No one in the gallery has seen Trinity or talked to her since she left."

"All right. I'll call you. I promise you I'll find out something."

"Thanks, Terrence. Call me," she said and hung up.

What the fuck was going on? I threw on some jeans and a T-shirt, so I could leave if need be. When I tried her cell and the call went straight to voicemail, worry crept in. I had had a GPS tracking system installed on both of our vehicles. I needed to log in to find out where her car was, so I hurriedly switched to the tracker app on my device and located her vehicle. I found her car at a shopping plaza. Perhaps she'd forgotten and left her phone in the car, but I wasn't gonna sit around and wait. I decided to go to the shopping plaza and see if I could find her. On the way, I made a call.

"Yo, Aaron, I know you ain't talking to me, but I may need your help to locate Trinity. I know you care about her, even if you don't care about me. So call me. I'm trying to find her, and it may be nothing, but in my gut, I feel like something ain't right. Call me." I hung up and prayed he would actually listen to the message.

Twenty-five minutes later, I pulled up in the parking deck where Trinity's car was located, and I found her Mercedes in a parking spot. I breathed a sigh of relief, thinking she had to have left her cell phone inside the car. Still, I got out and walked to the car. I damn near had a heart attack when I found that not only was her cell phone in the car, but so, too, was her purse. And the keys were still in the ignition. Now I knew something was wrong. Ain't no way she'd leave her purse in the car or the keys in the ignition. *Shit. Shit. Shit.* Pacing, I didn't know what to do.

"Think, Terrence. Think," I said aloud, hitting my head.

I ran up to the security booth and tapped on the glass. "Excuse me."

"Yes, sir?"

"Have you seen this woman?" I asked, pulling out my phone and showing the guy a picture of Trinity.

He shook his head. "No. Somebody that fine I would remember." He laughed.

I sucked my teeth. "Well, I'm her husband, and her car is over there, with the keys in the ignition and her purse and cell inside. But she ain't there."

"You sure she ain't steppin' out?"

"Muthafucka, look! I'm the only nigga stickin' my wife. You need to get on your fucking job and secure this place. She's missing, and I need to find her."

He put his hands up. "I apologize, sir. How long has she been missing?"

"She left her job damn near three hours ago, and she was supposed to be back two hours ago."

"Well, sir, I would call the police, but a person has to be missing for twenty-four hours before they fill out a missing person's report," he said, coming out of the booth.

"Do you know what all could happen to her in twenty-four muthafucking hours?"

"Sir, calm down. It is suspicious that her personal items are still in the car, but I'm telling you

what I know. Are you sure she wasn't meeting anyone?"

"I'm fucking positive. I can't wait that fucking
long. I'm calling the fucking police myself." Just as
I began to dial 911, my phone rang. It was Thomas.
I picked up.

"Yo, Thomas! Did Aaron get my message? I
really need his help. Trinity is missing."

"Man, I don't know what he got, but I know what
I found."

"What?" I asked, curious.

"Look, man. I don't know what is going on with
my brother, and I hope he forgives me for telling
you this, but I was at his house today, and I found
a photo album. He's collected pictures of Trinity
over the past two years, bunches and bunches of
pictures. Some were cut out of other pictures, and
he put them in an album, but it was all photos
of her. It's almost like a fucking shrine or some
shit. It's like he's obsessed with her. Then I found
two very odd things together, and I have no idea
what it means, but it can't be good. First, I found
paperwork on a storage rental for storage unit
two-two-four-five at Quality Warehouse Storage.
Why he needs that I don't know, because he has
a storage shed with nothing in it." He paused.
"Lastly, I found some shit you ain't gonna like. It
was some paperwork to release Vernon 'Pooch'
Smalls."

My mouth flew open. This muthafucka was insane. I knew good and fucking well he didn't get Pooch released. I didn't know what the fuck was going on, but I knew damn well that storage unit and Pooch had something to do with my wife, and I was gonna find out what.

"A'ight," I said plainly. "I gotta go."

"T, I know you're pissed, but we're family. Just remember that."

"Cuz, if your brother has done some ignorant shit and got my wife caught up in it, then I can let you know the blood line stops there. My wife and kids are my first priority, not Aaron."

Thomas sighed. "Do what you gotta do, then, man."

I ran back to my truck and drove like a bat out of hell back to the house. I jumped out, leaving the truck running, and ran inside the house. I grabbed both of my chrome-plated .45s and extra ammo. When I got back in my truck, my cell phone rang again. It was Mama Tracy.

"Terrence, have you heard anything?" Trinity's mom asked me when I picked up.

"Just make sure you take care of my babies, Mama Tracy. That's all I ask," I said and hung up on her.

Chapter 21

Pooch

It felt good as hell to say that I was a free man. I sat down and waited to be out-processed in fresh new clothes, courtesy of Big Cal. I had one mission and one mission only—to get my hands on Trinity. I couldn't even fully enjoy being free, knowing that I'd probably end up right back in there, but I didn't give a damn.

I couldn't wait to see the look on that bitch's face when she came face-to-face with me again. I bet when she woke up this morning, she never imagined running into this nigga. Oh well. She wanted to be a dirty broad, then I could be an even dirtier nigga. I was gonna force her to give me that good pussy and then strangle the life outta that ho. I deserved to see both come to fruition. All those nights I'd imagined bangin' the one chick I thought was true to me and I had risked everything for. She was gonna make every last one of them fantasies come true. I was about to bring new meaning to the words *till death do us part*.

"You ready to get the fuck outta here?" Big Cal asked me, hitting my arm.

I one-arm hugged him. "You know it, man."

"It'll just be a few more minutes," he said, then turned back to the officer.

Just then, I saw them walking Wolf by in handcuffs on the other side, and I turned my head.

"Pooch! Pooch!" he screamed.

"Shut up, inmate," one of the COs yelled.

"Pooch! Man, you gotta tell 'em it wasn't me. Pooch, come on, man," he said in desperation.

I got up and walked to the bars. "What's going on, Wolf?"

He looked me up and down. "Where the fuck are you going?"

"You didn't hear? I got sprung. I'm imperative to a new case."

"Whose?"

"Yours."

He looked at me. "Pooch, they are gonna put this drug shit on me, man. I can't do another ten years in here. I can't. I was up for parole, and my girl is waiting on me. Adrienne ain't gonna wait another ten years. You gotta help me," he said, looking at me with tears in his eyes.

"Can y'all give us a second?" I asked the COs.

They shrugged and backed up. They were on Big Cal's team anyway, so it really didn't matter if they heard what I said or not, but appearances were made to be kept up. I motioned for Wolf to lean forward as I did the same.

"Don't worry. Ten years is easy to do. You've already done it before. As for testifying, well, dawg, you know I tried to tell you that dealin' drugs inside the prison was wrong."

He frowned up. "What? Me? This shit was your—"

"And don't worry about Adrienne. She ain't checking for you. Since you're gonna be in here a while, you should probably know that her and Flava fell in love, and your chick is a certified lesbo now. Oh, and the only man who she's gonna let fuck is me. Don't worry, dude. I'll write you and tell you how the pussy tastes." I laughed. "But by then, you probably won't even care, 'cause you'll be Cock Diesel's bitch the moment I step outside this hellhole. You can go full-fledged now and take it up the ass too, 'cause that's about as close to sex as you'll get for the next ten years."

"You muthafucka!" he yelled angrily. "I'ma tell 'em it was all on you."

"Don't waste your breath. I've got all my bases covered, and if you try to do that, your ten years will be short. Real short. I'm sorry to have to do this to you, Wolf, but it was me or you, and I always come first. Every war has casualties. Keep ya head up. If you still feel raw about it in ten years, come get at me. But for now, don't drop the soap unless you really want to, cowboy," I taunted him. I turned around. Then I looked back, throwing up my index and middle fingers. "Deuces!" I laughed and walked off.

"You son of a bitch. I'm gonna get you and that bitch Adrienne. You wait. Wait, you dirty bastard. You wait," he said as the COs carted him off.

"Should I worry about him?" Big Cal asked me.

I fanned it off. "Maybe in ten years." I laughed as I signed my release papers.

"You're a free man, Pooch, but you'll be back," the officer said snidely as I threw the pen down.

"You might be right, Officer." I pointed at him as Big Cal and I left.

We got in his SUV, and he began to drive.

"So what's the plan?" I asked.

"Let me worry about the plan. When we get where we're going, you'll have your fun. We both will," he assured me.

"So where's my heat?"

He pulled the lid on glove box down. "In there."

"Where's your heat?"

He pointed to his armrest. "In there."

I opened the armrest and took out his two guns. "Thanks, man."

"I thought I told you that your heat was in the glove box."

"Do I look like Boo Boo the fool? I trust your ass about as far as I can throw you. Agreement or no agreement, you had a part in gettin' my black ass locked up, and you're still a pig. Fuck what you sayin'. We doin' this nigga in, and after that, we partin' ways. All I'm gonna say to you is don't come around me no more after this. The only reason I ain't puttin' one between your eyes right now is that you sprung me, and I'd like nothing better than to put that fire in Terrence's dome. After this, I have no problem puttin' fire in your dome. However, we can call it square if you stay the fuck away from me and my new organization."

"You're talkin' real reckless for a nigga who can go right back to prison at the snap of my fingers."

"Send me back. I'm loaded with way too much information to stay, *Officer*."

"So you're a snitch now?"

"Snitchin' on cops ain't never fucked up nobody's street cred."

He relented, realizing I was right. "Fine. Take the heat, and after this, me and you—we're done. Just leave my name outta your mouth."

"My sentiments exactly," I agreed. "How long is this drive?"

"Sit back and take a nap. I'll wake you when we get there."

"Bitch, please. And end up in the river? Bullshit. I'll sit back, but my eyes ain't closing until I'm away from your ass."

"Same ol' Pooch." He shook his head.

"And I ain't never gonna change. Remember that shit."

I didn't know what happened next, but apparently, my dumb ass did doze off. It was from all those nights I had stayed up watching my mouth and ass from Wolf. I was tired as hell, and riding and rocking in that big SUV put me to sleep like a baby. It was the first time since I could remember that I rested. Damn. Being free felt good.

"We're here," he said as we pulled up to some storage place.

"Glad I didn't wake up in a river," I said, looking down to make sure I was still gripping the same heat.

"I told you that you could trust me. Settling this shit comes first to me. Me and you are in the past, and I don't give a fuck what you do after this," he said as we drove around the different storage units.

"So, what did that nigga Terrence do to you?"

"He crossed the line."

I chuckled. "I can understand that completely."

"I know. You're the only nigga who can, since he stole your girl and your money."

I gripped the heat tighter. "Thank you for reminding me."

"You're welcome," he said, parking and getting the heat out of the glove box. "Now come on."

We got out, and Big Cal unlocked one of the storage units. When we walked in, I saw that it had been soundproofed. Trinity was tied to a chair, with a bag over her head and a bandana tied around her mouth. *Bitch*. Her muffled screams ignited my fury.

Big Cal looked at me and put his index finger up to his lips. Shit. No problem. I could be quiet. I wanted to surprise this bitch more than he did. He walked up to her. "I'm gonna untie this. If you scream, I'm gonna punch you in the face. Are we clear?"

She nodded slowly. He lifted the bag and undid the bandana. When her eyes adjusted to the light, she gasped loudly and started scooting the entire chair backward at the sight of me.

"Surprised to see me, baby? Did you miss your man?"

"P-Pooch," she stuttered. "How did you—" She looked at Big Cal. "Big Cal, please. He's gonna kill me. You can't let this happen to me. Please," she cried.

"Now, why would I do that?" I asked, getting in her face as she began to cry hysterically. "Perhaps because you lied to me about loving me? Maybe it was because you ran off and married your Dreads? Or maybe it's because my son—you know, the one you were pregnant with—was really Dreads's?

She cried out, "Big Cal, please! Pooch, I'm sorry. I'm so sorry—"

"Bitch, you ain't sorry," I yelled and backhanded her across the face. "You left me in that fucking hellhole to die so you could run off and be Mrs. Dreads. Lied to me about my son and got my fucking daughter being raised by Terrence. *Fuck you.* As much shit as I did for you? Fuck you, Trinity."

Lifting her eyes to Big Cal, she pleaded with him between cries. "Big Cal, why? Why are you doing this to me? What about my kids? What about me?" she pleaded, her face covered with tears and sweat.

"What about *you*, Trinity? What about *me*?" he asked, swallowing back emotion. "I was there for you. I had your back, and I looked out for you. *Me!* What about me?"

I looked at him strangely. I was totally confused. "What the fuck are you talking about?"

He started pacing and hitting himself in the head with the gun. "It was always me. Always in the background. Protecting you, guiding you, talking to you, being there for you. From this nigga here to Terrence. It was me. The friend. Nobody cared about my feelings. Nobody saw my pain. It was always about Pooch and Dreads."

"Nigga, what's wrong with you?" I asked, looking at him like he was stupid. "What? Are you in love with this bitch or something?"

"Shut up," he yelled.

"Big Cal, I didn't know. Honest, I swear to God. I didn't," Trinity cried.

"Bullshit! Couldn't you see the way I looked at you? Didn't I show you with how I talked to you and was there for you? There wasn't nothing I wouldn't do for you. *Nothing!*"

Muthafucka. He was in love with Trinity. No wonder he had a beef wit' Terrence. This nigga had to have had a beef wit' me too. This nigga was setting all of us up. I pointed a gun at him.

"Nigga, you better not even think about doing shit to me," I yelled at him.

"Trinity!" I heard a nigga yell from behind us.

Terrence!

We all gripped our heat and stood in a triangle, each with a gun pointed at two separate people.

"It's a muthafucking reunion. Now it's a party," I muttered.

"Trinity, baby, are you okay? Did they do anything to you?" Terrence asked, keeping his guns and eyes focused on me and Big Cal.

"No, baby. Just leave. I'll try to get out of this on my own. Please," Trinity cried.

"Even now, you choose him," Big Cal yelled. "Will you still love him when his brains are scattered at your feet?"

"What do you mean, choose him?" Trinity asked, confusion etched on her face. "He's my husband, Big Cal."

"Even after he shot me, I called you to check on you, and you wouldn't even talk to me, because Dreads said so. You damn everybody for your fucking Dreads," Big Cal shouted.

"So, it's like this, cuz? You wanna take me out over *my* wife?" Terrence asked him. "And you'd bring Pooch back to do it?"

"*Cuz*? This nigga is your cousin?" I asked, in shock.

"We were cousins until he shot me over her ass," Big Cal yelled.

"And you ain't got a gun pointed at me over her ass now?" Terrence bellowed. "Come on, Aaron. *Think*. Pooch don't give a fuck about none of us. He'll just as soon put a bullet in all our heads."

"We have an agreement. That won't happen," Big Cal yelled.

"You think this grimy nigga is gonna honor an agreement, knowing you were responsible for locking him up? Don't let this shit gas you up, dawg," Terrence shouted.

I gripped my heat a little tighter. "Nigga, I'm a man of my word."

"Baby, please," Trinity cried. "Dreads, just leave. Please, y'all, let him leave."

"At least I finally know where your heart lies," I said to Trinity. "You good-for-nothing bitch," I yelled. I noticed Terrence's finger tense on the trigger. "No, sir," I said to him, shifting my aim from Big Cal to Trinity. "Romeo and Juliet will die together this day if you think of pulling that trigger."

Ignoring me, Terrence focused on Big Cal. "She's my wife, Aaron. Come on," Terrence pleaded.

I shifted my aim from Trinity back to Big Cal, unsure of his motives.

"But I love her," Big Cal screamed. "How come you couldn't love me back? After everything."

Amazed, I almost admired that bitch for her ability to command every nigga in this storage unit. That Oshun energy she had over men was otherworldly. "Damn, your pussy power is the bomb, girl. You've got muthafuckas who ain't even hit it ready to kill for it."

Big Cal laughed. "Don't you remember, Trinity?"

"Remember what?" she screamed. "Please stop this, Cal."

Big Cal eyed her with pain in his eyes. I knew then that he was about to reveal some shit that was about to tilt the axis in this storage room. "Back when Terrence was locked up and you got wit' Pooch. He was drunk, and he made you get on the pole in front of him and his boys at the house, in the king suite. Afterward, you ran to your bedroom, crying. You had been drinking heavily, and I came to check on you . . ."

Terrence and I both looked at Trinity. "Bitch, I know you didn't," I boomed. "In my muthafucking house?"

She gasped as the memory came back to her. "*Oh my God.* You said that I didn't . . . that we didn't . . ." She could barely get the words out.

Terrence swallowed hard. "You fucked my wife, Aaron?"

"Yes! And it was the best fucking sex of my life. I told her I loved her and everything," Big Cal screamed. "You don't remember? The next day I told you that we didn't, so you wouldn't feel bad and tell Pooch. I didn't think you would honestly not remember. How could you not remember? The next month you were pregnant with Princess," he cried, becoming unhinged. "I played the back to keep you safe. When you finally got away from Pooch and got with my cousin, I was willing to put my feelings aside, but you were smiling at me, confiding in me, and getting close to me. I knew it was a sign. I was just waiting on the signal. I thought you were finally gonna let me be with you. I thought you were finally choosing me. So me, you, and my baby, Princess, could be together."

"*You bitch.* So Princess ain't mine, either?" I thundered.

"Don't you fucking pull that trigger, muthafucka," Terrence yelled, noticing my trigger finger twitching after I heard the news Big Cal had spit.

"I remember now, but I was so fucked up then, I didn't remember that, Big Cal. Besides, back then, you told me nothing happened, and I believed you.

So I pushed it out of my mind because there was nothing to remember. I never had feelings for you. You were my friend. That's it. And no, Princess isn't your daughter. I was already pregnant. That next month, when I found I was pregnant, I was already eight weeks along."

"Liar!" Big Cal screamed.

"It's the truth," she cried, eyeing me. "Pooch, remember when Princess got sick when she was an infant, and they thought she was gonna need a blood transfusion? They checked your blood. You were a perfect match. You're her father."

I calmed down as the memory came back to me. "She's right, Big Cal. I was a match. Princess is mine."

Big Cal let out an agonizing scream. "All this time, I thought that possibly she was mine. To have a baby by the woman of my dreams," he cried.

"You slept with him?" Terrence said, heartbroken.

"Baby, I don't remember it. He said nothing happened. I was drunk," Trinity pleaded. "I love you. You're my husband. Please forgive me. Even if I did, I didn't know he was your cousin back then. I'm not sure if he's lying or not now."

Big Cal shot a glare at her. His eyes danced with anger. "Lying? I should—"

He moved to attack her, but I trained my gun straight at his head. "I should kill all you sons of bitches. Ain't no fucking loyalty in friends, families, or foes." With my other gun pointed at Trinity, I sneered, "And your slut ass has been through all of us."

"Fuck you, Pooch!" she screamed.

"Fuck you, Trinity!" I yelled.

"Baby?" she pleaded to Terrence. "Dreads, please. I'm so sorry."

"You muthafuckas make me sick," Terrence seethed. "Talkin' about how Trinity wronged you. She was my lady since high school. Not y'all's. *Mine*! I lost her to you, and you're my fam, supposed to be takin' this nigga down, and you fallin' in love with my lady and fucking her while she's drunk. You bitch-made niggas disgust me."

"You fucking bitch!" Big Cal belted at Terrence.

"Please, y'all. Please let Dreads go," Trinity begged. "Pooch, you can kill me. Cal, do what you want to me, please. Just let Terrence go," she cried.

Damn. This bitch really rode hard for Terrence. She had proven that she was really a loyal, down-ass bitch for that muthafucka. She was willing to lay down her life for him. It was the first time that I had ever seen anybody who was willing to do that. Hell, I couldn't even say that I was willing to do that for anybody. This bitch truly loved fuckin' Terrence.

Out of the corner of my eye, I saw Trinity wiggling her hands out of the ropes. "This bitch is gettin' loose," I yelled, getting ready to point the gun at her, but I heard a gun click.

"*Run, Trinity*," Terrence said.

The only thing I heard after that was a hail of gunfire.

Chapter 22

Trinity

"*Nooo!*" I screamed as I dove out of the chair and hit the floor. The sound in the room was deafening as gunfire rang out. Then silence. After a few minutes, I realized that I was safe and that I hadn't been hit. Grateful that I'd survived the massacre, I jumped up. I had to get to Terrence. I ran straight for my baby.

"*Terrence!*" I yelled, running to where he lay on the floor. I got on my knees and held his head in my lap. "Baby, please wake up! Terrence, please. Please wake up. Baby, I need you. I love you. *Please, wake up,*" I cried hysterically as I rubbed his forehead.

I saw the blood smears that my hand left on his face. My entire body started to tremble as I lifted my hand. Blood oozed down my forearm and hand. My hand shook ferociously as I screamed and screamed.

Please stay tuned for . . .

Never Again, No More 5:

Game Over